———————————— ★ ————————————

When he reached for his gun, my heart pushed so heavily against my chest I thought it would come through my jacket and land in the empty mug in front of me on Martha's tray. But Francis didn't take aim. He simply waved the gun around as he talked, as if he needed a cigarette and this was the closest he could come.

"Mark my words," he said, using an expression I hadn't heard since my youth. "You'll be sorry if you continue to harass me or my family."

"Don't you want to know who killed your father, Mr. Deramo?"

Francis looked at me with impossibly narrowed eyes and a look of torment on his face, as if the question I'd asked him was more difficult than he'd seen on his Massachusetts state bar exam.

"I can't afford to know," he said, "and you can't, either."

———————————— ★ ————————————

Forthcoming from Worldwide Mystery by
CAMILLE MINICHINO

THE BERYLLIUM MURDER

The Lithium Murder

Camille Minichino

WORLDWIDE®

TORONTO • NEW YORK • LONDON
AMSTERDAM • PARIS • SYDNEY • HAMBURG
STOCKHOLM • ATHENS • TOKYO • MILAN
MADRID • WARSAW • BUDAPEST • AUCKLAND

THE LITHIUM MURDER

A Worldwide Mystery/August 2001

First published by HarperCollins Publishers Inc.

ISBN 0-373-26394-5

Printed in U.S.A.

PROLOGUE

MICHAEL DERAMO straightened his tie in front of his cracked hallway mirror and tried to imagine how many buckets it would take to hold one hundred thousand dollars. More rusty pails than all the janitors in Revere, Massachusetts, stored in their closets, he figured. He looked at his callused, liver-spotted hands and wished they had more life left in them to enjoy the leisure all that money would bring.

In less than an hour he'd have the last laugh on those stuck-up scientists with their briefcases and their pockets lined with pens and pencils, as if they were so important. He'd cleaned up after them for almost forty years over at the University Physics Lab on Charger Street.

Michael screwed up his craggy Roman nose as he thought of young John Hammer, leaving the men's shower room a holy mess after his lunchtime workout. Sweaty clothes and smelly, wet towels everywhere. Muddy tennis shoes on Michael's clean tile floor and puddles of water on the benches. Behaving as if Michael were his mother, or his wife.

And the big engineer boss, Fred Laughton, lording it over Michael. He acted as if he were doing Michael a favor, letting him work beyond the official retirement age of seventy, instead of giving him a gold watch and a decent pension. A big party wouldn't have been bad, either.

Michael's supervisor, Carlo Massimo, wasn't much better, even though he was also Italian. Michael's dark rheumy eyes swept across the main room of his rickety little bungalow and took in the shabby coffee table and worn-out easy chairs that Massimo had donated to him when they redecorated the lab's reception area. Probably Massimo had meant well, but he should have known better, Michael thought.

A converted garage with hand-me-down furniture, and a fifteen-year-old car that had been a lemon in the first place—this was not the life he and his father had envisioned as they'd crossed the Atlantic Ocean together when Michael was just a boy.

Well, things will be different soon, Michael told himself. He still couldn't get over how lucky he was to have overheard them in the conference room that night a week ago. If he hadn't gone back to get the jacket he'd left in the supply closet, it never would have happened. But there they were, four of them, huddled around the big walnut table that Michael kept polished and shiny as an undertaker's shoes. He'd stood in the hallway and peeked through the glass partition, its frosted texture making their faces a blurry jumble.

"About our lithium issues—we certainly don't want this to get to the public," Fred Laughton had said, both hands gripping his pencil as if he were trying to break it in two. "Let's just not worry right now about the impurities in the battery—we'll lose millions if that patent is delayed."

"What about the environmental problem?" Michael heard from a man with a deep voice he didn't recognize.

"If that gets out, we're dead in the water. We'll be hit with major fines from every keep-the-earth-green agency you can think of," Laughton said. "Then we'd never get this project off the ground."

"Not that we don't deserve a little slap on the wrist. A little lithium accident could ruin your day, to put it mildly," Hammer said, with a laugh that sent shivers up and down Michael's spine. He wished he had the nerve to poke his head in and ask them what was going on right then, but he kept still.

Michael listened carefully, catching phrases like "environmental hazard," "high-risk disposal," and "impatient patent attorneys.'' He didn't understand everything, but he could tell this was an important meeting. He had no idea what lithium was, except that he'd seen the word once on a can of grease he'd bought to get rid of rust on the iron hinges of the old wooden trunk his father had brought from Italy.

Michael had stood outside the conference room, quiet as a sponge mop, behind his favorite ficus. Without thinking, he leaned over and pulled a crisp green leaf toward him and plucked a piece of lint from it, as if he were still on his shift. When he let go, the whole branch snapped away from him and scraped across the glass panel. Michael jumped back, as if his vacuum cleaner had just started up on its own. His eyes widened as he saw the four men in the room rise to their feet at once. He walked away, his keys rattling on the big metal ring at his waist, his heart pounding in his chest.

"Mike?"

Laughton had stepped into the corridor and called after him. Michael hated the nickname and wished he had the nerve to call Laughton Freddie.

"Oh, hello, Dr. Laughton," he said instead. He hoped he sounded casual, as if he were just passing by and hadn't heard a thing.

"Have you been here long?"

Before he could stop himself, Michael locked eyes with Laughton and realized he couldn't get away with a lie. He took a deep breath.

"Long enough," he said.

To Michael's surprise, the tall, gangling man didn't seem angry. Instead, he seemed to shrink to Michael's five feet one inch right before his eyes.

"Come by my office and see me in the morning, will you, Mike?" Laughton said, putting his hand on Michael's shoulder as if they were buddies. "I'd like to have a little talk with you."

When Michael showed up the next day, Laughton had it

all worked out—Michael's silence in return for a load of money. Michael smiled as he remembered Laughton's words.

"Not that there's anything bad going on, Mike. We just don't want anyone to get the wrong idea."

"You don't have to do that, Dr. Laughton," Michael said. "I wasn't really planning to say anything to anybody about what I heard. Doesn't really make much difference to me."

"I know, Mike, I know, but this is a very big deal to us and we just want to make sure you don't run into any temptation to let this information slip into the wrong hands. So, we'd all feel a lot more comfortable if you'd just let us make a contribution to your favorite charity, or whatever."

Before their little talk was over, Michael had agreed to accept exactly one hundred thousand dollars.

Now it was time for the payoff. Michael switched off the lights in his cottage and headed out the door for the meeting place that he'd chosen himself, a place where he'd feel safe. Eleven o'clock, at the pavilion, about half a mile from the old brick bathhouse on the Boulevard, and far away from his nosy landlord. He'd chosen the biggest of about a dozen pavilions on Revere Beach, each with rows of worn wooden benches under a black pitched roof. Michael walked the Boulevard every night, and he knew it by heart. Some people had fancy offices with big picture windows and thick carpet, but Michael had his ocean. It was only right that he'd collect his money as the tide came in.

The beach was the one good thing in Michael's life. His flimsy little house was on prime real estate, set back from the Boulevard, in the shadow of expensive new high-rise apartment buildings. But they all had the same ocean in front of them, Michael thought, and the same salty air that seemed crisper than usual this mid-May evening. He walked slowly, trying to match the rhythm of the crashing waves, for good luck.

Michael could hardly wait to tell his landlord, Joe Bargello, that he'd be moving soon. Or maybe he'd try to make a deal— have them turn the ex-garage he'd rented into a fancy little villa for him right on the spot. Bargello lived in the ritzy front house, painted white, with a wide lawn that Michael was not supposed to set foot on. He had to walk around Bargello's flashy new silver Buick just to get from his own place to the sidewalk.

Michael had his story all ready for when they asked how come he could afford this new life all of a sudden. His son, Francis, the lawyer, he'd say, had just won a big case in Boston and had decided to share the wealth with his old man. Never mind that he hardly ever saw his boy any more. Evidently Michael's low-class job had been good enough to put Francis through school, but not good enough for the high-and-mighty Sylvia, his new wife. Sylvia and her brother, Barry Richards, and all their ritzy friends on the North Shore did everything they could to keep Francis away from his father.

Michael remembered when he used to play the drums, marching down the Boulevard with the Sons of Italy band every Sunday. Francis had been so proud of his father then, waving to Michael from the crowd, pointing him out to all his little friends. Michael knew the money he was coming into would make Francis proud again.

Nowadays, only Andy Palmer, Sylvia's son by her first marriage, seemed to like him. Even though the kid was spoiled rotten, he was always nice to Michael. Maybe to get back at his parents, Michael figured. He chuckled at the memory of Sylvia and Francis fighting with Andy over whether he should have a fancy race car to play with. One time, right in front of his parents, Andy had invited Michael to go with him to Pennsylvania to watch some big-time races. Michael knew Andy was inviting him just to annoy his mother, so he politely refused.

Michael slapped his thigh—maybe he'd use some of his new money to buy Andy a race car and really annoy his daughter-in-law.

Michael walked the hundred or so yards to the pavilion. There was only a trickle of traffic behind him on the Boulevard, but he knew that would change as soon as the evenings got warmer. He looked at the cars that passed him as if he were in a moving automobile showroom. Which one would he buy when he had a wad of bills in his pocket? Not that old junker rattling by. Not that low-rider pickup that needed a paint job as much as his own old Malibu did. Maybe that sleek black Ford with the glitzy hubcaps, but a newer model.

Michael tilted his head and smiled as he listened to the rustling of his knobby fingers in the pockets of his new windbreaker, dark blue with red and white trim. Red, white, and blue for the United States of America, the land of opportunity. For the first time in his life, Michael hadn't even looked at the price tag when he'd picked the jacket off the rack at the Brooks Brothers store in the mall, a sign of good times to come. He ran his hand down the smooth fabric of his new polyester tie. Like the way a real businessman dresses, he thought, thinking he might take back that money clip he'd rejected from Francis on his seventieth birthday.

When Michael reached the pavilion, he found its benches cold and wet from the sprays of high tide. He walked past them and leaned on the railing, facing the ocean. He took a spot next to a square of new cement, careful not to disturb the stubby three-inch-high plywood construction wall that surrounded it. Michael shifted his weight from one leg to the other every so often so they wouldn't cramp up.

He thought of Elena, his beautiful wife, who had died so many years ago, during the siege of pneumonia that hit the city. Michael banged his hand on the railing and clenched his jaw as he remembered that awful weekend. It wasn't as if you could just drive to a clinic in those days. And you didn't call a doctor just because an otherwise healthy twenty-six-year-old woman had a fever.

He wondered what Elena would have thought of his deal with the scientists. He guessed she would not have been happy. She probably would have thought there was something kind of shady about it. Besides, money had never mattered to her.

"As long as we have each other," Elena had told him over and over when they were struggling to make ends meet. Now, with his eyes on the tiny sliver of moon over the ocean, Michael explained it all to her—why he needed the money, how he'd worked hard all these years and raised their son without her, how he deserved some self-respect and comfort in his old age.

In the middle of his speech to Elena, Michael heard soft, scratchy footsteps on the sandy asphalt behind him. He turned around, anticipating his big moment with a grin that took over the corners of his mouth. Michael studied the form walking up the ramp to the pavilion benches, set two feet above the sidewalk. He—if it was a he—was shrouded in dark clothing and had probably come from the car parked in front of the mustard-colored fire hydrant. Michael could hear the motor running, competing with the sound of the Revere Beach banner flapping over his head.

Michael squinted, his eyes searching for a briefcase like the kind he saw on TV shows, when some wise guy showed up with half a million dollars to close a drug deal or to keep a witness quiet. But this figure had no baggage weighing it down. It headed right for Michael, passing the long rows of empty benches, not saying a word, nor raising an arm in greeting.

Who is this? The wrong person? What could that be coming out of his pocket? It had better not be a check, Michael thought, or a one-hundred-thousand-dollar bill, if there is such a thing. How would I explain that to Mr. Russo at the bank?

No, it wasn't a check or a money order. Whatever it was gave off a faint glint as the figure passed through a thin cone of yellow light from the streetlamp.

Michael looked around him. A strong fishy odor reached his nostrils, as if a dead sea creature had suddenly washed up on the beach behind him. This shadowy person was intruding on his meeting, or maybe trying to cut in on his deal, or— Michael shuddered—coming to shut him up for good.

MICHAEL COULD NOT even see the thin wire his murderer flipped over his head. He struggled against the force pinning him to the railing, against the arms tightening the wire around his throat, but his hands kept slipping on the slick fabric of his killer's jacket.

With his last, tiny spark of energy, Michael ran his fingers through the patch of new cement where he'd fallen, his nails shouting words his voice could not.

ONE

"THIS IS NONE OF your business, Gloria. Michael Deramo was a custodian, for heaven's sake," Rose said to me. She straightened the pile of papers and books on my coffee table and brushed crumbs of wheat bread from her skirt, as if in sympathy with the deceased cleaning professional.

"But he didn't sweep just any floors," I reminded my best friend. "He didn't work at the mall. He worked in an important science facility. They have a lot of government contracts there. Even a janitor might have had a Q-clearance, just like the engineers and scientists."

"So?"

"So, there'd be lots of possibilities for getting himself into trouble. He could have found an important document in the trash. He could have overheard a conversation or seen an equation on a blackboard."

"Gloria, listen to yourself."

"Or maybe he was an industrial spy posing as a janitor."

"Where do you come up with these wild ideas?" Rose asked, picking at a crust of bread. While Rose nibbled at her tuna sandwich, I took large bites of mine, fully aware that our different eating styles accounted for the difference in our clothing sizes. "Now that you're officially going steady with Matt," she added, "you don't need to invent reasons to work with him."

If we weren't sitting in my own living room, above the funeral parlor that she owned and operated with Frank, her husband of nearly forty years, I might have walked out on Rose Galigani, or asked her to leave. But since it was my apartment and her building, I stayed put, took a deep breath, and launched into my defense.

"'Going steady' sounds like high school," I said, with a grin that told Rose I was pretty satisfied with my new life—retired from physics research, back in my hometown after three decades, a consultant to the Revere Police Department, and a homicide detective's companion. I resisted thinking of myself as his "girlfriend" and had tried in vain to come up with a more mature-sounding synonym for our relationship.

My new vocation, working on murder investigations when a victim or a crime scene involved science, provided almost as many thrills as my former career in crystal spectroscopy. At fifty-six, my life was going so well, in fact, that I almost didn't hear the voice of my dead mother, warning me against the perils of contentment and optimism.

Don't get all wrapped up in this good luck, Josephine was saying, from the general direction of the window in my sunny living room. *God knows you haven't done much to deserve it.*

Since returning to Revere, I'd made great strides toward ignoring Josephine's criticism of me—ironic, since the move had brought me back to the site of my life with her. A mother in name only, Josephine had made sure I knew what a nuisance my birth had been for her and for the world at large.

I shut out her voice for the moment and turned my attention to my present company, comfortably seated on my blue-green corduroy sofa. Rose and I had been eating lunch together in front of the noon TV news. I looked forward to this routine that we'd fallen into whenever I was home and she could get away from her office, one floor below me in the Galigani Mortuary building. Our friendship was in its fourth decade, having survived long-distance while I lived in California.

At the end of the commercial break, I unmuted the TV and leaned forward, tuning Rose out and May Coster in, the latter being an impeccably groomed anchorwoman. Coster had promised more details on Michael Deramo, the lab custodian who'd been murdered the night before on Revere Beach Boulevard, about a mile from my mortuary home.

"Seventy-two-year-old Deramo, a native of Bari, Italy, but a longtime Revere resident, was found strangled to death not far from his Point of Pines cottage," Coster said. "His wallet contained no credit cards or cash, and he was wearing no watch or other jewelry. The police suspect robbery."

"Ha," I said. My tone, one of disbelief, earned me a slap on the knee from Rose.

The "in-depth" Deramo segment went on for only another minute or so, without much substance. Deramo had lived alone. His one son, Francis, was an attorney who lived with his family—his socialite wife, the former Sylvia Richards, and stepson, Andrew Palmer—in Marblehead, an affluent community a few miles north of Revere.

"They say he worked as a janitor. They don't say *where* or what he worked *near*," I said, "or what he might have heard." I clicked off the television set with a motion that dismissed it as a source of meaningful information.

"He worked near floor wax and brooms, and he heard his vacuum cleaner," Rose said. She'd wrapped more than half her sandwich in plastic and put it in my refrigerator "for later."

We both knew that Rose would never get around to eating the rest of her lunch. I looked at my own plate, empty of even the smallest crumb, and decided that Rose had earned the right to her energetic size-six body. Today she'd dressed it in a linen suit of dark green, the perfect complement to the carefully placed red highlights in her hair.

"I'd better get back to work," she said. "I'm behind on everything, as usual when Martha's out for a week."

I walked her to the door. A question burned on the tip of my tongue, and it wasn't about why Martha Franklin, Rose's assistant, was away.

"Are you busy downstairs?" I asked, my hands playing with the cord of my navy-blue Cal Berkeley sweatshirt hood, as if I'd already lost interest in the answer.

Rose laughed out loud. "I was wondering when you were going to ask," she said. "And the answer is yes, Galigani's is the mortuary of choice for Mr. Deramo's services. His daughter-in-law was here this morning making arrangements."

Although Rose's voice carried no hint of unpleasantness, the word "arrangements" coming from her lips conjured up images of corpses in the prep room, hooked up to noisy embalming equipment, three floors below me in the basement of the building. Nevertheless, I gave her a broad smile, not even trying to contain my delight that a murder victim would once again have his wake at my address.

Galigani's first-floor funeral parlors had served me well in the past few months. They'd been as good as formal police interview rooms for two homicide cases that I'd worked on with RPD's Sergeant Matt Gennaro, my "steady," as Rose called him. The wakes of the victims gave me legitimate and unique access to all the principal suspects. I sometimes wondered if this was not the single most compelling reason that I hadn't moved from the "temporary" quarters Rose and Frank had offered me when I returned to Revere a year ago.

"There's something else," Rose said.

"What?" I asked, choking on my speedy reaction.

"I don't know why I do this, Gloria."

"Do what?"

"Encourage you."

"Out with it," I said. I used my considerably larger body to advantage, putting it between Rose and my door. "You know you want to tell me."

"Okay, for what it's worth, here it is. Sylvia Deramo, the daughter-in-law, is a name-dropper. She made it clear to me that there were no janitors among the Richardses, *her* side of the family," Rose said, throwing her tiny shoulders back and raising her nose in the air to illustrate her point. "But I think she's new North Shore rich trying to look like old money."

"And?"

"And when I said how awful it was that it might not be safe to walk the Boulevard these days, she said her father-in-law was not a very smart man and he shouldn't have tried to play with the big boys. Those were her words, 'play with the big boys.' She was sort of talking to herself and stopped short when she became aware of me again."

I let out a long breath. "That's it. She's practically telling us her father-in-law's been the victim of foul play, Rose. Why were you giving me such a hard time before?"

"Well, you know I don't like your poking into dangerous places. I'm always torn between trying to help you and protect you at the same time."

"I appreciate that," I said, as we hugged each other. "And you know I'll be careful."

Rose laughed, her head shaking from side to side in exaggerated frustration as she walked toward the stairs to the second floor. "Why don't I believe you?" she asked.

I called after her, "Just because I've had run-ins with a double murderer, a hit man, and a killer now in prison for life?" And that's just in the last eight months, I added silently.

The sound of Rose's laughter was uninterrupted until I heard her office door close.

TWO

WITH ROSE GONE, I tried to settle down in front of my computer to work on my final presentation as a guest speaker in Peter Mastrone's Italian class. My boyfriend for a brief time when we were teenagers, Peter had been teaching European history and Italian language and literature at Revere High School for more than thirty years. He'd lived with his mother until her death a few years ago.

The reunion between Peter and me when I returned to Revere was disastrous, but we'd finally reached a point where we could be civil to each other after what he called a series of miscommunications and I called a gap to be measured in light-years. Although I'd had almost no contact with Peter during all the time I was in California, except for a card or two, he behaved as if I'd come home just to be with him. In spite of my efforts to establish our relationship as simply friends, he'd given me a gold heart-shaped pendant last Christmas. It was still in its red velvet box at the back of my dresser drawer, unworn, and likely to be untouched until my next serious housecleaning.

I did enjoy talking to Peter's students, however, and looked forward to my class for them on the eighteenth-century Italian mathematician Maria Agnesi. I'd planned the presentation to coincide with her birthday, May 16, which gave me only a few days to edit my transparencies and collect a few more anecdotes. My favorite was the story of how she came to be known as the Witch of Agnesi, thanks to a mistranslation of the word "versiera," meaning "versed sine curve" but also an Italian word for witch.

This afternoon I felt uncharacteristically restless, glancing at the clock every ten minutes and getting up often to nibble at the lemon cookies Rose had brought to lunch but ignored. I searched through my jewelry box and chose the pin I'd wear to Peter's class—a small bronze replica of the statue of Garibaldi that stands in the center of an enormous square in Milan, Maria Agnesi's birthplace. I'd bought it on a trip to Italy with Rose the year I'd received my doctorate. The Italian patriot and general lived a hundred years after Maria, but lacking a pin with her image, I decided it would do.

After an hour of fighting temptation, I gave in to what I really wanted to do—I went to work on the Michael Deramo murder case. No matter what the RPD and Ms. Coster of television newsland might be thinking, I smelled a murder, and a research opportunity.

Falling into my old habits, from years of experience in scientific investigation, I took a new spiral-bound notebook from my desk drawer, wrote DERAMO in large red letters across the cover, and made a list of what I knew so far. Not much. Sadly lacking in data, I made a plan for gathering information.

I thought about my technical contacts at the Charger Street lab. It took some effort to come up with someone that I'd dealt with who wasn't either in prison or angry with me for suspecting her or him of murder. No wonder I don't have many friends in Revere, I realized. I've made myself about as popular as a street-corner police informant.

There was one young lab technician I hadn't alienated—Andrea Cabrini, whom I'd met while I was working on a contract with Matt in the fall. I called the main lab number and an operator transferred me to Andrea's extension. As I waited for her to pick up the phone, I pictured her overly wide body and puffy cheeks and recalled her distress at the murder of her only friend, Eric Bensen, a physicist I'd met during his brief residence in California. What Andrea Cabrini needed was a pal, and who better than me for that role?

"Hydrogen lab, this is Andrea."

I knew Andrea to be naive and trusting, and as soon as her small voice reached my ears, I was embarrassed at my intentions to pump her for information. Too late, however.

"This is Gloria Lamerino," I said. "You may not remember me—"

"Oh, yes, Dr. Lamerino," Andrea said, sounding happy to hear from me, thus increasing my guilt-to-comfort ratio. "I remember you. How are you?"

"I'm just fine. And you?" I asked, not knowing quite how quickly to proceed to the reason for my call. I remembered how little respect Andrea earned from her patronizing colleagues in the hydrogen research program at the lab, although, from what I'd seen, she was a competent technician. I had no data to support my conclusion, but I suspected that she was ostracized because of her bulky, unfashionable appearance and her lack of social graces.

By the time I was able to formulate a reasonable introduction to my questions, Andrea came to my rescue.

"I'm fine, too," she said. "Is there something I can do for you?"

"I'm sure you're very busy, Andrea, but I did have a couple of questions I wanted to ask you."

"I'm really not that busy. Do you want to come over? We could have lunch." Andrea's voice had taken on a lightness I hadn't heard when she first answered the phone.

Now what, I asked myself—do you want quick answers to suit your needs, or are you really willing to spend some time with this woman? Years of catechism classes about charity toward others took over and I made a plan to meet Andrea for lunch the next day at the lab cafeteria.

"Maybe if you tell me the topic, I could be thinking about it," Andrea said, as if she were asking her teacher if she could write a term paper for extra credit.

I forged ahead.

"I was wondering if you knew Michael Deramo, the man

who was killed on the Boulevard last night. He was a custodian at your lab."

Andrea drew a quick breath.

"Are you on the case with the detective?" she asked. I thought I heard a chair squeak and imagined her changing position on her seat.

Another dilemma for me. This call was turning into a stress test, I thought, as my fingers tightened around my phone.

"I'm doing some preliminary work," I said, checking the tip of my nose for signs of enlargement.

"I barely knew the man," she said. "Honestly, I don't know where he lives or anything."

Hearing her anxious gasp, I realized that poor Andrea probably thought she was a suspect again. Not for the first time I became aware of how awkward I was when I tried to pass myself off as a law enforcement professional. I rushed to reassure her.

"You're certainly not a suspect, Andrea. I just thought you might know something about the department Mr. Deramo worked in. You have such a good grasp of everything that goes on there."

"Well, thanks. I do know he worked in the new lithium program, where they're doing battery research," she said, in a much calmer voice. "Dr. Laughton and Dr. Hammer run it. And I know they're close to filing a patent application. They're over in the classified wing."

The word was enough to start my heart racing. "Classified" meant Deramo did have government clearance to be around restricted discussions. That could mean anything from weapons-related information to industrial secrets. I told myself not to get too excited, that Deramo probably wouldn't have understood what he heard day after day anyway. Most likely he didn't know about the environmental hazards of lithium waste disposal, nor the technical difficulties involved in getting patents. But there was always the possibility....

I was heading down an interesting mental path when Andrea's voice over the phone and a simultaneous knock on my door brought me back to the present.

"So I'll see you tomorrow?" Andrea was saying.

I carried my cordless phone to the door and looked through my new peephole, a testimony to a couple of recent guests who shouldn't have been admitted to my apartment. I jumped back from the eyepiece at the sight of Sergeant Matt Gennaro, as if he'd come to arrest me. Not that I didn't like it when Matt dropped by. I simply preferred that it not be while I was attempting to impersonate a police officer.

I said, "Can you hold on a minute?" to Andrea, and "I'll be right there" to Matt, using the glass front of my San Francisco poster at the same time to check my hair. Too curly from the humidity, and more gray than yesterday, but otherwise acceptable. I screwed up my nose at the stale tuna smell coming from my kitchen, but shrugged off the impulse to scrub the counter before opening the door. *Sorry, Josephine,* I told the ghost of my mother, hovering over me with a sponge and a can of cleanser.

I opened the door to Matt, my phone at my hip. He smiled and signaled that I should continue with my call. I swept my arm across my living room in a make-yourself-comfortable gesture and turned back to Andrea, feeling like a sorority girl caught in a breach of house rules.

"That's probably enough for now," I said to Andrea. "I'll see you tomorrow."

"Great. I'll see what I can find out in the meantime," she said.

"At this point, it's very informal," I said, racking my brain for a way to tell her to keep this to herself, without alarming either her or Matt.

"I won't say a word, Dr. Lamerino," Andrea said in a soft voice. I hung up and silently thanked her for catching my drift.

I turned to Matt, a little like the way Lucy approached Ricky Ricardo when she'd been caught sticking her nose where it didn't belong.

"Hi," he said, handing me a cappuccino in a paper cup and giving me the hello kiss we'd established as our official greeting. In the nearly four months that we'd been dating, the kiss had traveled around, from cheek to cheek, to occasional lip contact. At five-six, Matt was only a couple of inches taller than me, so it was a comfortable posture for us. Our standard goodbye kiss was the same, except that it lasted slightly longer. Not bad for two middle-aged people whose combined dating experience was less than that of the average high school sophomore these days.

"I hope I didn't interrupt anything."

"Not at all. I was just working on my Maria Agnesi talk for Peter's Italian class," I said, staying close to the truth.

Matt took out the half-glasses he'd acquired recently when the focal length of his dark brown eyes finally exceeded the length of his arm.

"Interesting," he said.

I thought he was referring to my fascinating Agnesi transparencies, decorated with her beautiful mathematical functions, but when I turned around I saw that he'd picked up my notebook, the one with DERAMO on the cover. The ink from the red marker was barely dry, and I suspected that the color matched my cheeks.

"Is this a crime scene?" I asked him.

"This is what we call in reasonably plain view," Matt said.

"I love it when you use search-warrant language."

Matt laughed, and I was able to unlock my jaw and relax my fingers. I looked at his slightly rumpled clothes—Thursday was gray suit day—and indulged myself in feeling his presence. I liked the idea that I knew him well enough never to give him anything with raisins in it, or any clothes with red, not even a thin stripe from that end of the color spectrum.

And he knows I love cappuccino California style, I mused, with a thick dusting of chocolate, not the cinnamon topping that's more common in European and East Coast coffee shops.

"Have you had lunch?" I asked. "Let me make you a tuna sandwich."

Apparently Matt was dwelling on the business at hand— my incriminating notebook.

"So you've already found a way to relate this to science?" he asked, waving the book in the air as if he were in the Flag Day parade on the Boulevard.

I had much too little to offer Matt by way of evidence or data—twice-removed hearsay from Rose about the mumbling of Deramo's daughter-in-law, Sylvia, and a comment from Andrea that he mopped a classified hallway. With so little to go on, I chose to ignore Matt's question and repeat my own.

"How about that tuna?" I asked.

"How about I'll make my own sandwich while you tell me what you've got."

"Pardon me?"

"You probably heard the story on the noon news," he said, checking his watch. "So I figure you've had almost two hours to think about it and start your inevitable investigation. If you have something, I want to know."

I nearly gave him a middle-of-the-visit kiss, which would have been a first.

"I'll take that as a green light," I said.

"Make that yellow," Matt said, opening the correct cabinet for a plate. I liked sitting in one of my matching blue glide rockers while he made himself at home in my kitchen. I wondered briefly what Josephine would have thought about having a guest make his own tuna sandwich.

In deference to the confidentiality required by my friends in the mortuary business, I skipped over Rose's gossipy report on the former Sylvia Richards and went straight into a lithium tutorial.

"Deramo worked in the classified wing, where they're investigating lithium. That's the metal with the lightest weight and the highest energy density. There's a blossoming market for lithium ion batteries, but one type that uses a liquid to carry the charge is a high-risk technology. You can have leaks, flaming…"

Matt held up his hand in the way he usually did when I sounded like an overzealous professor. He might have been posing for a statue in the Rubens period, when ample body shapes were in vogue. All in all, with our identical Roman noses, unenhanced black-and-gray hair, and generous girth, Matt and I could have passed for brother and sister.

"I'm probably going to need something more basic," he said. "You know, your usual technology-for-cops approach." When he lowered his napkin I saw the crooked smile that I'd liked since our first meeting—several murders ago.

"Do you want your science lesson now or later?"

"Later. Right now, I need to go to Deramo's house on the Boulevard. Do you want to come?"

Does Newton have laws, I almost asked, but kept my composure.

"I do," I said, and we smiled at the game we were playing. "Not that I'm ungrateful, but why are you so amenable to this theory of mine that Deramo was murdered?"

Matt's pleasant countenance faded as he delivered his report.

"Deramo wasn't just strangled," he said. "He was garroted. We're asking ourselves, what casual mugger carries a piano wire around with him?"

I sat back to absorb this information, but Matt wasn't finished.

"And his house was broken into," he said.

THREE

I CONVINCED MATT that I should change my clothes before beginning a new contract with the Revere Police Department. My position was that women under thirty, or Rose Galigani at any age, could get away with sweat suits even at a corporate board meeting, but I needed all the help I could muster to look professional.

"No one else will be there, except possibly a couple of uniforms," Matt said.

"I don't think well in fleece," I said, pinching the thick fabric of my Cal sweatshirt for emphasis, and closing my bedroom door.

I hadn't been outdoors since an early-morning walk, a modest 1.3-mile gesture toward fitness. I opened my window for an informal temperature reading, looking over the tops of the elm trees in front of my building on Tuttle Street, toward St. Anthony's Church.

As a child, I'd labored over Sunday-school definitions in St. Anthony's basement classrooms, memorizing the laws of the church and the distinction between mortal and venial sins. I examined the fair-weather cloud formation above the towering Romanesque structure and imagined old Monsignor Vitale scrutinizing the state of my soul from his place in the sky. I wondered if I was earning extra points for joining the fight against the mortal sin of murder, a violation of the fifth commandment—and whether that made up for missing mass on Sunday for many years.

When Matt and I finally left for the Boulevard, I was wearing my new cranberry knit two-piece dress, chosen by Rose in her campaign to get me out of black and shades of gray, a wardrobe relieved only by my summer whites. She was doing better than my best California friend, Elaine Cody, who had failed a similar attempt. My signature pin for the day was an Italian flag, the red, white, and green emblem a reminder of the victim's homeland.

I picked up my expensive-looking soft black leather briefcase, realizing that it gave me away as an amateur at police work. Matt carried a small, well-used notebook, stuffed into his back pocket, but I hadn't learned to do without three zippered compartments and two side pockets.

Matt drove his unmarked blue RPD sedan along the Boulevard, and we reminisced, as we always did, about the missing amusements. No matter how many high-rise apartment buildings and boutiques were added each year, in our minds we would always see the Ferris wheel and roller coasters that had made Revere Beach Boulevard the playland of New England for decades. We rode with the windows open, the spring breeze from the ocean feeding our memories of pepper steak sandwiches and exciting trips through the mock horrors of Bluebeard's Palace.

"On this Deramo contract, Gloria—I don't expect a lot of involvement on your part," Matt said, with only the slightest smile.

"Of course not." I brushed aside the memory of Matt's anger on several occasions when he'd thought my "involvements" had gotten out of hand. He was kind enough not to remind me of decisions that had put me in danger in the recent past.

"If this janitor did have some science papers in his house, I'm sure that's what the burglary was about and we're too late."

"But there could be something they missed."

"Exactly. And if it turns out the homicide was related to his connection to the lab, we'll need to know about—what is it? Lithium?"

"Lithium. The third element on the periodic chart. Think of it as battery material. The old nickel-cadmium batteries that used to be favored by industry are too bulky to meet the new requirements of smaller components, like laptop computers and cell phones. There's a lot of competition in the personal computer business at the moment, and lithium is at the heart of it."

"Is that the same lithium they use in the drug?"

"The formula for the drug does contain the same lithium we're talking about, but it's a complicated powder—lithium carbonate. The molecular composition would be Li_2CO_3."

"Oh, right. And here I thought I was smart knowing it's given to manic depressives."

"I don't know much more either. Once we get into pharmaceuticals, I'm out of my league."

"Thanks for not making me feel stupid. I know I've told you this before, but I wish I'd paid more attention in science class."

"It's never too late. Don't be intimidated by the fact that Maria Agnesi was only seventeen when she published her commentary on Isaac Newton."

"Seventeen, huh? What was I doing at seventeen? Not much."

"Me either."

"Well, at least this time around, I like the teacher."

His remark and the accompanying glance silenced me, and just when I thought I was becoming adept at flirting. I did my best not to turn away.

"There's a contract for you in that folder," Matt said, as we passed the site of what used to be the world's best frozen custard stand. He tilted his head toward the backseat of the car. A widower for more than ten years, Matt was not much better than I was at sustained intimacy.

I reached over the console between us, pulled a manila folder onto my lap, and opened it, expecting to see a page of small print and a line for my signature. Instead, Michael Deramo stared up at me with the one eye that was visible as he lay on his side. His throat was bruised and messy, incongruously mismatched to what had probably started out as a neat shirt collar and tie. His lips were contorted, and if I didn't know how unlikely it was, I'd have said he was caught smiling. Michael's left hand, next to his head, rested in a patch of new cement, his wrist held up by a thin wooden construction wall a few inches high.

I thought I'd controlled my gasp, but Matt looked over and shook his head.

"Jeez, I'm sorry, Gloria," he said, rubbing his forehead. "I completely forgot. I meant to take those photographs out."

"I'm fine," I said, shifting the photographs to the bottom and slipping the crisp, clean contract to the top of the pile. I thought of a line from a Woody Allen movie—"I'm not afraid to die. I just don't want to be there when it happens."

In one moment, my feelings about Michael went from neutral to overdrive—I realized I'd also switched to a first-name basis in my mind. And it's about time, I thought. Until I was faced with the reality of what one human being had done to another, it had been too easy to think of murder as an intriguing puzzle, a new RPD assignment, a chance to exercise my analytical skills. And, I admitted with reluctance, an opportunity to spend time with Matt.

I balanced the contract on my lap, signed two copies, and closed the file. Neither Matt nor I spoke until we'd pulled up in front of the old and famous Kelley's Roast Beef stand, one of the few links to the past still in operation on the Boulevard. Here was something we could count on—an endless supply of green-and-white paper plates and cups, thin slices of roast beef, tuna salad with overly generous amounts of mayonnaise, prize-winning lobster roll specials.

"Let's get a drink and sit for a while," Matt said. "I wanted to go over the preliminary police report with you anyway. Then we can walk to Deramo's house from here. It will take us past the scene.''

Pacing, I thought gratefully. Matt excels at pacing. He wouldn't insult me by calling off this task, but he acknowledges my anxiety in a way he knows I can handle.

We got coffee at Kelley's and sat in the car, the pigeons offering too much competition for space on the benches. We were parked in one of the spots along the ocean side of the Boulevard, the time-honored place for necking. My own experiences of coming here at night to watch the submarine races were completely vicarious, however, since I had not been in the dating crowd in high school. Thanks to a shy personality and Josephine's strict rules, I did my homework instead. The regimen got me all A's, but no date for the prom.

"Too bad I didn't know what this place was for in 1956," Matt said, as if he'd been reading my mind. We'd already had the conversation about how pitiful our dating résumés were. Matt had been too short and chubby for jock status as a teenager, and thus out of the running for popularity contests or flings with cheerleaders. He told me he hadn't dated at all in the years since his wife had died of heart disease, and I had no reason not to believe him.

For me, besides my casual tenure as the girlfriend of the overbearing Peter Mastrone in high school, I'd been engaged briefly, right after college, to a man ten years older than me. He was killed in a car crash three months before we were to be married. I took off for California on what would have been our wedding day, and focused on my graduate studies and my career. I'd had few dates as an adult, most of them arranged by the vigilant Elaine Cody, until my combination lunch/contract-signing meeting with Matt more than thirty years later in Revere.

"Maybe we should come back when it's dark," Matt said, reaching for my hand.

"Is that a proposition?" I asked, my voice a little shaky. "Or are you trying to lighten the mood?"

"Both," he said, leaning toward me.

"But there's no policeman around to shine a flashlight on us."

WHAT WAS GOING ON, I asked myself, that our first middle-of-the-day necking—which was a notch or two more intense than our usual level—came in conjunction with a visit to a crime scene and the burglarized home of a murder victim? I decided to start a new notebook when I got back to my apartment, labeled COURTSHIP.

We walked along the Boulevard to the place where Michael's body had been found. The bright yellow tape around the north end of the pavilion had attracted about a dozen people, standing around like sightseers from a tour bus. Mostly women, they were all older, from a generation that obeys rules—at least that was my guess as to why they stood as close as they could get without touching the tape. Their chatter was in whispers, as if they were in the vestibule of St. Anthony's Church waiting for Tuesday-night novena services.

Matt held up his badge in a discreet gesture, and the mild-mannered rubbernecks filed away, this part of their field trip ended. I was grateful that we weren't looking at a bloody scene, then realized that Matt wouldn't have brought me if it had been too gruesome. Even so, as I looked at the outline of Michael's body, the full-color image of his brutalized neck came unbidden to my mind and I tensed my arm muscles to control a shiver.

The section of pavilion surrounded by the tape stood out from the rest—except for the chalk drawing, it was immaculate, swept clean of sand and debris by the police, as if Michael had overseen the maintenance job himself. We stayed only a few minutes, leaning on the railing, facing the endless ocean, without speaking. The breeze lifted my cranberry skirt in swirls around my legs, and the crashing waves seemed to wash away the signs of violence at my feet. I fingered the tiny metal Italian flag on my collar and hoped I could make a small contribution toward bringing Michael's killer to justice.

As we left the pavilion, I looked once more at the cement, remembering the position of Michael's hand in the photographs I'd seen.

"Is that a mark in the new cement?" I asked Matt.

"Looks like several marks."

"I mean the one right near his hand."

"Most likely kids," Matt said, leaning over the patch. "We learned the cement was poured at the end of the workday, around four-thirty. I'm sure some budding artists came by soon after."

"Right," I said, wondering if that was too easy an answer.

We resumed our walk toward Michael's home, and Matt continued his briefing on the details from the police report. The early-morning joggers who'd found Michael, both elementary school teachers, had known him from the neighborhood. He was a longtime resident and a familiar sight walking along the beach, at different times of the day or night, depending on the shift he worked.

A police canvass had determined that none of his neighbors had seen Michael leave for his walk on Wednesday night, however, so the recorded time of death, between ten and midnight, was just an estimate.

"For a while we thought we had something," Matt said. "His son's car—that's Francis Deramo, the lawyer—was seen on the Boulevard around eleven-thirty. He says he was on his way home from a late meeting with a client in Winthrop and thought he'd stop by to see his father. When he didn't see lights, he figured his father was asleep or working a night shift and he just kept going."

"Does the Winthrop meeting check out?"

"We're working on it. Francis is still at the station as far as I know, with Berger."

"Does George know I'm working on this case?" I asked, wondering what Matt's partner's current opinion of me was. I thought I'd successfully convinced George Berger that I wasn't after his job, and that I didn't think he was stupid, and that I respected his knowledge of science, but I wasn't sure I'd covered all the bases.

"He's fine with it," Matt said. "You've definitely won him over. Don't be surprised if he asks for your help with this new computer software he's using. Supposedly it does the crime scene drawings for you. All the big cities have it, and we've been asked to be part of some pilot program."

"You're beta-testing a graphics package?"

"Isn't that what I said?"

We both laughed at that, and I was so glad we'd reached the point where we were comfortable with our respective awkward moments.

"So far we have no reason to talk to the scientists at the lab, except for general background," Matt said. "It's not as if we have anything that points to any of them."

"The house visit might change that."

"Wouldn't that be a break?" Matt was flipping through his notebook as he talked. "We don't have a whole lot more. Deramo's supervisor at the lab, Carlo Massimo, lives over near you, behind St. Anthony's Church. He hasn't seen Deramo since they worked a shift together last weekend."

"I didn't hear any mention of grandchildren."

"Just a step-grandson, Andrew Palmer, Sylvia Deramo's son by her first marriage. We're talking to him, too," Matt said. "He has a sheet."

"A bed sheet? A sheet of paper?"

Another laugh, and a "Touché" from Matt, getting caught in jargon of his own.

"Actually, it's more like a racing sheet," he said. "Andrew

is a race car driver wannabe. He got picked up for battering the winner's car after he lost a race. Wrecked a door with a tire iron. Knocked the driver around a bit. Also, there's a drug possession charge that Barry Richards, his big-time lawyer uncle, got him out of.''

''Not your average janitor's family.''

''Not hardly.''

MICHAEL'S RESIDENCE, a small white clapboard bungalow in the Point of Pines section of Revere, was set back from the Boulevard, barely visible from the street. His landlord, Joe Bargello, lived in the much larger house in front. He'd also been questioned, but according to the report had neither seen nor heard anything unusual.

I'd never personally been part of a police canvass, but with my recent loose connection to detective work I got to see the RPD force in action. I was amazed at how quickly the police gathered information about a person's background, his relatives, friends, and neighbors, piecing together the life of a man who could no longer speak for himself.

While Matt talked to a uniformed officer sitting in a patrol car, I waited at the edge of the asphalt driveway taking in the neighborhood, a mixture of new high-rise apartments and old-style single-family dwellings. The area was marked by a labyrinth of small alleyways, with many closely packed bungalows that were probably used only in the summer months.

A piece of crumpled yellow paper caught my eye, disturbing the otherwise carefully manicured lawn of Michael's landlord. The scrap was relatively clean, so I picked it up and stuffed it into an outside pocket of my briefcase, where I'd already stashed the extra paper napkins from Kelley's.

Matt turned just in time to see this maneuver, and he added one more to my growing list of clues that he understood me.

''Josephine would be proud of you,'' he said, as we walked back toward Michael's house.

FOUR

MICHAEL'S ROOMS WERE strangely silent, as if his death had cut off some pipeline of energy to their unadorned walls and thin carpeting, the lifeless brown couch and the multicolored plastic dishes.

None of Michael's furniture had been overturned, and nothing appeared broken, but the contents of his dresser drawers had been spilled onto his neatly made bed and the doors of the cabinets in his tiny kitchen were all ajar, as were his closet doors. The hallway mirror was cracked, but not in a way that indicated the intruders had done it, since it hadn't been toppled and nothing around it was disturbed.

On the whole, the inside of his house didn't look as bad as my own apartment did when it had been trashed a few months earlier, a direct consequence of my first contract with Matt. Or maybe things just seemed worse when it was my rocker with its rungs in the air and my underwear drawer that was in shambles.

As one whose desk, files, and bookcases contained the equivalent of a medium-sized California redwood, I was surprised to see the little table that seemed to serve as Michael's desk completely free of paper. There was a black plastic holder containing a couple of pens and pencils and a pair of scissors, but the dark brown surface of the table was bare and shiny, as if it had just been polished by an expert.

"There's not even a note pad or a calendar," I said to Matt.

"Not that he'd have much paperwork to deal with in his occupation."

"Still," I said, "not even a scrap of paper in the wastebaskets? I wonder when trash is collected around here."

A set of photographs that Michael had mounted on the largest of his walls caught my eye as the only wall hangings. The prints were apparently all by the same photographer—four identically framed black-and-white shots, with labels in smooth calligraphy, indicating their significance in the architectural history of Bari.

I stood in front of the wall as if I were at a shrine, a testimony to Michael's love of his hometown in Italy. Three small prints, about eight by ten, were arranged at eye level—photographs of the Basilica of San Nicola, the Svevo Castle, and the convent of St. Scholastica.

The fourth print, about sixteen by twenty-four, was set apart from the others—an aerial view of Bari's port, Porto Vecchio. I allowed myself to enjoy the artistic composition of the photograph. Neat rows of square white buildings formed a top and left side border, with small boats looking like radii coming and going from a triangular land base at the center of the picture.

I'd been to Italy several times, though not to Bari, and my mind wandered back to those trips. I remembered my astonishment at seeing the Leaning Tower of Pisa. The angle of tilt was much more dramatic than I expected. I pictured Galileo performing his legendary experiments from the top of the tower and made a note to check the latest research about whether he'd actually done them. Expert opinions about that seemed to vary from year to year.

"Here's something," Matt said, interrupting my meditation on the history of science. He pulled a note from under a refrigerator magnet shaped like a bunch of grapes and showed me a small piece of paper that appeared to have been torn from a yellow lined pad. I recognized the handwriting as that of someone from the old country, with differences in line width showing up even though it had been written with a felt-tip pen. The paper had one phrase on it, "Martello, 11," with an initial that could have been an I or an L in front of it.

Matt riffled the pages of his notebook as if it were a child's flip book. "Don't see a name like that, and it doesn't ring a bell," he said, sticking the scrap of paper into the binding of the notebook.

Matt and I stood in the center of Michael's kitchen, on his worn but spotless linoleum, and addressed a series of rhetorical questions and answers to ourselves as much as to each other.

"If he were blackmailing someone named Martello, would he write it down and post it on his refrigerator?" I asked.

"Maybe just as a reminder of what he thought was a windfall coming his way," Matt said. "But if the breaking and entering was done by the murderer, would he or his people have missed this note? It's in plain sight."

"Or *she* or *her* people."

"I can see why you'd say that, considering your recent collars."

I smiled at Matt's reference to my service record in uncovering female felons.

After about an hour of searching through Michael's meager belongings, we left the house. I was especially disappointed that we hadn't found a single equation scratched out on a napkin, or perhaps a lithium battery schematic with incriminating words underlined. As it turned out, the only thing we carried away from the house was the Martello note and a piece of trash from the lawn. Not only had we nearly struck out on clues to Michael's killer, but my RPD contract was in jeopardy.

By the time we finished, it was past four o'clock. I considered asking Matt to dinner later, but it wasn't our usual pattern to see each other on weeknights. Even though I was retired and Matt's job was not based on a nine-to-five, Monday-to-Friday week, we kept to a standing arrangement for getting together on weekends—Friday nights and Sunday afternoons—as if it were a crime for us to abandon 1956 protocol.

So far we'd only been interrupted by Matt's pager a few times as we ate dinner or sat in a jazz club or played cards with Rose and Frank.

"I'll see you tomorrow night?" Matt asked as he pulled up to Galigani's, putting an end to my half-formed, crazy idea of a Thursday-night date.

"Tomorrow night," I said. "Wild and furious canasta."

BACK IN MY APARTMENT, once again in navy blue and gray fleece, I put off starting a COURTSHIP notebook and opened the one I already had, labeled DERAMO. I recorded my few impressions from the afternoon's work. I wrote "L./I.? Martello" at the top of a page and listed the possible relationships to Michael. It seemed likely that it was someone named Martello that he went to meet the night he was murdered. I didn't bother with the phone book, since I knew that Matt would have people on the obvious trails right away—relatives, neighbors, the workforce at the lab. I couldn't seem to dismiss the idea that there was somewhere else to take that lead.

I finally noticed a blinking light on my answering machine and played back three messages. I was happy to hear Elaine Cody's voice, not so happy to hear Peter Mastrone's, and neutral about my cousin Mary Ann's. I indulged myself, taking a cup of coffee to my rocker, and called Elaine first. I punched in her number at work in Berkeley, where it was only two in the afternoon.

I pictured Elaine at her desk, dressed in a sharp power suit, even though she worked in a low-bid government facility with mass-produced, colorless steel furnishings. Elaine was a technical editor, the most well-read of my friends, who'd tried in vain to expand my reading taste to include more than scientific biographies and magazines like *Physics Today* and *Technology Update*. Once she'd talked me into taking a night class with her in contemporary fiction, but by the third week of reading "experimental novels" I'd strayed across the hall to listen in on a statistics course.

"Well, I have another contract with the RPD," I told her in response to "What's new?"

"Has Revere's homicide rate always been so high, or is it just your good luck?"

"Are those my only choices?"

"No, I guess not," Elaine said with a laugh. "And my real reason for calling is to see if you have time for a visitor. I have some frequent-flyer miles that I'll lose if I don't use them by the end of June."

"Wonderful. Of course I have time. You mean you're willing to come back to this apartment?"

Elaine had visited me in Revere only once, when I first returned to the East Coast. As it happened, that week the Galigani Mortuary had an extra-high client count, with wakes overflowing into the rooms usually reserved for showing caskets or storing extra chairs and supplies. Elaine proclaimed her distaste for funeral homes as places of permanent residence and vowed not to return until I had a "real apartment."

"Maybe I can help you pack?" Elaine asked.

I knew immediately that Elaine was talking about my returning to California, not simply moving to another building in Revere. My time was almost up, she'd reminded me often in the last few weeks, since I'd promised to reevaluate my move after a year. I'd kept my resolve not to visit the West Coast for at least that long to give myself an even chance to make a good decision about where to spend my next thirty years.

In my mind, I'd flunked decision-making all my adult life, thanks to Josephine, who'd allowed me no practice as a child or a teenager.

"You don't want to go roller skating," she'd say. "You'd be no good at it. You're so clumsy." I wished she'd explained what I found out much later—that we couldn't afford roller skating, or piano lessons, or whatever else I thought I wanted—instead of using a tactic that destroyed my self-confidence and my ability to decide things for myself.

I knew in the end I'd make the choice about where to live the way I made all the big decisions of my life—impulsively, in direct contradiction to my professional training in mathematics and science. When I was twenty, I'd become engaged to a man who was entirely wrong for me, then run three thousand miles away when he died. I often wondered if I'd come back to Revere thinking I could start over, resetting my counter to zeros. I might as well have used a dartboard to plan my life, I thought.

"Are you still there?" Elaine asked. "Don't hang up. I'll stop pressuring you, I promise."

"It's not that. I'm a little distracted right now. And things are going well with Matt," I said, as if that were the answer to the question about where I wanted to live. At the idea that I might be making a decision based on my relationship with Matt, I felt a flush of red that Elaine probably could have predicted.

"Going well, huh? Does that mean you've finally gone past the theory stage and into experiments?"

"Elaine." By this time I felt my flush had spread far enough to span the distance of the forty-plus states between us.

"None of my business, I know. I just want to keep up on things. Besides, if this is getting serious, I'd better come and check him out personally. We'll see if he passes my 'good husband material' test."

Our laughter came so quickly I didn't have a chance to remind her that I'd been her maid of honor at two weddings. She'd married, in turn, a Berkeley lab engineer and a struggling artist from San Francisco. My personal favorite was a third man, to whom she'd been engaged but had never married—a French chemist in California on sabbatical leave from his Parisian university. Neither of the marriages, nor the betrothal, had lasted more than a year or so, and Elaine had vowed there'd never be a fourth engagement.

I knew for a fact, however, that Elaine didn't blame her mother for her poor judgment in husbands. Apparently I was the only one with a clear vision of where my faults came from.

Elaine and I talked for another half hour, discussing mutual friends and setting a tentative date for her visit. When we hung up I was in a pleasant mood, unwilling to spoil it by returning Peter's call. I assuaged my guilt over this by planning to work on his class instead, right after a call to my cousin.

Mary Ann Sarno was a widow, about the same age as Michael Deramo, it occurred to me, in her early seventies. She'd moved out of Revere when her husband's job with the Massachusetts Correctional Institution took them to Framingham, Massachusetts, near Worcester—"Wusta," as my Revere friends called it. Too bad cousin Louie Sarno wasn't still alive to tutor me on the penal code and related criminal procedures, I thought. I was sure I hadn't appreciated him and his professional knowledge enough in my youth.

I guessed Mary Ann and I both thought we'd see more of each other when I returned to Massachusetts, but it became clear on my first visit to her home that we had little in common. Worcester, about thirty miles from Revere, was as far as Mary Ann had ever traveled, and her thinking had stayed put also. She didn't approve of my new lifestyle, which she saw as dangerous and unbecoming to a woman. And she didn't know the half of it, I thought, since I never gave her any details about the physical confrontations that had marked the conclusions of my previous RPD contracts.

Mary Ann's answering-machine message to me was short and jerky, a sign of her discomfort with technology.

"This is your cousin. Uh, call me back," she'd said to my

computer chip in a halting, staccato cadence with several in-
tervening throat-clearing sounds.

I punched in Mary Ann's number and reached her on the
first ring.

"Your friend Rose called and invited me to your party,"
Mary Ann said.

Leave it to Rose, I thought. I hadn't officially agreed to her
idea of an anniversary party for me, to celebrate my one year
back in Revere. One way to guarantee my consent was to
have already invited the guests.

"Do you think you'll be able to come?" I asked, fairly
sure of the answer.

"Oh, no. It's too late in the day. And you never know what
the weather will be like."

"Well, maybe some other time." No use reminding Mary
Ann that it would surely break records if there was a snow-
storm on Route 9 in the middle of May. "Have you been
feeling all right?" I asked her.

"My arthritis is getting worse. I can hardly climb the few
stairs to the church, and I don't know how much longer I'll
be able to knit. My fingers are very bad."

"I'm sorry to hear that."

I hung up with Mary Ann soon after she finished with her
inventory of ills. I chose to think that her negative attitude,
which she'd had as long as I'd known her, had less to do with
her age than with her outlook on life, formed at a time when
women had few choices and little to keep their mental abilities
alive. I made a note to tell Rose that her plan to seal the fate
of the anniversary party by inviting a guest from far away had
failed.

Now that it was Peter's turn for my attention, I booted up
my computer to work on my notes for his class, a much more
pleasant prospect than talking to him.

I surfed the net for a quote by Maria Agnesi, disappointed
to find only discussions about her, nothing attributed to Maria

herself. I made a note to mention that Maria had written a mathematics text for her younger brothers. Fifty years later it was still the most complete mathematical text in existence, covering what was known at the time of algebra, geometry, and the newly invented calculus. She accomplished this when she was only twenty, about the same age I was when I became engaged to a man I later learned was tied to organized crime. I didn't plan to include that personal comparison in my talk.

Before I could finish my visual aids, I needed some notes from my briefcase, and, in the familiar chain reaction that usually motivates my doing housework, I had to clean out my briefcase before I could locate the notes.

I pulled out the napkins from Kelley's, some cough drops that were permanently stuck to their wrappers, and stray tissues decorated with pieces of black lint from the lining of the bag. Eventually I found the Maria Agnesi notes I was looking for in one of the zippered sections, but I finished cleaning out the briefcase anyway. The last thing I extricated from the side pocket was the piece of paper I'd found on the lawn in front of Michael's house.

Curious, I smoothed out the yellow lined paper into an eight-and-a-half-by-eleven sheet. I noticed the same style of script as that on the scrap of paper from the door of Michael's refrigerator. This note was much longer, however. Its sentences were choppy, with many words crossed out and written over. It was what Elaine would call a rough first draft.

I remembered how my father—uneducated, like Michael—wrote drafts like this when he sent letters to his relatives in Italy, or even if he was writing a postcard. He'd practice first, on a piece of scrap paper, then copy it onto the stationery or card. I wondered what my father would have thought about the clean, swift editing made possible by word processors.

I looked at the paper in front of me, picturing how it must have spilled out of Michael's confiscated trash.

"Dear Francis," it read, "I'm comming into some money."

The next words that were legible were "you won be ashamt of me," and farther down on the page, "if they ask you tell them you give it to me."

Although it was a stretch to go from this letter to the conclusion that Francis Deramo had murdered his father, it seemed clear that he was being told about a payoff scheme that would ultimately affect his own career as a patent attorney and his standing in his profession. If it had been a payoff, and if Michael had lived to finish the letter, and if he had ever mailed it. Even with all the ifs, I was very excited about a possible lead and picked up the phone to call Matt.

"I have something you should see," I said, explaining the evidence and how I came to have it in my briefcase.

"I wonder which of my uniforms is not as good a housekeeper as you are," he said. "I'll come and get it. Uh—do you have plans for dinner? It's almost that time."

"I guess it is," I said. "I could do a ratatouille."

"Sounds good. I'll pick up a few things to go with it and be there in a half hour."

So soon after midday smooching, another breakthrough, I thought. A Thursday-evening dinner date.

FIVE

I LOADED A CD of Charlie Parker, one of Matt's favorite jazz artists, while I sliced zucchini, tomatoes, and eggplant. My choice of music was a response to Matt's playing a collection of Verdi arias for me on the one occasion that I'd visited his house. Our own game of trying to please each other.

Matt told me he'd lost the habit of entertaining guests, having let his house go to ruin, in his words, since his wife's death.

"I've cleaned it out a little bit for you," he said, after inviting me in for coffee one afternoon.

"You don't have to do this," I'd said. "We can go to Sabrine's, or to my place."

"I want you to see where I live. Just don't expect much."

Matt's home, near the center of Revere, not far off Broadway, was more or less what I pictured a bachelor environment would be, with not much attention to adornment, or to good lighting for that matter. I saw no photographs and wondered if he'd removed those of his wife, Teresa, on my account. I'd allowed myself a moment of mental redecorating, picturing the two of us brightening the decor and cleaning out the cluttered corners.

Back in the present at my cutting board, I mulled over whether to tell Matt about my meeting with Andrea Cabrini at the lab the next day. Not that there was any big deal about having lunch with an old friend, I told myself, nearly choking on my rationalization. I took out a large aluminum bowl and watched the vegetable colors mix as I tossed them, as if they represented my choices. Zucchini green was yes, tomato red no, and eggplant purple maybe.

My pattern had been to keep Matt in the dark about any activity that was borderline as far as my contract duties, or anything that might cause him to worry about my safety. By the time I heard his knock on my door, I hadn't come up with any reason to change that pattern. Before I let him in, I did a quick visual sweep of my apartment, checking for telltale signs of my undercover work. I hoped that the aroma of oregano masked the fishy odor of my deceit.

Matt brought bread and salad ingredients, a six-pack of nonalcoholic beer for himself, and sparkling cider for me. From our first dinner together, we'd realized that we might be the only two Italian-Americans we knew who didn't like wine. Matt's reason was more dramatic than mine—he'd watched his father die of liver disease from alcohol abuse. I simply didn't like the taste, probably because the wine my father made in our cellar when I was a child burned my tongue.

"You've done it again, Gloria," Matt said, picking up Michael's draft letter from my desk.

"I was just there first," I said. "You would have seen it eventually."

"I don't know. I didn't have Josephine's neatness training."

"Well, what do you think of it?"

"I've just read Francis Deramo's statement to Berger. It certainly doesn't fit with his receiving a letter like this from his father. But we don't know that it was ever completed, or mailed, either."

"But it does suggest that Michael was involved in some kind of blackmail scheme," I said, "which would most likely be related to the lab." I stopped short of saying "and thus my business," but Matt seemed to know what I was getting at.

"It does. And, yes, it's probably a good idea to have you

come out to the lab when I talk to Fred Laughton and John Hammer."

"To whom?" I asked, not wanting to reveal that Andrea had already told me about the lithium program leaders. I wondered if it showed on my face that I'd already started a mental search of the web for their curriculum vitae.

"Drs. Laughton and Hammer are the two investigators Deramo spent the most time with. That is, his main assignment was to clean their offices and labs. Would you be free for a noon meeting tomorrow?" Matt asked, as we sat in front of my new blue placemats. "These guys are busy and can only spare their lunch hour."

I probably would have dropped the fork anyway, but it seemed to coincide with my sharp intake of breath at the mention of Friday's lunch hour. Oh well, I thought, I guess it's the zucchini option.

"I'm already booked for lunch," I said. "I have a meeting with Andrea Cabrini."

It took Matt a minute to register Andrea's name and search his brain for a match. I hoped he'd be pleased that I was building up my informant base. Then, for the first time in weeks, I heard his peculiar laugh, the one that sounded like "whoa." I considered it his equivalent of "aha."

"I was going to tell you," I said, covering two thirds of the options I'd entertained. "I thought she might be able to tell me about the lab's lithium program."

"Sometimes I think I'm working for you," he said.

My eyes widened, but as I was about to press for details, my phone rang, and I had to be content with the sight of Matt's smile, which I took as a sign that I wasn't in serious trouble.

Peter Mastrone's voice came as an unwelcome intrusion into the pleasant domestic scene I'd been relishing. As I heard the edge of annoyance in my "Hello, Peter," I felt guilty.

For this feeling, I blamed Pope Pius XII and Sister Claire Marie of St. Anthony's, both long since dead.

"Did you get my message, Gloria?" Peter asked, as no thoughtful person would have, in my opinion.

"Of course I got it," I wanted to say. "My answering machine works. You can always count on technology, but never on me."

"I've been busy working on your class for next week, Peter" is what I actually said.

"That's why I'm calling. I thought we might get together this weekend and talk about it."

"It's the same group of students, isn't it? Italian 401?"

"Yes, but it's the last class of the year, and I thought we'd do something special."

"I'm in the middle of something right now," I said. "Will you be home later?"

"How's your vocabulary review coming along? Are you ready for a new list?"

"Not yet, Peter, but thanks for reminding me to study. Can I call you back?"

Peter had been instrumental in my rediscovering the language of my ancestors. Four years of Italian grammar at Revere High School gave me a good foundation in sentence structure and the sequence of tenses, but I'd lost nearly all my vocabulary skills during my years away. In my California neighborhood, I could have done all my banking and grocery shopping in Spanish, Mandarin, or Cantonese, but not Italian.

I was grateful to Peter for setting up a self-study program for me, somewhat more sophisticated than a "word a day" calendar. But not so grateful that I could suppress my feeling of annoyance. I tried to think of the Italian word for "pest," but could only come up with *insetto*, which referred to the tiny airborne kind.

"You have company," Peter said, in an accusing tone.

"Yes, I do."

"The cop?"

I decided that Peter had his own notebook, labeled AG-GRAVATIONS. Not that there was anything wrong with cops, or the word "cop," but when Peter used it to describe Matt, the word sounded more like "lowlife."

I swallowed hard and tried again.

"Can I call you later?"

"I thought that was just a weekend thing," Peter said, as if he were referring to required military reserve duty.

"Or maybe tomorrow morning?" I was proud of myself for staying on track and not treating Peter like the cranky adolescent he sounded like, but this time I had a tentative plan to hang up if he didn't answer appropriately.

"I have a free period at ten," he said, finally responding directly to my question. "I'll be in the faculty lounge. You have the number."

"I'll call you at ten," I said. When I hung up the phone, my fingers ached as if I'd just finished a round of tightening bolts on my lab bench.

I looked at Matt, who was wandering around my apartment, his habit when I was on the phone. I'd stopped wondering if he approved of my eclectic decor, simple and comfortable, with not too many matching pieces other than the glide rockers I'd brought from California. And I hardly cared anymore if I'd left a piece of underwear in view. When I organize that COURTSHIP notebook, I thought, I'll record these milestones.

"Peter?" Matt asked.

"Yes."

"Should I be feeling guilty?"

"No, he should," I said, putting the finishing touches of garnish on a platter of ratatouille and noodles.

We covered several topics unrelated to police business while we managed to finish the entire bowl of vegetables and pasta and nearly half a loaf of bread. Matt had heard from

Rose that I was resisting the idea of an anniversary party, and he appeared to be on my side.

"I'm not much for parties," he said, telling me nothing I didn't know, and nothing I didn't feel myself. With Mary Ann a "no" on the guest list, we thought about keeping the celebration to a simple dinner for the four of us in Boston.

"Rose is easily manipulated," I said.

"Any particular strategy?"

"I'll promise her a shopping trip for new dresses for both her and me, for one thing."

Matt laughed at my solution, but the end of the meal seemed to be his signal to get down to business.

"So, where were we?" he asked. "Andrea Cabrini."

"Oh, yes, you remember her—the technician we met last fall."

"I remember her. Do you have lunch with her regularly?"

"Uh, I'm sure I can change the time to free myself for a noon meeting with Laughton and Hammer. I just thought I'd see how she was," I said, waving my glass of water in the air to give a breezy feel to my statement.

Matt's sideways glance told me he wasn't convinced. I wasted no more time.

"The truth? I thought she might have some inside information about how the lithium scientists are handling the waste from the battery research."

"And waste handling is a good candidate for blackmail?"

"I'm glad you asked," I said, pushing my chair back from the table. "Are you ready for after-dinner science?"

Matt blew his breath into his cheeks. "I'm more ready for a nap, but I'll give it a try."

I heard him snicker as I dragged out a small easel and a pad of newsprint I'd bought for just such occasions in a moment of optimism about my future as a police consultant. One of the best parts of my new career was the chance to cultivate science literacy among Revere's law enforcement professionals.

"You should have been a teacher, Gloria."

"I don't think so," I said. "I'm only comfortable one-on-one. It took me quite a while to get used to talking to Peter's class. And once a month is plenty for that."

I drew circles to represent the lithium atom, with three electrons surrounding the nucleus, and explained how a lithium ion was different from lithium metal. I drew an X through one electron to show that the lithium ion had lost an electron.

"Lithium ion batteries are safer than ones using lithium metal, which is highly reactive," I told Matt, "but for either kind, you need to follow strict guidelines for safety."

"What about the battery in my car? Is that hazardous material?"

"That's not a lithium battery, but all batteries are potentially hazardous to people if they're not used with care, and they pose great risk to the environment if they're not disposed of properly."

Matt stifled a yawn, but I continued, confident of the exciting material I was covering.

"One big difference is that your car battery is consumer-friendly. It's been packaged for maximum safety, unlike the battery systems researchers work with. Commercial batteries are manufactured with features like special circuits and fuses to protect them from overdischarging. They also have safety valves, and a device to stop the flow of electricity when the temperature exceeds a certain level."

Matt put his fist to his mouth to hide a second yawn, so I put down my marker, which had turned out to be not as useful as my hands during my presentation.

"Ready for dessert?" I asked him. "I have lemon cookies and biscotti, both from Luberto's." Matt and I were big fans of Luberto's Bakery, located perilously close to the police station.

"With a little sugar, I can take another few minutes. I'll make the coffee."

"I just want to cover one more point," I said, while Matt opened a package of biscotti. I continued in spite of the delicious, distracting odor of anise overwhelming my nostrils.

"Here's one possible way the Charger Street lab might be in trouble—they could be ignoring disposal regulations. Right now there are two ways to deal with expired batteries or the waste from battery research that are safe and legal."

I turned over to a clean sheet of newsprint and wrote

1. Recycle.
2. Treat.

"Many private companies will pick up your waste and recycle it for you. And some will chemically treat your lithium waste or any other waste, for that matter, so that you can then dispose of it safely."

"If it's so easy, why would anyone not follow the regulations?"

"Sometimes it's even easier to cheat, and certainly less expensive. I guess it's the same reason anyone breaks a law, big or little. And for scientists a key issue is time. It takes time away from research to deal with safety concerns."

Matt brought coffee and a plate of biscotti to the couch, and I was ready to relinquish my podium. I had one more answer to his last question, however, and it was one I hated to admit.

"There's ego, too," I said, "and elitism. Researchers have traditionally considered themselves above the law, as if their work were more important than the rules and regulations, especially ones made by nonscientists. Sometimes scientists think they know better than the lawmakers."

"I'm thinking of the Manhattan Project," Matt said.

"Those guys didn't have to answer for anything. It was as if they were priests."

"Those days are over."

"For both scientists and priests," we said almost in unison.

OUR FIRST weekday-evening date was cut short when Matt's pager started to vibrate, soon after the lithium lesson.

"I'm still not used to this thing," he said when he finally realized what was tickling his middle.

I cleared the remains of our meal while Matt called the station.

"Berger needs some help downtown, so I'd better go," he said when he'd hung up. He pointed to the counter full of dirty dishes and screwed up his nose. "Sorry to leave you with this," he said, and then, with a smile and a hug, "I'm sorry to leave you at all."

I felt as if I were wearing an electronic receiver, too—a full-body pager that had just gone off. When Matt left, I stood leaning against the door for a long time.

SIX

I CALLED ANDREA first thing Friday morning, the perfect excuse for skipping my exercise bicycle routine—if you could call anything as sporadic as my fitness sessions "routine."

"Thanks for being so flexible," I said to her, after rescheduling our meeting for ten-thirty.

"There's a new cappuccino wagon in the main cafeteria," she said. "I'll meet you there. I did some checking around and I have a few things to tell you."

I was more excited about the "few things" than about the espresso machine. In my experience, institutional coffee, with or without foam, was for emergency use only.

I put on my black suit and a white silk blouse. One of my nun outfits, as Rose called them. I was sure the pendant I looped around my neck brightened the presentation dramatically. From a distance, it looked like a simple piece of multicolored glass circled in a gold frame, but when you got up close, a hologram of Albert Einstein's head came into view. I knew I was overdressed for the lab, but at my age and weight, I couldn't wear anything too casual without looking like a street person.

It was a perfect seventy-five-degree spring morning, I was on a case, and I had a canasta date for the evening with the Galiganis and Matt, the three people I cared most about. I was feeling so good that Josephine felt she had to make an appearance. *Don't get too cocky,* she whispered, as I locked my apartment. *You could get hit by a car. And these friends of yours could turn on you at any minute.* Though I no longer fully believed her, I relaxed the wide smile on my face and slowed my pace as I walked down the stairs and into the Galigani garage.

I drowned out Josephine's voice, at least temporarily, by a touch of the FM button in my Cadillac, surrounding myself with magnificent music that sounded familiar but I couldn't identify. I was finally getting used to the enormous car Rose and Frank had handed down to me when they bought a new fleet in the fall. For the first few months, I was embarrassed to be seen in the long black luxury vehicle. Or maybe I was thinking of its history, carrying grief-stricken widows and perhaps an occasional newly deceased "client" of the mortuary.

"You need a serious car," Rose had said, using her hand to wave away my objection and drying her carefully painted fire-engine-red nails at the same time. "Don't you remember how people drive around here?"

"Everyone will be expecting a prom queen to exit," I told Rose.

"Never mind. You wait. Someday that car will protect you and you'll be grateful."

The radio announcer told me that it was Vivaldi's *Four Seasons* coming out of the six speakers in my car as I headed north to the Charger Street lab, where I had not one but two meetings of the kind I liked. *Think about that, Josephine.*

I parked my Cadillac in a single, normal-sized, close-in spot, another sign that I was becoming accustomed to its girth and to stepping from it in public, and entered the building by the cafeteria door.

I was greeted by stale lunch smells—a mixture of mustard and raw onions and mashed potatoes with gravy—like the aroma in institutional cafeterias from coast to coast. The walls were painted the usual gray of schools and asylums, with tables and chairs to match.

I saw Andrea Cabrini, in a long-sleeved purple tunic top, standing at the coffee wagon, paying for a drink and a croissant. Her black-and-purple-print pants were wide and shapeless, as if she'd stepped into two bolts of fabric standing side by side. She greeted me with a big smile, half hidden by her cheeks.

"Dr. Lamerino," she said, offering me one hand, her pastry and drink miraculously balanced in the other.

"'Gloria' is fine," I said. "How are you Andrea?"

She looked at the hologram hanging from my gold chain, her smile tilting a bit to the left.

"Eric loved Einstein trinkets," she said, as if that were the answer to how she was, as if she felt only as strong as the memory of her friend, physicist Eric Bensen, who had been murdered in the fall.

"I remember Eric's Einstein statue," I said, putting my hand on her shoulder. I hoped my pendant hadn't reminded her how the statue had made her a suspect in Eric's murder for about an hour.

Andrea had unlawfully entered the Benson crime scene and retrieved the small plastic likeness of Einstein that she'd given Eric for his birthday. I figured that was probably one of the most adventuresome things she'd ever done.

I ordered bottled water—the red-and-white-striped canopy over the wagon didn't trick me into ordering a coffee drink—and we took a table away from the few other patrons. Andrea's long, stringy, dark hair came within a centimeter of dipping into her coffee. I wondered what her reaction would be if I were to suggest a different hairstyle or more stylish clothes. She needs a Rose Galigani in her life, I thought, or an Elaine Cody, and I'm lucky enough to have a personal groomer on each coast.

Andrea took a lab-issue black-and-white faux-marble notebook from her striped canvas bag and opened it to the first page. I was pleased to see the sheet covered with writing, and also happy that she got right down to business once I convinced her I didn't want half her croissant.

"First, the personal stuff," she said. "Michael's son, Francis, is about fifty years old. He's a lawyer and lives in a fancy house in Marblehead, right near the golf course. This is his first marriage but her second. She has money, plus a twenty-year-old son, Andrew Palmer, who's in trouble a lot. He thinks of himself as some kind of star race car driver. I think he's been arrested for assault and battery. Plus, Sylvia, the wife, was a debutante and ashamed of Michael's occupation.''

So far, in spite of her pluses, Andrea hadn't told me much that I didn't already know, but I nodded appreciatively, impressed that she'd put all this together in the short time since our phone call. I was curious about how she'd learned it all, especially the part about Andrew's arrest record, but I didn't want to distract her by asking. Like a good researcher, she came through with her sources voluntarily.

"I got most of this from Nino Sartori, the guy who cleans my wing," Andrea said. "He was good friends with Michael. They both belonged to the Sons of Italy, and they used to eat lunch together all the time."

She had a bite of croissant and a sip of coffee and turned the page in her notebook. Another full sheet, I noticed with pleasure.

"Oh, before I forget. I copied these clippings for you," she said, removing an envelope from deep in her purse. "You can look at them later if you want. Two are about Andrew and two are from the lab's internal newsletters, about the lithium program in general."

"Thank you, Andrea. You've done a wonderful job."

Andrea gave me a broad smile and smoothed down the pages of her notebook, ready for more action.

"Francis is part of his brother-in-law's firm, Richards and Deramo it's called now—that's for Sylvia's brother, Barry Richards. They have an information technology practice. I see them around here a lot."

High-tech patents, I translated to myself. That I didn't know, and Andrea probably noticed that I sat up straighter on my gray metal chair, because she did the same and smiled her awkward smile again. I remembered Rose's quote from Sylvia, about how Michael was playing with "the big boys," certainly an apt term for technology transfer lawyers, or lawyers of any kind, I thought.

A perfect blackmail scheme was taking shape in my head. And Andrea hadn't even finished.

"Their law firm is on line to patent the lithium battery from Laughton and Hammer's program."

"Very interesting, Andrea," I said in a conspiratorial tone, meaning every syllable. Probably not standard police practice, I thought, but certainly acceptable for two women friends at a coffee klatch.

Andrea continued in a softer voice, as if we were moving on to a more sensitive topic.

"Michael told Nino he felt that Francis was turning against him, his own father, just to stay on Barry Richards's good side."

"I wonder what he meant," I said.

"Nino said Francis hardly ever invited Michael to his home anymore. A few times he showed up in the wrong clothes and drank too much, they told him, so he wasn't even included at a big family reunion at the Richards estate last Christmas. Michael found out about it accidentally through his stepgrandson. Things like that. I guess Andrew was the only one who liked Michael."

Unpleasant as it was to hear, the Richards family's reaction didn't sound extreme to me. It didn't seem that long ago that my own father had been told not to wear his work shoes when we visited relatives who'd made it to the suburbs.

Andrea and I agreed on how important all of this would have been to someone of Michael's generation—being accepted by children with more education and financial resources.

"Just because you're in college," my aunts and uncles

would tell me, "don't think you're better than we are." Later I wondered why they worried, knowing of my early training from Josephine, and her daily reminders that I wasn't even as good as anyone else she could think of, let alone better.

I wondered at this new image of the victim, however—arriving in work clothes and getting drunk on expensive champagne. I needed more verification before I'd buy it.

"Maybe I could talk to Nino sometime," I said.

"Sure. I can introduce you."

I took out my notebook to add Sylvia's brother, Barry Richards, to my suspect list, which so far consisted of generic lithium physicists and an unknown person from a note on a refrigerator door.

"Do you know anyone named Martello?" I asked Andrea. "The first name might begin with an I or an L."

Andrea chewed on her white plastic spoon and shook her head. "I can think of a Monatello, but that's the closest. And her first name is Marie. I'll look in the lab phone book," she said, making a note on a new page.

"Do you need a break?" I asked her. "Another coffee?"

"I'm fine. This is the most exciting thing that's happened to me in ages," she said, then covered her mouth and drew in her breath. "That sounds awful. Michael's dead. I didn't really mean it that way."

I thought about how often I'd been in the same situation. It was so easy to hit the "undo" button on a computer, and so impossible to undo anything in real life. I patted her hand, hoping she wouldn't dwell on her indiscretion.

"I know what you meant," I told her.

"I'm sorry about Michael," she said. "But since you called I keep thinking maybe I can help you find his killer. I always wished I could have helped you on Eric's case."

"You're a good technical person, Andrea," I said. "I can see why you're excited to be doing this kind of research too. That doesn't mean you don't feel bad. The best way to help the police is to do the job well, and you can't do that if you're overcome by emotion, so you shouldn't worry if you forget the reason for the research.''

Andrea thanked me for understanding. She was probably unaware that the speech was for me, too.

WE DID TAKE A BREAK for another drink after all, and when we returned to our table, Andrea was ready with what she called ''the technical scoop.''

''Fred Laughton is the head of the lithium program. He's been having a couple of problems lately. Some of this is in the clippings I gave you. The first is technical; the second is environmental. You might say political.''

I took notes as Angela spoke, appreciating how well organized she was.

''The technical problem has to do with their original bonding process for the battery. Evidently there are some impurities that stay trapped at the top of the battery, so they can't honestly market it as viable for the four C's.''

''Computers, cell phones, and…?''

''Camcorders and cordless tools,'' Andrea said. ''Sorry, that's how they talk around here.''

''Every field has its jargon,'' I told her. ''I'm just impressed that you'd know the inside language of another program.''

''I move around a lot,'' she said. ''That's what makes a technician's job interesting. That's how I heard about the impurities. We talk, you know. And we're always looking for new things to do. We read each other's department newsletters, in case there's a job posting we'd like to apply for.''

''I'm impressed anyway.''

''Thank you,'' Andrea said, then quickly moved on, apparently no better than I was at handling compliments. ''The second problem is the waste—you know, the usual trade-off between by-products of research and environmental hazard. Dr. Laughton doesn't understand what all the fuss is about.

He never had to worry about it in the early days of the lab, I guess. He is kind of old."

Andrea had hardly spoken the last words when a look of regret crossed her face.

"Gray hair?" I asked, touching my own, with a smile to put her at ease. I didn't want a second round of self-recrimination.

"I meant old compared to his assistant, John Hammer, the latest technical genius on his staff. The Hammer is a little younger than me, in his mid-twenties, but he already has his Ph.D. and is moving up."

I blinked and shrank back in my seat, as if Andrea had swung a hammer at me.

"What did you call him?"

"Oh, sorry. That's what everyone calls John. 'The Hammer.' Not only because of his name, but because he's so aggressive about his work, his funding efforts. His whole personality is like—well, a hammer."

I'd lost track of Andrea's explanation, my mind deep into an Italian dictionary. I could picture the page of *m*'s as if it were in front of me on the coffee-stained cafeteria table instead of on my own maple end table in my apartment.

Martello, the Italian word for hammer.

It wasn't an I or an L. It was both: Il Martello—the hammer.

SEVEN

IT WAS ALL I COULD DO to bring my meeting with Andrea to an orderly close, at about eleven forty-five. Besides the obvious distraction of having figured out whose name Michael had left under the magnetic grapes on his refrigerator door, my interaction with Italian vocabulary reminded me that I'd promised to call Peter at ten o'clock. I couldn't remember why I was supposed to call him, but I knew he wouldn't be happy with being stood up, whatever the topic.

I struggled to pay attention as Andrea reviewed information she'd collected on an environmental task force assigned to investigate Laughton's waste disposal practices. I was focusing instead on how to contact Matt, and possibly Peter, before our noon interview. Meanwhile, I felt as though hammers were located throughout my body, pounding on my head, my chest, even my knees. My brain reeled at the idea that we might have come up with Michael's killer so quickly.

Getting up from my chair in the middle of one of Andrea's sentences, I apologized and told her that I needed to prepare for my next meeting.

"I hope I've been a little help," she said. "Maybe we can get together again?"

I assured her that I'd learned more from her than I could have imagined, and that I'd be in touch. I was in such a frenzied state that I found myself inviting her to a party.

"A couple of friends of mine are planning a little anniversary celebration for me," I said. "I've been back in this area for a year. It'll be in two weeks or so. Would you like to join us?"

"I'd love to," she said, her face brightening.

Her apparent delight at being asked to a party made up for the distress I felt at my impulsiveness. I hoped Rose would never find out how I'd finally made the decision to go ahead with her celebration—based on my guilt at leaving Andrea so abruptly, and my desire to provide entertainment for a woman I perceived to be a social wallflower.

We gathered our things, and as we moved away from the table, Andrea pointed across the cafeteria at two men entering the do-it-yourself sandwich line.

"There they are, Laughton and Hammer," she said, her elaborate arm gesture reminding me of a late-night television host introducing a team of acrobats.

My eyes followed her arm and her gaze to what looked like a father-and-son duo, both tall and lean, both in khakis and dark polo shirts set off by their fair skin. A major difference was the amount of hair on each head, Laughton's being close to bald. Their lab badges hung from long chains around their necks. In my mind the silver links turned into murder weapons, growing into thick wires, first in Hammer's hand, then in Laughton's. I reasoned that if one of them was involved in a blackmail scheme with Michael, so was the other.

"I can introduce you to them," Andrea said, moving toward the men.

"No. Thanks anyway," I said, shrinking back. "I have to make a phone call first, so I'll wait and meet them when Sergeant Gennaro gets here."

"Your life seems so exciting, Dr.—Gloria," she said, and at that moment I had to agree with her.

I went to a pay phone on the back wall, next to the rest rooms. I turned away from Laughton and Hammer, as if I already knew that they were a murderous team, bent on strangling me in full view of the lunch crowd. I'd started to push the buttons for Matt's pager when I saw him enter the cafeteria, coming through the door beyond the cashier's stand where my suspects were paying for their sandwiches.

In my frustration, I wanted to scream, "Why is everyone early today?" I hung up the phone and walked toward Matt, still hoping to have a moment alone with him, but Laughton and Hammer had already reached him. I caught up with them in time to hear Laughton address Matt.

"Only a visitor would be wearing a suit and tie around here," he said, with a pleasant smile. "I'm Fred Laughton and this is my associate, John Hammer." I looked down at my tuxedolike outfit and realized that they'd probably ID'd me, too.

I pulled out my best professional smile as Matt introduced me as his technical consultant. "Dr. Lamerino is a retired physicist who works with us occasionally," he said.

The two other physicists wrinkled their brows simultaneously, in a response that I was used to. They looked more than ever like a team, and I was surprised that neither of them asked the question written on their faces—something like "Her, a physicist?"

"I tried to call you just now," I said to Matt in a low voice, wrinkling my face, as if I could give him a message with comical eye and jaw movements. We need to develop a private code, I decided, too late for this occasion.

If Matt knew I was itching to give him important news, he didn't let on, and a few minutes later the four of us were seated around a small square table not far from where I'd first heard about the Hammer. To my dismay, Matt declined an offer of lunch, ruling out a private chat in the sandwich line.

As Matt took out his pen and prepared his notebook, a shadow came over the table from behind me. A tall man in a very expensive brown suit—a lab visitor if I'd ever seen one—had joined our group.

"This is Barry Richards," Laughton said. "We thought we should have our lawyer here while we're being questioned by the police." At that Laughton laughed at his own joke, and Hammer and Richards joined him.

Matt and I were introduced to the overly pleasant Richards, in his late fifties like Laughton, I guessed, and also balding. His smile was not unlike that of the man on television who tries to convince you that you need aluminum siding or more life insurance.

"Fred and John invited me to your meeting to stand guard over our little industrial secrets," Richards said, nodding to Laughton and causing another round of laughter among the three men. I noticed that Richards had a long, narrow birthmark on the side of his neck, and I wondered if that was why he was wearing a shirt with an extra-high collar.

"I know you're all busy," Matt said, clicking his pen. He hadn't joined in either of the laughing sessions, maintaining a pleasant but businesslike expression. "We'll make this as brief as possible. I'd just like to get a feel for the kind of work you do, since Mr. Deramo worked in your area. Dr. Lamerino is here to help me with any questions I might have later, so I don't need to bother you again."

The two blackmail victims, as I thought of them, had started eating from their plates of thick sandwiches, pickles, and potato chips. Hammer had enough light brown hair for all of the men at the table, and he kept brushing it back from his forehead.

"He didn't exactly work with us," Hammer said, with a laugh that annoyed me.

Just what the world needs, I thought, another haughty physicist. Richards had brought a cup of lab coffee to the party and squeezed in on Matt's side of the table.

"Even janitors contribute in their own little way," Richards said, hitting a ten on my personal Richter scale of condescending behavior.

Matt seemed able to ignore the comment even though their shoulders were touching and Richards was leaning his large head into Matt's notebook.

"Is there anyone you can think of who might have had a grievance with Mr. Deramo?"

"I thought it was a routine mugging," the young hammer said.

No mugging is routine, I wanted to tell him, my fists clenched on my lap, especially if it ends in the death of an old man. Matt said no such thing.

"We like to cover all bases," he said. "I'm sure you can understand that."

"Mike was a nice old man," Laughton said. "I know Carlo Massimo, his supervisor, liked him a lot—gave him our used furniture and time off whenever he wanted it."

Matt wrote in his notebook, as if everything his interviewees said had enormous weight.

"We're wondering if there's anything Mr. Deramo could have heard or seen during the course of his work in your building that might have gotten him into trouble," Matt said.

"Not a thing," Laughton said, shaking his head. "As John said, he wasn't an associate. He cleaned the building. And the police have already been through Mr. Deramo's locker and broom closet."

Hearing Laughton spit out the word "Mr.," as if Michael hardly deserved the title, I decided I'd had enough of the kind of behavior that gives scientists a bad name. Also, as unappetizing as I found the smell of pickles, the food under my nose was making me hungry enough to want to speed things along so I could leave to have lunch with Matt in a real restaurant.

"What's the status of the investigation into your waste disposal practices?" I asked. "I understand there's a task force examining your program and procedures."

The four men looked at me with different degrees of surprise. I gave Matt what I thought was an apologetic look, as if to say, "I know this is your interview, but I have some hot news." After more time than one might expect from the two

sharp people to whom my question was addressed, Laughton
answered.

"The investigation is routine."

Like a mugging? I wanted to ask.

"They do this every time new regulations come along,"
Hammer said. "And in any case, I can't imagine what it
would have to do with a janitor."

For about ten minutes, I quizzed Laughton and Hammer on
how their program accounted for the wastes they generated,
trying to determine how far they would go to protect their
potential for entering the worldwide lithium market. I watched
Laughton, Hammer, and Richards for telltale signs of nervousness, but I had only limited resources to call on as far as
interview techniques went.

I remembered reading that guilty people often fiddle with
their jewelry, cross and uncross their legs, and have difficulty
maintaining eye contact. When I saw Laughton tapping his
fingers on the table and Richards picking at the edges of the
handkerchief in his outside breast pocket, I gave them one
guilty point each, but then abandoned the project. I found I
couldn't keep track of my own part of the conversation and
scrutinize the suspects at the same time. Did Matt and his
colleagues have special training, I wondered, or were they
natural multitaskers?

Thanks to Andrea's insight into their technical problems, I
had ammunition for a new tack and opened the subject of
impurities in Laughton and Hammer's research batteries. My
goal was to intimidate them, thus making them more vulner-
able when Matt moved in with the tough questions, like what
were they doing between ten and midnight on Wednesday.
This was more or less our version of bad-cop-good-cop,
which had served us well in the past. I enjoyed it a bit more
than usual this time.

For some reason, Matt seemed to take only a casual interest
in the conversation, not picking up my cues. He made a few

notes, while Laughton and Hammer became more and more animated about their impeccable research practices. Richards kept himself busy writing in a small book and drinking coffee, but didn't add anything to the conversation.

I kept trying to jog Matt into action with comments like "I suppose a hefty fine for noncompliance would set your research back dramatically." He didn't even budge when I mentioned possible delays in the patent for the battery.

Finally I figured out a way to play my ace.

"Dr. Martello," I said, looking at John Hammer, "do you have a copy of the new federal regulations for hazardous waste?"

Hammer and Laughton squinted at the name I used. Matt and Richards put down their pens and stared at me.

"Oh, I'm sorry," I said rotating my head to take in all the men at the table. "I'm studying Italian vocabulary as a kind of hobby, and I got confused for a minute. Did you know that the Italian word for 'hammer' is *martello?*"

Matt cleared his throat and straightened his tie, giving me a slight nod.

"Did you know that, Dr. Hammer?" he asked.

Hammer shook his head, apparently oblivious to the significance of the translation.

"No, I didn't," he said, screwing up the side of his mouth as if this were one more nuisance question from a dumb cop and his sidekick. To me his answer meant that he could have been in Michael's kitchen, not recognized that the note on the refrigerator had his name on it, and thought it harmless enough to leave behind. Maybe he thought Michael was reminding himself to buy beer, I thought, with a slight feeling of superiority.

"One more question and we'll be through here," Matt said. "Just routine. I need to ask you both where you were the night Mr. Deramo was killed."

"We were—" Hammer began.

"Exactly when was that?" Laughton asked, putting his hand in front of Hammer's chest, as if to restrain him from a sudden stop.

"Wednesday night, sometime after dinner, probably before midnight," Matt said.

Laughton and Hammer strained their necks in their tieless shirts, their faces flushed, their jaws tense. Even without interview training I could pick up on those signs.

"We were here, working late," Laughton said.

"Both of you?"

"Yes."

"Was anyone else around?"

"No, just the two of us," Laughton said, his attitude much meeker than at the start of the interview. "It happens a lot. We have the major portion of the responsibility for the entire lithium program. The people under us have regular hours, but we don't." Laughton's voice trailed off in the manner of someone who realizes he's trying too hard to defend himself.

"Mr. Richards?" Matt asked, winning a rare look of shock from a lawyer.

"I… I'll have to think a minute," Richards said. "Let's see. I was watching the eleven-o'clock news."

"Anyone with you?"

"My wife was upstairs. She had a migraine and went to bed early."

"Then that's it," Matt said, with a cool flip of his notebook. "I'll be in touch."

Matt and I stood and left the men at the table, pickle juice and crumbs on their plates and worried looks on their faces.

As we walked toward the parking lot, Matt put his hand on my back.

"So, I take it your ten-o'clock meeting with Andrea went well?"

"Very well," I said, and then I took a daring step toward self-congratulation. "Say it, say it," I said.

"Nice work, Gloria," Matt said, with a grin.

"You, too. Did you do that deliberately? Give them such a wide range for the time of death?"

"I did."

"So when Richards pinned down what he was doing at eleven o'clock, that might mean something."

"It might."

We smiled all the way to our separate cars, satisfied with our own and each other's performances.

"WHAT'S NEXT with the inimitable Laughton and Hammer team, plus lawyer?" I asked Matt, sitting across from him at Anzoni's Italian restaurant a half hour later. No rancid mayo and pickle smells here—just the sweet aroma of garlic and roasted peppers on warm focaccia bread.

"I have a feeling I'll be hearing from them," Matt said. "It's pretty clear that Hammer was Michael's eleven-o'clock appointment. I'm going to give him a chance to think things over and see what he comes up with. But even if that's who Michael thought he was meeting, we still have nothing that puts Hammer at the scene, and it doesn't make him the murderer. Nor does it mean either Laughton or Richards was involved."

"You know me," I said, nodding in agreement. "I never want the scientist to be the murderer. I'm happier when it's a little old lady."

"This is a new talent, Gloria—using your knowledge of Italian to decipher a clue, instead of science. Maybe we should add 'bilingual' to your contract. I don't know anyone in the department that's kept up with the language, though a lot of us are first- or second-generation Italian."

"I think it's rare in our generation. Our parents were so intent on having us be Americans. I guess I have Peter to thank for bringing me back to my roots."

No sooner did I get those words out than I remembered

again that I hadn't kept my ten-o'clock appointment to call Peter. I figured a police contract emergency was a good excuse for my delinquency and made a mental note to call right after lunch. Whatever repercussions I'd get from my tardiness, another hour wouldn't make much difference, I figured.

While I was on my Italian track, partly from the old Roman atmosphere of Anzoni's and partly from my victory with Il Martello, I had another idea to pursue.

"That reminds me," I said to Matt. "Do you still have those photographs I saw yesterday—the ones of the crime scene?"

"They're back in my office. And this is related to Italian because...?"

"I want to have another look at the mark in the cement near Michael's hand."

"You think he wrote something in Italian?"

"Why not?"

Matt sat back and waited as our server removed the now spotless plates that had once contained our large sandwiches and replaced them with coffees.

"I'm not about to argue with success," Matt said. "I'll get you copies of the photographs and you feel free to meditate on them. But I am going to ask you to keep your distance from Laughton and Hammer and their lawyer."

"I know—if they are involved, they might not like me at this moment."

"At this moment they don't like you anyway."

"Right. I'll be careful."

Matt sipped his coffee and looked at me, his forehead in a frown, his eyes narrowed. With Anzoni's faux Tiffany lamps behind him and a creeping fern within tickling distance of his neck, the sight reminded me of a typical restaurant scene in a gangster movie, minus the red-checked tablecloth.

"And I should believe you because...?"

"This fill-in-the-blanks is making me tense," I said.

"What's the best way for me to make this clear to you? You can't go around doing police work on your own. You have a short memory."

"Meaning?"

"Meaning how many times in the past year have you been threatened, shot at…"

"I was only shot at once," I said. "And I don't deliberately seek out murder suspects to hang around with."

"So you're not going to Deramo's wake tomorrow afternoon?"

"What can I do, Matt? I live there," I said, showing him the palms of my hands, in a gesture of helplessness.

EIGHT

DRIVING HOME FROM Anzoni's, I rehearsed several different versions of what I'd say to Peter when I finally called him back. Why did I care if he was unhappy, I asked myself. I don't even like him very much anymore. I was annoyed that I'd lived most of my life trying to please everyone I came into contact with, whether I liked the person or not—even waiters and flight attendants, who supposedly got paid to please me. Failing to win Josephine's approval, my inner psychotherapist told me, I struggled to earn it from the rest of the world's population.

I parked on the street in front of my building, since I knew I'd be leaving again in the evening to drive to Rose and Frank's for canasta. I tried to avoid pulling into the garage more than once a day, since it involved the difficult task of squeezing my elephantine car in between the hearse and the mortuary van.

I sneaked a glance into the main parlor as I passed it on the way to my apartment two floors above. A cafeteria-like sign in the doorway, black felt with small white plastic letters, announced the wake for Michael Deramo the next day, but as far as I could see, the large, chair-lined room was empty of people, dead or alive.

I pictured Michael's body still downstairs on a narrow metal table in the prep room where the embalming process took place. I had no happy memories of the basement of the Galigani Mortuary, and I quickly replaced the image with that of Matt in the gray crewneck sweater he'd probably wear to our card party that evening.

I wasn't surprised to find a message from Peter on my answering machine.

"Gloria, it's two o'clock in the afternoon on Friday, and I'm working in the faculty lounge until three," he'd said. "Call me there if you hear this in time. Otherwise at home this evening."

Although there was no "please" in Peter's request, the absence of a snide remark put me in a better frame of mind. I picked up my phone and punched in the number for the faculty lounge.

"I'm so sorry, Peter," I said, as soon as I heard his voice on the line. "I had two meetings, back to back, and this is the first chance I've had to call."

"No problem," he said, to my amazement. "I really just wanted to go over some special plans I have for next Tuesday's class."

"Fine. I'm almost ready with my part. I think you'll all enjoy some of my Maria Agnesi stories."

"I thought we might meet for a short time this evening. I know it's Friday and you play cards later, but we could have an early dinner at Zollo's."

"I'd have to be back here by seven-thirty."

"That won't be a problem. I'll meet you at the restaurant, so you can leave whenever it's comfortable for you. Shall we say six o'clock?"

"Six is good," I said.

As I hung up, I wondered what spell had been cast over me while I accepted Peter's invitation. I attributed it to a combination of Peter's new "no problem" tone and my gratitude to him for the Italian vocabulary lessons that had served me so well earlier in the day. I decided to keep my tuxedo outfit on for dinner. Who knows what I'll give away, I mused, if I'm in my relaxed-fit jeans?

I sat in my rocker and reviewed my Maria Agnesi notes. I thought the students would get a kick out of an anecdote about her adventures as a somnambulist. Often, it was said, she'd go to her study while walking in her sleep and solve a mathematics problem she'd failed to complete when she was awake. In the morning she'd be surprised to find the solution carefully worked out on paper. I wondered if a person could force such a state on herself, the better to solve crimes.

It's worth an experiment, I thought, and closed my eyes to simulate sleep while mentally reviewing the suspects in the Deramo murder. My suspects, I reminded myself, not necessarily the RPD's. Since professional courtesy required me to rule out scientists whenever possible, and I couldn't bear to think that a son would kill his father, only Francis's wife, Sylvia, and her brother, Barry Richards, the family from moneyed Marblehead, survived as potential murderers.

On the fringe of my suspicions was Sylvia's son, Andrew— too young, I thought, and without motive, since, as far as we knew, Michael had died before he collected any money. Michael's landlord, Joe Bargello, and his supervisor, Carlo Massimo, were other possibilities, but also with no apparent reason to kill him. On the whole, however, I decided that it was a good idea to keep everyone on the list for the time being.

My exercise reminded me that I still had another source of information I hadn't tapped—the news clippings Andrea had given me. I found the envelope on my desk and returned with it to my rocker.

The first two were stories from the *Marblehead News* about Andrew Palmer. At the sight of him in a photograph that accompanied one of the articles, I realized it was probably not quite the image a former debutante would wish for her son's debut onto the society pages. A grainy black-and-white shot of Andrew caught him getting into what could have been an overgrown cart, low to the ground and completely open, like a stretched-out motorcycle with four bulky wheels. Andrew was clutching a helmet in one hand, waving at the camera with the other. He appeared trim and fair-skinned, although it was hard to tell from the poor photocopy.

The caption under Andrew's photo read "Local boy wins regional kart title." So, I thought, it is a cart, but how did they let that typo slip by? My question was answered by reading the whole article. Since "kart" was mentioned no fewer than ten times, each time with a *k*, I took it for race car vocabulary. From the context I guessed that karts were the beginners' level of racing car, and that Andrew had excelled at this phase, no doubt with dreams of a spectacular career. The second article told of a skirmish Andrew had gotten involved in at a race, nearly wrecking the car of a driver who beat him in competition. Another cause for a migraine in an upper-crust family.

Sports news always had a numbing effect on me, and reading about race car driving was no exception. I dozed off before I had a chance to read the lithium articles.

I managed to snap myself awake in time to set out for Zollo's. The pseudo-experimental sleeping session had provided no additional insight, leaving me even more impressed by young Maria Agnesi's special powers.

On the way to the restaurant, I played the tape of my most recent vocabulary assignment from Peter, in case he had a pop quiz in mind. As I said the words and phrases out loud, following Peter's recommendation, I had the feeling that there was a connection with Michael Deramo—not any particular idiom, just the nagging idea that I should be paying more attention to a clue. Probably just because this was Michael's language, I decided. But even as I continued my infinitives drill, repeating after Peter's taped voice—*Valere la pena:* to be worth the trouble, *Non cedere di un palmo:* not to budge an inch, *Mettersi nel branco:* to follow the crowd—I found myself hoping Matt would bring the crime scene photographs with him to our canasta date. I needed another look at the graffiti in the cement.

UNLIKE MOST NEW Italian restaurants in Boston and vicinity, Zollo's in Winthrop didn't try to look like the old country, with armless plaster statues and artificial fountains. Zollo's decor was high-tech, its supporting beams exposed, its fixtures chrome and Lucite. Floating shapes of mixed metals hung from the high ceiling and hovered over the tables, giving the appearance of a multivehicle space landing.

Peter, in dark flannel slacks and a starched sport shirt, had taken a table at the back, under a large copper kidney-shaped object. His Sicilian heritage gave him five to six inches over most of my Neapolitan friends, including Matt and Frank Galigani, and when he stood to greet me, he nearly crashed into the modules above him. He bent his lean frame, another Sicilian benefit, and kissed my cheek.

"I hope you didn't get all dressed up for Zollo's," he said.

Oh-oh, I thought, here comes the barb, maybe about looking good to play cards with the cop. But I was wrong. Peter finished with, "You look very nice, Gloria."

I ordered only espresso, in deference to my digestive tract, which needed rest between my large Anzoni's sandwich at my late lunch with Matt and the irresistible dessert I expected at the Galiganis'.

"I want to have a little graduation ceremony for my seniors," Peter said, twirling his linguini with an expertness that didn't surprise me. "They've been with me for four years. I have the music that they'd hear at a graduation in Italy. I've been talking to the people at Luberto's to see about a special cake for after the program."

"I love that idea, Peter. What can I do to help?"

"Well, that's why I've been wanting to talk to you. I hope it's not too late, but it's been hard to get you. I'd like you to make your presentation more like a keynote address at a graduation. You know, stand behind a podium, maybe even wear your doctoral robes?"

"No transparencies or handouts?"

"I suppose you've already prepared them."

"Yes, but it doesn't matter," I said, genuinely moved by Peter's interest in his students as well as his atypical good humor. "I'll rework the presentation this weekend. From what you're saying, I can still keep the Maria Agnesi theme. She was a teenager when she did her greatest work, after all, so it will fit right in."

"Perfect. I really appreciate this, Gloria. I know it will mean a lot to the students."

We talked for a while about individual students that I'd come to know as a result of my monthly visits. I told Peter about one young woman who'd handed me a note privately after a class. She'd written to thank me for inspiring her to continue in science. It was my dream response.

We checked our watches at seven-ten.

"Let me walk you to your car," Peter said, "then I'll come back and settle the bill."

I wasn't too happy about having to adjust my preconceived idea of how my meeting with Peter would go, but I resigned myself to the possibility that he had reformed. In the back of my mind was the nagging feeling that my life would be a lot easier if he hadn't.

MY PLAN WAS to run upstairs and change and leave again in a few minutes, so I parked my Cadillac on Tuttle Street, taking the closest two-car-length spot, about half a block from the mortuary.

As I started the trip to my building, I saw someone out of the corner of my eye, a figure that seemed to literally come out of the bushes at the intersection of Revere and Tuttle Streets. I had the distinct feeling that it was an unfriendly presence. Out of some reflex, I found myself estimating the distance between us and came up with six or seven meters. I resisted turning around to look, although I'd read in an RPD booklet on personal safety in the streets that you should make eye contact with a person you think is following you. The brochure also recommended changing directions and going into a store or public place—useless advice for Tuttle, which was not a through street, and where the only building close to a public place was the mortuary I lived in.

I convinced myself that I was paranoid, still reacting to the Hammer's shifty gray eyes. At seven-forty, it was barely dark. There was enough traffic traveling east, in the direction of the beach, to give me a partial sense of security, but I found myself arranging my car keys in my sweaty hand in the weapons position—the largest key held out straight between my thumb and index finger.

As I turned into my driveway, I had a better look at the figure—definitely male, I decided, not too tall, and a bit on the heavy side. I could see that he was wearing a dark jogging suit with shiny white stripes down the leg of his pants. His hands were in his jacket pockets, the hood pulled low over his forehead. In my opinion, the mild sixty-five-degree May evening didn't call for bundling up that way, except to hide devious intentions. And he wasn't jogging. He seemed to be pacing himself to enter the building with me. The building that was empty, I reminded myself, except for Michael's bloodless corpse.

I had to make up my mind in a few seconds which risk to take—making a fool of myself by screaming, or quietly becoming a killer's next victim. He was closing the gap, and I could swear I heard stalking music in the background, but it was only heavy metal from a passing car stereo.

From the recesses of my mind, where memories of junk television programs have been stored since I was a teenager, I remembered a key phrase: create a diversion. I pushed the red square button on the transmitter attached to my key chain—the panic button—and immediately my trusty Caddie came to life. Its horns blared an incessant, loud monotone and all of its lights—front and back, inside and out—flashed, like the end of World War II.

A young couple walking on the other side of the street stopped to see what was happening and a pickup truck rounding the corner onto Revere Street slowed down, holding up another car behind it. Although it lasted only forty-five seconds, the commotion was evidently enough to discourage my alleged stalker. He took off at a trot down Tuttle Street while I rushed into the building and locked the door behind me.

I congratulated myself on a pretty decent diversion, but not until my breathing returned to normal and my heart stopped pounding. I even managed a smile when I remembered Rose's words as she'd talked me into taking the Cadillac, something about the car protecting me someday.

I went into the main parlor and looked out the window, feeling like what turn-of-the-century Bostonians called "the lace-curtain Irish," snooping on their neighbors. I looked down Tuttle Street as far as the width of the window would allow and couldn't see the "jogger." I pulled up a straight-backed Galigani chair and sat there for another ten minutes, watching the traffic on the street and sidewalk, before going up the stairs and entering my apartment.

As I changed from my black suit into slacks and a sweater, I tried to talk myself out of the queasy feeling in the pit of my stomach. My self-inflicted speech included a reprimand for being so unaware of my neighborhood that I couldn't distinguish one of the residents from a stranger on the street. What would a police safety brochure say about that?

I considered the possibility that the man who'd sent me and my car into hysterics was simply out for a bit of harmless exercise. But then why had he taken off when the car acted up? Everyone else—the innocent people—stopped or slowed at the Caddie's tantrum.

My next hurdle was the walk back to my car. As I tied the lacings on my black suede oxfords, I pictured myself sprinting along Tuttle Street, my thumb poised over the panic button. I was tempted to call Matt and invent an excuse for him to pick me up, but I knew that would be only a short-term solution. I shouldn't even mention this nonincident, I told myself. The only sensible plan was, one, to stop being afraid of my own shadow, and two, to keep working on the investigation and get the real murderer off the street.

It wasn't by coincidence that I scrapped the sweater idea and chose to wear instead the navy-blue RPD sweatshirt that Matt had given me for my birthday in February. Protection by association, I thought. There was no question of my matching the fashion sense of Rose and Frank, anyway, both with impeccable taste in clothes and trim bodies to show them off.

I got to my car without incident, or perceived threat, and locked it immediately. The Galigani home was on the other side of town, close to the Revere-Chelsea line, and I realized I'd be about twenty minutes late, uncharacteristic of me. I had my excuse all ready for when Rose criticized my tardiness— a last-minute meeting with Peter, I'd tell her—but I didn't need it.

"Gloria," she said, greeting me with a hug. "You're never late. You must have been held up at gunpoint."

"You're not far off," I said, smiling as if I'd made a joke.

FOR THE MOST PART, with the good company and the irresistible flaky Italian pastries the Galiganis provided, I was able to take my mind off my supposed stalker. Whenever an image of the person in the jogging suit slipped through, I brushed it off as an unlikely threat. After all, it wasn't as if I'd intimidated anyone to the extent that he or she would want to attack me. So far, except for a bit of harmless questioning at the lab cafeteria, I'd kept a low profile in the investigation of Michael's murder.

Looking at Matt sitting next to me at the card table, I remembered other murder investigations and other, real threats to my life. I had the wild thought that one of the two people I'd helped put in prison on earlier cases might have escaped and come back for revenge. The physical characteristics were too far off, I decided, and gave my attention to arranging a meld from the thirty cards I'd accumulated.

Not for the first time, my partner, Rose, and I lost at canasta, but I went home with winnings that meant a lot to me. Matt had brought me copies of the crime scene photographs; Frank had given me an unedited version of Michael's newspaper obituary, which he'd obtained from his younger son, John, the editor of the *Revere Journal;* and Rose had slipped a plastic container of leftovers into my tote bag as I was leaving.

NINE

ON SATURDAY MORNING, I sat in my bed with coffee and a *svogliatella*, the rich Italian pastry reminding me of a pleasurable evening the night before. I read the longer text of Michael's biography, which contained a few more bits of information than the edited piece that had appeared in Friday's paper. I'd decided to save the gory crime scene photographs for a time when I wasn't involved in food or drink.

The full obituary John Galigani had retrieved for me listed Michael's home town as Bari, a seaport in southern Italy. He'd come to the United States in 1936 when he was a teenager, with his father and younger sister, Lina, three of the nearly twelve million immigrants landing on Ellis Island during its sixty-two years of operation. Lina Deramo had died of tuberculosis shortly after they'd arrived in Revere to join the relatives who'd sent for them. Apparently none of that generation was alive now. Michael had been married briefly to Elena Fiore, who died of pneumonia in the 1940s, leaving Michael with a one-year-old son whom they'd named after Saint Francis of Assisi, the patron saint of Italy.

Francis Deramo, now fifty years old and a successful attorney, had chosen the single-session format for viewing his father's body. Visitors were welcome from one to three o'clock in the afternoon on Saturday, after which there would be a private burial at Holy Family Cemetery. As I read the names of Michael's survivors, Francis and his new family, I thought about how to interview them at the wake without their knowing it. Also, without Matt's knowing it, I reminded myself, since I'd almost promised that I'd keep away from fieldwork this time.

I was convinced Francis had received a rewritten copy of Michael's letter, and I was still very curious about what his wife, Sylvia, meant by Michael's "playing with the big boys." Another big problem I had was the connection between the Laughton and Hammer lithium team and the law firm run by Barry Richards and Francis Deramo. The only thing that wasn't fuzzy in my mind was that Michael's murder was at the center of this maze.

Shifting my files around, I moved on to the two clippings about the lithium program, which I still hadn't read. Andrea had cut them from one of the lab's internal newsletters, written more in the form of technical memos for each department, rather than a newspaper.

The first item referred to a serious decrease in battery efficiency if improvements could not be made in the process used to bond lithium metal and plastic together to create a battery. I figured this was the cause of the impurities Andrea told me about, at the top of the batteries.

The second bulletin had to do with a new vacuum chamber process to deposit lithium, molecule by molecule, onto plastic, creating a spool of lithium battery film. This form of battery held promise for being twenty times more powerful than a conventional battery, the bulletin said. But it was also many years from being viable for commercial use, I guessed, knowing a little bit about the long road from research to development.

As I licked the last *svogliatella* crumb from my finger, I heard the buzz of the intercom in the living room. I got up to answer it, slightly embarrassed, as if Rose could see that I was still in my pajamas and bathrobe while she worked downstairs.

"Are you up?" Rose asked.

"It's almost ten-thirty."

"I guess you're not," Rose said, with a laugh.

"I'm working in bed," I said, feeling justified as I glanced back at my spring-weight maroon-and-white comforter, strewn with papers, clippings, and file folders.

"How would you like to work down here?" Rose asked.

I bent down, closer to the intercom unit and cleared my throat as if to hear better.

"What do you have in mind?"

Not last-minute assistance with Robert Galigani and the embalming fluids in the prep room, I hoped.

"Here's the problem," Rose said. "All the flowers for Michael Deramo have to be rearranged. Evidently there's some pecking order that Martha missed, and the ones that should be on top are on the bottom and et cetera."

Even if I hadn't stopped correcting Rose's grammar a long time ago, I would have let that slip past, eager to hear the bottom line. I wasn't even deterred by the trouble I'd gotten into the last time I'd pinned a black Galigani staff ribbon to my lapel.

"And Martha and the rest of us are all really busy, with the viewing being only a couple of hours away."

"You want me to rearrange the flowers?"

"Essentially, yes," Rose said. "It means you'll have to spend some time with Sylvia, Michael Deramo's daughter-in-law. She wants to personally oversee the job. Are you interested?"

"Only if it will help you out," I said, while neither of us tried to contain our laughter.

I PERFORMED A level-of-effort grooming operation in record time, appearing in Frank Galigani's first-floor office only twelve minutes later. Sylvia Deramo was sitting in the chair across from him, her small frame clothed in a stunning mourning outfit—sheer black stockings and patent leather pumps, and a simple black dress in a warm, draping fabric that looked soft enough to sleep on. I glanced down at my own attempt at stunning simplicity, a black knit pantsuit, and realized that even if I'd had a solid eight-hour day to get ready, I couldn't share a stage with the grieving daughter-in-law.

Frank, on the other hand, was a match for the highest of high fashion, in a dark blue suit, one of his Italian imports. I felt as if I'd been hired for the honor of serving coffee and sweeping up after the two of them.

I wondered how Frank would introduce me, and marveled at his ability to say nothing incriminating, untrue, or offensive, while sounding informative. It was a talent I'd noticed before, which in no way made him less honest in my eyes. More than once as I stumbled through the negotiations of my life, I'd thought of taking lessons from him.

"Gloria Lamerino is our best aide at times like this," Frank said. "She'll work with you until Mr. Deramo's presentation is exactly the way you want it."

"Indeed," Sylvia said in a crisp tone, clearly appraising my imitation clothing. I wanted to tell her I'd just come in from washing the cars in the Galigani motor pool.

I gave her a smile that I hoped inspired confidence and followed her out the door toward the main parlor. I looked back over my shoulder at Frank, who remained standing behind his desk. He gave me the most surreptitious thumbs-up I'd ever seen.

"I'm so sorry about your father-in-law," I said to Sylvia's back, with no smoothness whatsoever.

"Yes," Sylvia said, with the same sharpness as in her previous word to me. In retaliation, I studied the back of her head to see if I could spot the true color of her intensely frosted hair.

We entered the parlor together and walked past rows of chairs arranged on a deep red carpet, with a center aisle, as if we were in an old-fashioned theater like the kind Edward Hopper painted. At the end of the aisle, where the stage would be, Michael Deramo was laid out in a rich dark brown suit and an off-white shirt with a matching tie, the whole outfit looking more expensive than any Michael would have had in his closet. I wondered if his family had ever bought him a new suit while he was still alive.

It was the first time I'd seen Michael, except for the gruesome photographs of his murdered body. He looked so much like my own father and all the old Italian men that I'd grown up with that I wanted to call him Uncle Mike.

I also wanted to kneel down in front of him and tell him how sorry I was that he'd met a violent end on Revere Beach, which we both loved, and that I would try harder to find his killer. Sylvia, however, was ready to work.

"This basket is from Barry Richards, my brother and my husband's law partner. It should be right here," she said, sweeping both her arms in an arc that ended at Michael's head.

I moved the arrangement of gladioli, tall and peach-colored, from its ignominious location on the floor to a place on the higher of the two steps that made up the flower platform. To do this I had to adjust the positions of several other pieces, according to instructions from Sylvia, who used her long coral fingernails to communicate exact coordinates. I felt like the lowest of day laborers, but I was determined to make the most of it.

"It's so awful that this could happen to Mr. Deramo in his own neighborhood. I walk around there a lot myself at night," I said, stretching twice into "a lot." "I've always thought it was pretty safe."

"That wreath of red and white roses from the associates in Francis's firm needs to go on the top step on the other side," Sylvia said.

"Especially the place where he was found," I said. "Not that far from a streetlamp. It makes you wonder if it really was a random killing."

"A few more inches to the right," she said. Her voice was

so cool I imagined a white-robed servant fanning her face from above.

We were both speaking in near whispers, as if Michael were sleeping and shouldn't be awakened by feuding women. I continued to fuss with pots and baskets, keeping my remarks in a casual tone.

"I know the police are working hard," I said, breathing heavily from the exertion of lifting a large basket of geraniums.

Sylvia didn't bother to respond to that remark. I was running out of tricks, and becoming increasingly uncomfortable having this conversation so close to Michael's dead body. As soon as I figured out how to phrase my comment without getting Rose involved in an ethics violation, I decided to up the ante.

"I heard they think your father-in-law may have been murdered because he'd gotten on the wrong side of some people in high places," I said.

That seemed to get Sylvia's attention, and she moved to put an end to the game.

"I've heard about you," she said, brushing the palms of her hands against each other as if she'd been the one lugging heavy, wet floral pieces up and down steps.

I straightened myself up from a gardening position and faced her, but she stared me down and I blinked. It's a good thing I'm not on any corporate boards, I thought.

"My family's business is not your business," she said. She probably didn't mean "business" as used in fiction like *The Last Don,* but that's what it sounded like. "I'll tell you what I meant, because I'm sure your little friend up there told you what I said in a moment of grief over my father-in-law's death. When I referred to his playing with the big boys, I meant that he had the confidence of a much younger man and went out without taking precautions."

Unprotected Boulevard walking, I thought. Is that what killed Michael?

"Mrs. Deramo," I said, "I'm sure you want to do everything possible to help the police find your father-in-law's killer."

"I have nothing more to say to you."

Before I could formulate a response, we were interrupted by an early mourner. A man about my age, in his mid-fifties, stood in the doorway, his hands folded near his chest, not unlike the posture of the deceased. His outfit looked like an older, cheaper version of Michael's, rumpled like its wearer.

"Excuse me," he said in a gravelly voice that reminded me of Matt's. "Is Michael ready?"

I took a deep breath, glad to be relieved of my self-imposed duty of cross-examining a hostile witness. It was time to show myself a helpful, courteous member of Galigani's staff.

"The viewing doesn't start until one o'clock," I said, adjusting my tone to one more befitting a funeral parlor employee. I hoped I sounded kind yet authoritative, like Frank Galigani and his son, Robert. "However, I'm sure Mr. Deramo's family wouldn't mind if you came in."

A glance at Sylvia told me she was paying no attention to me or the visitor. She had stepped back and appeared to be making one last assessment of the floral tribute to her deceased father-in-law.

"I'm Carlo Massimo," the man said. "Michael's supervisor over at the lab. I just wanted to pay my respects, but I have to go work soon. To fill in for Michael."

Massimo pulled out a large handkerchief, white and useful, unlike the decorative beige one that Barry Richards had fiddled with during our interview in the lab cafeteria. Massimo sniffed into his hanky as he finished his sentence. I put my hand on his shoulder in a sympathetic gesture, partly to make up for Sylvia, who didn't acknowledge Massimo in any way. She'd taken the opportunity to strut out of the parlor and walk toward Frank's office, probably to leave a small tip for me, I thought.

I led Massimo down the center aisle, where he knelt on the prie-dieu in front of Michael's body, showing more reverence than Sylvia Deramo had. I took a seat at the back of the parlor, as if to monitor Massimo's visit—not that I could imagine how I might be needed or what I would do if Massimo suddenly pocketed a flower or two. But I was feeling some responsibility for allowing a visitor access before regular hours, and, I had to admit, the thought had crossed my mind that I might quiz Michael's supervisor when he'd finished his prayers.

The room seemed much quieter and more peaceful since Sylvia had left, and as I waited for Massimo to rise, I thought about Michael's poor fortune in life and in death. I hoped there was something more for his soul, and, by extension, for mine. I could hardly remember the days when I was sure I knew how it all finally ended.

As Massimo walked toward me, I stood up and invited him to join me in a cup of coffee at the table the Galiganis had set up in a small room across from the parlor.

"I'm sorry about Mr. Deramo," I said, pouring our coffees. "Were you good friends?"

"Oh, yes," Massimo said. "Michael and I belonged to the Sons of Italy. We played bocce on the weekends, and sometimes pinochle. We had some great times."

Massimo's brown, baggy eyes had a distant look, his mouth holding a wide smile as he talked. He seemed ready to share his memories in the way that I found common among close friends of a dead person, with every good time magnified and every shortcoming forgiven and cleansed.

I hated to intrude upon his memories, but I had police work to do.

"Do you think anyone might have wanted to kill Michael?" I asked him.

"You mean on purpose? Is that what they think?"

"I'm working with the police," I said, coughing slightly to diffuse the overstatement. "There is definitely a chance that Michael was murdered by someone who knew him."

Massimo blew a long stream of air my way, and I caught the smell of stogie cigars, the kind my grandfather used to smoke. Through valiant effort, and with the help of a layer of sweet aromas from the flowers surrounding Michael's body, I managed not to turn my nose away.

"Madonn'," he said, invoking the Blessed Virgin Mary, as customary when an old Italian hears something that strains credulity. "I can't believe that."

"Did he tell you anything unusual, or behave differently in the past couple of weeks?"

Massimo shook his head, so I prodded further.

"It might even be a small thing, a slight change of habit?"

"No, I can't think of anything. Unless you count that day he needed a stamp."

TEN

I PUT DOWN my coffee and folded my hands on my lap, as if that would help me wait patiently for the rest of Carlo Massimo's story. I pictured Michael with his letter to his son copied onto good paper, finally satisfied with its composition and his handwriting, ready to mail it.

"The stamp?" I asked Massimo.

"Yeah, he drove me crazy one day last week looking for a stamp to mail this letter to his son, Frankie. Michael never wrote letters. And we paid all our bills in person downtown. You know, at that drugstore near City Hall. They still have a window where you can get a money order. We used to go together. So, this was different. It was a big thing for him. He told me it was a very important letter."

I sat up and drew a long breath.

"Did you find a stamp?"

"We looked all over the desk in our trailer outside the building. Finally, Michael had to go back to work, so I told him I'd go to the lab's mail room and take care of it myself." Massimo held his coffee mug in both hands and raised it in the direction of the main parlor and Michael's body, like a priest blessing the congregation with a sacred vessel. "When I see Michael like this," he said, blinking away tears, "I'm glad I did him the little favor."

As moved as I was by this gesture, I wanted to get Massimo back on the track of the letter. I leaned forward and put my hand on his arm.

"I'm sure you did many favors for Michael," I said. "But this might have been the biggest one. Did you get any kind of receipt from the clerk?'' I was hoping for the miracle of a certified letter.

"Lucia—she's the lady in the mail room—she took care of everything for us. When I told her how important it was, she got this special envelope from her drawer. Big purple and orange letters on it. She had to fill out some labels."

While I was thinking "Federal Express," Massimo sat back and laughed as if he were picturing what must have been a unique transaction for him.

"Then she gave me this little strip of sticky paper with a long number on it. It stuck to my finger, so she put it on a piece of paper for me."

"Mr. Massimo." I said, "this could be very important in finding who killed Michael. Do you still have the little strip of paper?"

"Yes, yes, I think I do. I'll bring it to you if you want."

I leaned back in my chair. "That would help a lot."

My gaze wandered over Massimo's shoulder. I pictured myself bringing Matt physical evidence that Francis had received his father's letter. Unlike police professionals, I was able to make a smooth transition from Francis's reading the letter, realizing his own firm's plan for a lithium battery patent was in jeopardy, and killing his father to protect his career and his fortune. Case closed.

My triumphant image was disturbed only by my glimpse of Sylvia Deramo walking slowly past the doorway.

As soon as I could gracefully take leave of Carlo Massimo, I went upstairs to my apartment to call Matt. From Massimo's description of his trip to the mail room it sounded like the clerk had sent the letter Federal Express.

More than once in my research career I'd had to resort to an overnight messenger service to meet a deadline, but the paperwork had been handled by the office clerical staff. I had no idea how to determine who if anyone had signed for Michael's letter. What I did know was that someone had to interview the lab's mail clerk right away. Unless there was a tracking system, it would come down to Francis's word against that of a custodian, supervisor or not.

Matt's partner, George Berger, answered the office phone, and I debated whether to tell him what I'd learned, given the tenuous hold I had on his professional respect. Berger had resented me at first, and I didn't want to give him a real reason to think I was superfluous to the operations of the RPD.

Playing it safe, I decided against sharing this information with Berger, in case it turned out to be a totally useless lead, and distracted him in the usual way, with questions about his seven-month-old daughter. I realized I practically owed my new career, and maybe my thriving social life, to little Cynthia Berger—if her father hadn't been on paternity leave when I arrived in town, Matt might not have been so amenable to using my services. Had fate brought Matt and me together? Or an elaborate algorithm of statistical probabilities?

"Is she reading Shakespeare yet?" I asked, playing into Berger's insistence that his daughter showed early signs of genius.

"She loves books," he said. "Maybe it means she's going to be a famous author."

And maybe it doesn't mean anything, I thought. I was convinced that babies didn't know the difference between a book and a clock radio. But I wasn't about to tell any new parent my theory, let alone Berger.

"When are you going to bring Cynthia in again?" I asked, remembering the purpose of my conversation, which was to stay in the good graces of Matt's partner.

"We're planning to bring her to the Fourth of July picnic," Berger said. "She might even be walking by then."

We signed off after I promised to be at the picnic, omitting how I hated events that required eating among insects and balancing a paper plate on my slanted lap.

"No, thanks," I'd responded to his offer to take a message for Matt. "I'll try later."

I'd tried to give Berger the impression that I could wait for weeks to reach his partner, but I punched in the numbers for Matt's pager as soon as we hung up.

I listened for Matt's return phone call as I dressed for Michael's wake. I pulled out a black skirt to go with the jacket I was wearing, and thought about how I'd been to more funeral services than parties in the past year. Instead of a return phone call from Matt, I heard the buzz on the intercom, and Rose's voice.

"News," was all she said, giving me the signal that she'd be at my door in a minute.

Rose came into my apartment, dressed in her professional clothing. Her straight-line navy-blue dress was accented by a small pin shaped like a bouquet of flowers, with stalks made of antique gold and garnets arranged to look like blossoms. She was full of energy, her three-inch black heels having no apparent impact on her ability to walk quickly and gracefully.

Rose went straight to the kitchen and started my espresso maker as she talked.

"I've been making some calls for your anniversary party," she said.

"I just agreed to it last night, and you've been working here all morning. When did you have time for these social calls?"

"It's what I do, Gloria."

"Or did you start long ago, as with my cousin Mary Ann?"

"Oh, yes, well, I know Mary Ann doesn't get out much."

"She still won't," I said. "She can't make it."

"And you're glad of this?" Rose sighed and shook her head, as if I'd never understand the social world of adults.

"Well, no."

"Gloria, do you want to hear my news or not?"

"I do. I'm sorry."

"It's Peter," she said, carrying small cups of espresso to my couch.

The espresso maker and set of matching cups had been Rose's housewarming present. I knew the gesture was part generosity and part her distaste for drinking espresso from my motley collection of mugs. "Those are for beer at frat parties," she'd said of my assortment of ceramics stamped with college seals.

"Doesn't Peter want to come to the party, either?" I asked.

Rose shot me a look that said, "Fat chance."

"He's delighted to be invited. He's bringing a friend."

"Good."

"A woman."

Rose sat back and looked at me to get the full effect of her news. Her smile was the one she brought out when she had any kind of scoop.

"Peter and another woman," I said. "I should have known. I must be really full of myself not to have guessed."

"Why do you say that?"

I told Rose about our meeting and Peter's new friendly-but-not-pushy attitude.

"He was so reasonable," I said. "I'm relieved in a way. At least it doesn't mean he's trying harder to be my boyfriend. Then I'd have to give him another chance, and it would complicate things. I certainly don't need two men in my life. And I'd rather focus on Matt."

I stopped to evaluate my ramblings. Why am I talking so much? I asked myself. Surely I'm not hurt that Peter has a new romantic interest. I gave up on him first, didn't I? With no boyfriend for decades, did I now want two? What a hassle. My former single, romance-free life was looking better all the time.

"Don't you want to know who it is?" Rose asked, giving me a quizzical look. I hoped I hadn't been thinking out loud. "You're okay with this, aren't you?"

"Absolutely. I'm thrilled. Who is she?"

"Barbara Negri. She's a widow, about our age," she said, keeping to her pattern never to say the exact number—fifty-six for both of us. "Blondish-gray hair," Rose continued. "Nice choice of color. We buried her husband a few years ago. Prostate cancer. Two grown children. Works part-time in the high school library. Which is probably where Peter met her."

Rose sounded as though she were reading from a cue card propped up on my coffee table. She tapped her fingers on her knee between phrases, most likely unaware that few other people in Revere would have as many details as she had about Peter's party date. The Galigani Mortuary had been in operation for more than thirty years. That's a lot of wakes, and a lot of contacts, I mused. Add to that her son John's management of the local newspaper, and there's not much that could escape the Galigani database.

A knock on my door interrupted Rose's unauthorized biography of Barbara Negri. Matt was smiling into my peephole from the other side, holding up a cardboard tray of coffee cups.

"I see I'm a little late with these. I got your page, Gloria, and thought I'd answer in person, since I was on my way to the wake."

Rose gave Matt a wide smile. "Isn't it handy that she lives here?"

We all knew that Rose was ready to ward off the evil aura of anyone who tried to persuade me to move from her building, like Elaine Cody, for example.

"That reminds me," I said. "Elaine is planning a trip out here. Maybe the dates will coincide with the party."

"Oh-oh," Rose said. "I'll see if I can persuade Frank to reroute our business to Chelsea that week."

"So, the party's on?" Matt asked.

"The party's on," Rose said, punctuating her statement with two thumbs up.

And with that, she excused herself and went back to work.

MATT AND I had only a few minutes before the official start of Michael's wake. He seemed very interested in what I'd heard from Massimo, telling me that Francis had continued to deny that he'd received a letter from his father.

"This might give us some leverage," he said. "But we'll have to see what kind of receipt we have. I'll get someone over to the mail room right away."

After placing his call to the station, Matt sat on the couch with a handful of small butter cookies with cherry centers, popping them into his mouth, one bite each. Since neither of us was going to the burial service after the wake, we'd planned to have a late lunch together, doubling the number of dates we usually had in one week.

"Any other news?" I asked.

Matt waved his free hand in a "not much" gesture.

"Hammer confessed."

"What?"

It's a banner day for my apartment, I thought, a hotbed of news, personal and professional.

Having been rewarded by the desired effect of his words, Matt smiled. Like Rose in a similar situation moments before, I thought. Did all my friends take delight in surprising me?

"He confessed to setting up the meeting with Michael, as we thought he would after the little Italian lesson you gave him. But he says Michael was dead when he got to Boulevard, around eleven-thirty. So far there's no evidence that says he's lying."

"Did he say what the meeting was for?"

"Michael had overheard him and Laughton and two other scientists in the conference room one night about a week ago."

"And?"

"And they had been discussing the problems they've been having with the lithium program."

"And the problems were?" I asked, recognizing that Matt was not going to come right out and tell me that my initial theory was correct.

"Problems with waste, and problems delivering a certain kind of battery for a patent application."

"And when everyone realized the janitor had overheard this conversation?"

By now Matt was smiling broadly and moving toward me on the couch.

"They offered money."

"And?"

"And you were so right," he said, starting with a playful handshake and ending with a serious embrace.

ELEVEN

MICHAEL'S WAKE attracted a surprisingly large number of visitors, the ranks swelled by rows of representatives of the Sons of Italy and his local union of maintenance workers. Rose had told me that Michael's landlord, Joe Bargello, had rescheduled a vacation trip to Florida to attend the wake. He'd called her to ask what time he should come.

It was remarkably easy to distinguish Michael's cronies from his son's associates and in-laws. It was as if they all had their incomes stamped on their hands and price tags still attached to their garments—a two-pairs-of-pants-with-every-jacket deal for the union guys and hand-tailored shirts for the North Shore folks.

Robert Galigani, the oldest of Rose and Frank's three children, was on duty. As I watched him maneuver among the guests from across the room, I thought about the three Galigani children and the different directions their lives had taken. It was tempting to see their paths as parallel to those of their parents and me. Robert, looking so much like his father, even to the pattern of his receding hairline, had joined the family business. John had taken his mother's love of people and news to the editor's desk of the *Revere Journal*. And Mary Catherine, my godchild, was a chemical engineer.

Matt and I went our separate ways in the parlor. I stood at the side for a while, where I had a view of the front row of mourners. Sylvia sat between her husband and an empty chair, which I guessed was for her son, Andrew Palmer. I saw Matt talking to a young man who fit Andrew's description, except that he was nicely dressed in a dark suit and didn't match the image I'd created for him. Between the news features and

Matt's report on Andrew's "sheet," I pictured a drugged-out kid in a silky race car driver uniform.

As I rehearsed how I'd approach Andrew to express my sympathy and also acquire some information, I wondered if I'd ever again attend a wake merely to pay my respects to a grieving family.

At the end of the front row, attorney Barry Richards sat sideways on his straight-backed chair and carried on a long conversation with Fred Laughton in the seat behind him. I strained, without success, to hear what they were saying. I thought about learning to read lips as a handy skill for my new profession. Since, as far as I knew, neither man had an Italian heritage, I was further handicapped by a marked absence of hand gestures. Viewed from a distance, the two tall, balding men might have been sharing stories of their grandchildren, but my three-case career with the RPD put me in a frame of mind to think otherwise.

From the sidelines, I formulated a plan that would give me maximum return for the afternoon, without calling Matt's attention to my activities. I saw that he'd moved away from the young man I thought to be Andrew Palmer to sit in a row of old men in ill-fitting shirts and ties. With his inexpensive suit and humble, shuffling manner, Matt blended right in as a Son of Italy. Except for about twenty years' fewer wrinkles, I noted with gratitude.

I'll start small, I thought, and approached Michael's step-grandson. I intercepted him as he was leaving the parlor. I could see Andrew's sad expression, more like the ones on the faces of Michael's colleagues than those exhibited by Andrew's mother and stepfather. His blue eyes and reddish hair were a rarity in the room dominated by Neapolitans like me.

Faced with the choice between my self-appointed dual roles as pseudo-cop and professional sympathizer, I decided on the Galigani staff routine.

"Excuse me," I said. "Andrew Palmer, isn't it?"

"Yeah."

"I'm Gloria Lamerino. I'm with the mortuary. You're Mr. Deramo's grandson, aren't you?"

"Yeah," he said again, not correcting my characterization of him.

I'd chosen my opening deliberately, wondering how Andrew would take to being labeled a blood relative of a janitor. Up close, I noticed that his eyes were ringed with red, as if he'd been crying. Or on drugs, I told myself, before jumping to conclusions.

Two not-guilty points for Andrew, I thought, in my usual rush to judgment. He looks sad and doesn't mind my thinking he's directly related to Michael.

"Is there anything I can do for you?" I asked him.

"I'm okay. Thanks."

With such a benign response from Andrew, I regretted my choice of role-playing and made a slight move toward criminal investigator. We'd walked a few feet to a corner of the foyer, away from the steady buzz of low-level conversations from the parlor.

"I'm also helping the police on this case," I said. I grimaced at my own remark, feeling like half a comedy team pulling one-liners out of baggy pants.

"Really?" he said.

Andrew didn't seem to think anything was strange or out of line. He stared past me, looking far into the parlor in the direction of Michael's corpse. I'd gotten a grand total of five words from Andrew Palmer. I was on my way.

"I was wondering if I could ask you a few questions."

"Sure. What do you want to know?"

I gave Andrew one more point for not tightening up at the idea of being interrogated about Michael's death. Or maybe he could see through my thin veneer.

"Can you think of anyone who might want to harm your

grandfather? Someone who had a grudge against him for any reason?''

"Not really. He's actually not my real grandfather, you know, but we got along okay. He minded his own business."

He didn't mind it quite enough, I wanted to say, but deemed it inappropriate.

"Did he ever talk about being threatened or being afraid of anyone? Or worried that something bad was going to happen to him?"

"I didn't see him that often, you know? It's not like we had that much in common."

Andrew's voice cracked and he wiped his sleeve across his eyes in one rapid motion, suddenly looking much younger and more naive than I'd expect from a Generation Xer in the fast lane. He moved to the podium that held the guest book and leaned on it.

The foyer was empty except for Tony and Sal, the Galigani's strongmen, who strolled around the smaller parlors, far enough away to give their guests privacy, close enough if they needed assistance. Quite a staff Rose and Frank had trained, I thought with pride.

"I don't mean to upset you," I told Andrew. "Maybe that's enough for now."

I turned to leave, but Andrew touched my arm.

"No, wait. It's okay. Actually, I want to talk to someone. To tell you the truth, I kind of used Michael. I feel really bad now, you know. It was my way of aggravating my mother and my Uncle Barry. They hated me being nice to him."

"Oh?" was all I could get out of my mouth, fine specimen of an interviewer that I was.

"Yeah. They blamed him for making it hard to get into some snobby clubs. He didn't wear the right clothes and he didn't know their stuffy rules, you know? Just once he had a little too much wine and they called him a drunk. It drove them nuts that I actually talked to him like he was a human being. But now it's like maybe I was just as phony as them.''

"It's not that simple, Andrew. Don't be hard on yourself.''

"Yeah. I think I understood Michael a little bit. Like on his seventieth birthday a couple of years ago, my mother and Francis got him this silver money clip. A money clip. The poor guy didn't know what to do with it, and Francis ended up bringing it back home and using it himself.''

"There wasn't a party for him?''

"No, just me and Francis. We took him to this fancy Italian restaurant in Gloucester, and Michael kept saying he should open one himself if this is what they could charge for spaghetti. I was still in high school then. I felt bad for him and I tried to make it up by being, you know, nice to him that evening. Asking him about the old country and everything.''

"I'm sure Michael appreciated the attention, and maybe you did a lot for him. When someone is gone, we always wish we'd done more.''

"Yeah, I guess,'' Andrew said. "I better go.''

I reached into the small purse I carried when I was just two floors away from my belongings, an alternate to the large bag plus briefcase that I usually toted everywhere. I pulled out a thin brass case.

"Will you take my card, Andrew? I hope you'll call me if you want to talk some more. Anytime, you know.''

"Thanks,'' he said, and left the building.

AFTER THE WARM-UP with Andrew, I was ready to step to the front of the parlor and offer my condolences to Michael's son, the lawyer Francis Deramo. He sat in the first row, next to Sylvia, a small man with thick eyebrows over eyes lined with dark circles. He seemed only a couple of inches taller than she was.

His response to my brief expression of sympathy surprised me.

"Did you know my father, Dr. Lamerino?" he asked, stretching his short legs out in front of him.

"Not personally, no."

"And you're not a policeman—woman, whatever they're called these days?"

He kept his voice low and his forehead wrinkled. He had a menacing look that would have frightened me if we were in an empty parking garage instead of my friends' crowded funeral parlor.

"I work with the police on special contracts, Mr. Deramo," I said, gathering courage with a glance at Robert Galigani, and knowing that Tony and Sal were not far away. "I'd be happy to talk to you about it when the time is appropriate."

"It's appropriate now," he said, spitting out the *p*'s, and nearly knocking me over as he stood up. "Let's go somewhere."

"Why don't I see if I can find a private place for us to talk," I said, catching Robert's eye at the same time.

"You do that," Francis said, jerking his head around in the collar of his shirt, like a 1940s movie tough guy.

Sylvia, on the seat next to him, kept her eyes straight ahead, a thin smile pulling her lips into an unpleasant shape. It wasn't clear whether she was paying attention to my interaction with her husband or dreaming of club membership unencumbered by a father-in-law who was a custodian. She probably still thinks of me as the Galigani florist, I thought, only one step above a janitor, and not to be bothered with.

"What can I do for you?" Robert asked, approaching us with all the smoothness and authority of his father.

"We'd like a room for a private conversation, Robert," I said. "Is that possible?"

"By all means. Give me a minute to prepare Martha's office."

Robert arranged for Martha Franklin, Rose's assistant, to set us up at the work table in her second-floor office. Francis and I took seats opposite each other, across the wide metal surface.

Martha brought us a tray of coffee and pastries—miniature eclairs and napoleons. For once in my life, I wasn't the slightest bit tempted by their colorful, creamy presence. While I'd been maintaining a calm exterior, my stomach was taking up the slack, knotted in tension. I didn't usually clutch up at the prospect of talking to a murder suspect these days, and I wondered why Francis intimidated me. I decided it might be because this interview seemed to be on his terms, not mine.

Martha, who already thought I was single-handedly responsible for the rise in cleared homicide cases in Revere, was duly impressed that I needed an interview room. She winked at me as she left her office, and I was sure she was wishing she had a two-way mirror and an intercom hookup to follow the proceedings.

With Robert and Martha both gone, Francis closed the office door, reached into his jacket pocket, and pulled out a gun.

I swallowed my fear as unobtrusively as I could, giving reconsideration to a napoleon as a worthy candidate for my last meal. My hands gripped the edge of the table, just above my lap.

"Mr. Deramo," I said, swallowing again, "there are policemen throughout this building." I slid right past the exaggeration. "I don't know what you think you're going to do with that. I thought we were going to talk."

Francis placed the gun on the table, close to the edge in front of him. Its sleek gray lines blended into the surface of Martha's table. For a moment, my mind wandered and I wished I knew what kind of gun it was, as if it mattered whether its bullets were full-metal-jacket that would penetrate my body immediately, or semi-metal-jacket, designed to expand on contact. I've been reading too many of Matt's law and order magazines, I thought.

I looked at Francis, my eyes half closed, my whole body weak, pleading for its life.

"We *are* going to talk," he said. "I just want you to know who the big boys are."

For the third time in my one year back in Revere, a gun was threatening my physical being. I tried to take comfort in the fact that this time the killer was not pointing it directly at me, and help was only a scream away. Picturing Tony and Sal at my beck and call, and stretching common sense to the limit, I concluded that I wasn't in immediate danger, and could risk asking a question or two.

"Did you receive a letter from your father a few days before he died?" I asked the man in charge of the gun.

Francis seemed astounded by my arrogance, and I couldn't blame him. I wondered if I'd lost my survival instinct somewhere in the Rockies as I'd driven east from California in my Jeep. I couldn't think of any other way to reconcile this new me with the quiet, unassuming Berkeley physicist that I used to be. At that time, the word "gun" would have brought to my mind not the pistol variety, but the long tubes used for hydrogen research, called gas guns.

"Don't you get it?" Francis asked, frowning at me and throwing his hands in the air.

When he reached for his gun, my heart pushed so heavily against my chest I thought it would come through my jacket and land in the empty mug in front of me on Martha's tray. But Francis didn't take aim. He simply waved the gun around as he talked, as if he needed a cigarette and this was the closest he could come.

"Mark my words," he said, using an expression I hadn't heard since my youth. "You'll be sorry if you continue to harass me or my family."

"Don't you want to know who killed your father, Mr. Deramo?"

Francis looked at me with impossibly narrowed eyes and a

look of torment on his face, as if the question I'd asked him was more difficult than any he'd seen on his Massachusetts state bar exam.

"I can't afford to know," he said, "and you can't either." Then he left the room, pocketing his gun before he got to the door.

TWELVE

I SAT AT Martha's table for a few minutes after Francis left, still not trusting that my legs would hold me if I stood up. I gasped involuntarily when a shadow crossed the doorway. I looked up to see Robert Galigani, and breathed deeply.

"Are you all right?" Robert asked me. "I saw Mr. Deramo leave. He looked pretty flustered. And so do you."

"Everything is fine, really," I said, my voice cracking. Even someone without Robert's training might have been suspicious of that remark.

Robert sat in the chair recently vacated by Francis and his gun and looked at me.

"Was that police business?" he asked.

"Sort of."

Robert shook his head and frowned. I read concern in his wrinkled brow and tight lips.

"Aunt Gloria," he said, reverting to his childhood form of address and making me feel extremely old. "You don't have the training to do this on your own. Aren't you supposed to be working with Sergeant Gennaro?"

I nodded, partly because I was still too unsteady to argue with him and partly because I agreed with him.

"You're right, Robert," I said. "But don't worry. I'm not in danger and I won't do anything stupid."

"Let me take you upstairs," he said. "I'll make you some tea, and you can rest."

"Then I could have my daily nap?" I said with a smile.

"I didn't mean that, Aunt Gloria."

"I know. I'm just teasing you, Robert. You're so good at comforting people. No wonder we're all so proud of you." I held his hands across the table. "Thanks for your attention," I said.

I gave Robert a smile meant to reassure him that this was still his old Aunt Gloria, not ready for retirement to soap operas, but not some loose cannon of an amateur detective either.

I did give in to Robert in part. I let him escort me to my apartment and put a kettle of water on the stove for tea, which seemed better for my nerves than espresso. I sent him away promising to relax for a while, and that's what I did. I loaded a CD of Beethoven piano concertos, with Seiji Ozawa conducting the Boston Symphony Orchestra, and took a cup of chamomile tea to my rocker.

I hadn't slept well the night before, thanks to the real or imaginary jogging stalker outside my building. I'd had several bad dreams, including a vivid one of a hooded man driving a blood-red Cadillac onto the sidewalk and through the door of the mortuary building. When the Cadillac reached Galigani's foyer it burst into flames, the blaze having the same crimson hue that burning lithium imparts to a fire. I wondered what kind of nightmares Francis's pistol would inspire.

The tea, music, and my overall fatigue worked together to put me to sleep and I didn't hear anything until a knock on my door at three-thirty. I'd slept for more than an hour.

I staggered to the peephole and saw Matt, his hands in the pockets of his dark blue funeral service suit. I opened the door after a ten-second interval during which I ran my fingers through my hair and twisted my skirt back into place.

"I woke you up," he said, evidently putting all the clues together—my bare feet and baggy eyes, a lap robe in disarray on the rocker, and a CD at the end of its play time. "I'm sorry. I thought we were going to lunch after the wake."

"We are," I said. "I just need a few minutes. Were you downstairs all this time?"

"No," he said, focusing on me in a way that led me to

believe I looked even worse than I felt. "I slipped out and went to the station to compare notes with Berger and get an update on some things we're tracking down. Are you all right?"

"This is how I look when I wake up," I said, smiling. I deliberately omitted aggravating circumstances, like being the target of an evening stalker and a tough-talking daytime gunman.

While I changed into pants and a sweater, I made a pass at predicting the conversation we'd have if I told Matt about either the stalker or the gun or both. The gun was more real than the stalker, I reasoned, and would also cause Matt greater concern. I could see my contract being torn to shreds, and myself retired for good from crime-busting. It wasn't a welcome picture, so I put off the decision until I heard what information Matt might have to share first.

WE MADE IT TO Anzoni's in time for their early-bird special—vegetarian cannelloni and salad.

"What's new on Berger's end?" I asked, with a nonchalant air, in tune with shaking olive oil onto my crusty bread.

"The lab mail room's closed on weekends, and we're trying to locate the clerk who took care of the letter for Carlo Massimo."

"So where do you think we—you are in this investigation? What did you say the stepson's alibi was?"

Matt gave me a squinty look that told me I was coming close to exceeding the limits of my contract, but he opened his notebook and read to me.

"Sixteen members of Riders in the Sky—that's the Suffolk County race car club—swear that Andrew Palmer was at a meeting from about nine o'clock on Wednesday evening until the wee hours of Thursday morning."

"He did seem genuinely sad at his grandfather's funeral," I said, "but..."

Before I could finish my thought, Matt broke in.

"Let's talk about your anniversary party," he said. "I hear Peter's bringing a friend."

"I'm impressed. You really are a detective."

"Rose told me."

We both agreed that Rose Galigani was the truly relentless investigator in our foursome.

"I wonder why she thought you needed to know Peter was bringing a date."

"I think she wanted to reassure me," Matt said. "And you don't have to blush. I like being able to drop by without thinking I might be walking in on a private party."

"I like it, too."

"So maybe this means we're going steady?"

"You really have been talking to Rose."

We finished our coffee with no more banter, as if we needed time to digest this verbal advance in our relationship.

The mild weather and Anzoni's location on Revere Beach Boulevard made an ideal combination for an after-supper walk. Without discussion, Matt and I left the restaurant and crossed the street to the ocean side. For a while we walked in silence, as if we'd agreed not to compete with the seagulls' cries, the crashing surf, and the noise of passing traffic, some of it supplemented by the loud stereos of teenagers on a Saturday-evening cruise.

We passed several pavilions, identical in size and color to the one where Michael died, and it was hard for me not to think of him. We stopped at a concrete bench on the sidewalk and sat until it was too dark to make out the faces of the people sitting on the sand or walking their dogs at the edge of the water.

As far as I could recall, we'd never displayed our affection so openly. Sitting on a public bench, Matt's arm around my shoulder, we might have been mistaken for a couple married thirty years. I wondered how much this new stage had to do with the recent information that Peter's attention was directed elsewhere.

The only thing disturbing my comfort was the awareness that I was withholding information from Matt. Although I could chalk up the Tuttle Street jogger to my paranoia, it was hard to believe that Francis's behavior was unconnected to his father's murder. I knew Matt would want to know about it. I took a deep breath and started my confession, skipping past the opening sign of the cross.

"I have something to tell you about Francis Deramo," I said. "But you have to promise you won't worry."

Matt removed his arm from my shoulder and turned to face me—not a good sign, I thought, and immediately regretted my decision to tell him. I also bemoaned the fact that I hadn't prepared my remarks ahead of time, in my usual careful manner, with transparencies and research.

"Francis had—uh—a gun, and he—uh—took it out while we were talking. He did not point it at me, however."

Matt leaned over, his head in his hands, close to his knees, and I imagined a stiff Roman collar around his neck and a purple stole draped over his shoulders.

"He did not point it at me," I repeated. "He simply wanted to intimidate me. He told me I shouldn't be pursuing this investigation."

"And he's absolutely right." Matt sat up straight and faced me.

"I'm only telling you because it might be important, not because I'm afraid."

"You should be afraid."

"I'm here, aren't I?" I said, spreading my arms as if to show him that every inch of me was intact. "Do you think it means Francis participated in whatever got his father murdered, even if he didn't do it himself?"

"Tell me everything."

I gave Matt, almost verbatim, the entire short conversation

I'd had with Francis Deramo, and waited for my penance. I wished he'd give me an Our Father and three Hail Marys and let me go.

WE GOT IN THE CAR and headed back to Tuttle Street. This time the silence was uncomfortable, forcing me to rethink my idea that confession brought peace of mind. Matt pulled into the right side of the mortuary driveway, his headlights shining on the garage door and on the bushes along the edge of the building. I turned to face him, determined not to end the evening on a sour note.

"Matt, if you're angry, I wish you'd say so."

"I'm not angry. I'm worried."

"But the incident is over, and I was only one floor away from Sal and Tony. And you. There was nothing to worry about."

Even as I said it, I knew the explanation wouldn't hold water. Matt wasn't worried about what could have happened in the past.

"I'm worried about what you'll do next," he said, effectively finishing my thought.

"I don't want to be a source of worry for you. But I have to do what I think is my job in these cases. What do you expect me to do? Just turn off my brain after you've given me a puzzle to solve?"

I took a deep breath after what was probably the strongest pitch I'd ever made to Matt regarding my resoluteness once I started on a case.

"Here's what I expect you to do. When things get to a point where we're closing in on a killer, you need to back off. Is that hard?"

"So, I work with you on the easy parts? You might as well buy yourself a science textbook for all the good I'd do under those restrictions."

"You have a good point. Maybe what I had in mind when

I hired you was unrealistic. Maybe what we do is abandon the whole idea of your police work. No contract, no worry.''

Not the resolution I had in mind, but he is in charge, I reminded myself. Besides being my friend, he is the police.

"All right, why don't we discuss my future in law enforcement after this case is over. Let me see this one through, then we'll talk.''

"I can't believe what you're saying after you just had a gun pointed at you. What would make you stop pursuing this case?''

I thought it wise not to correct his depiction of a gun pointed at me, even though I'd told him twice that it hadn't been.

"Try to understand that it's hard for me,'' I said, making another attempt to get us out of the argument loop. "I did research for decades, Matt. You don't stop because you have a setback. When I was in graduate school I worked for eight months, every day, trying to get information on titanium crystal structure. It turned out the laser I was using wasn't designed to reach the power I needed for my specimen. I had to choose another crystal and start over from scratch.''

"I suppose someone told you to give it up?''

"As a matter of fact, yes. My adviser told me to quit. Who knows what I'd have done with my life if I'd listened to him?''

Matt shook his head.

"I admire your perseverance. I really do. But look at it from my point of view, Gloria. If something happened to you, I'd never forgive myself.''

Matt rested one hand on the wheel of his sedan and the other on my shoulder, squeezing it to emphasize his point. It was almost enough to weaken my resolve. Good thing he wasn't my thesis adviser twenty-five years ago, I thought. I might have quit and gone to hairdressing school.

I was about to explain further, admitting to both of us that

besides the intriguing puzzle a murder created for me, I'd
found myself becoming emotionally involved with the victims
in the cases I worked on. I'd never met Michael, but I felt I
knew him at least as well as his own family did.

Before I could formulate my new point, Matt shifted his
eyes to the ground in front of the car and made a sudden
movement toward the windshield to see more clearly.

When I strained my neck and followed his gaze I saw a
large dark shape crushing the stalks of the hedge and sticking
out onto the driveway, only slightly, close to the right front
tire of Matt's car.

"Stay here," Matt said to me, getting out of the car.

I remained in my seat, but rolled my window down, obey-
ing the letter if not the spirit of his instructions. All I could
see was a pair of dark, heavy work shoes, like the kind my
father used to wear, at the ends of short, thin legs clothed in
thick work pants, and crossed over each other at an unnatural
angle.

Matt came over to my window, putting his body between
me and the lump in the bushes.

"Gloria, I want you to move over and drive the car out of
here onto the street."

"What...?"

"Pull around to the right and park in front of that hydrant.
I'll be over in a minute."

I did as I was told, thankful that I didn't have to drive more
than two car lengths in the state of suspense I was in. I hoped
unreasonably that what I'd seen was roadkill—as if someone
might have dressed a raccoon in human clothes and thrown it
in the bushes. But in fact I was not surprised to learn that the
body was human.

Matt came up to me in the driver's seat when I'd parked.

"It's Massimo," he said.

I looked at him, my heart sinking to the brake pedal.

"Carlo?"

Matt nodded.

"Dead?"

Even one syllable at a time seemed too much effort for me to give voice to, as if my larynx and throat went out of service at their own will, upon hearing of another murdered custodian.

Matt nodded, grim-faced.

"Yes. Do you have your phone in your purse?" he asked, taking his own from his pocket.

I shook my head, not an easy task for my weakened muscles.

"It's broken. I had to leave it at the service center."

"Call Frank on this, then," Matt said, handing me his cellular phone. "Have him or Robert come over here right away. I'll get the dispatcher on the car radio."

As I pushed the numbers for the Galigani residence, I felt completely disconnected from the reality in front of me. When I allowed myself back into the present for a fleeting moment, I had the most frightening thought of my life—that I might as well have killed Carlo myself. I'd put him in danger by my ill-conceived, unauthorized questioning.

I heard Frank's voice, but by then Matt had finished his call, and he took the phone from me. Matt's words to Frank came to my ears as if they'd traveled across an ocean.

"There's a situation here that you need to be aware of," he said. "Can you come now?"

Matt hung up and got into the car beside me. He took my hands in both of his.

"Gloria, I'm sure you're upset. But you need to hear this. The medical examiner will have to confirm it, but it looks to me as though he was murdered somewhere else and deposited here."

Matt's tone was calm and matter-of-fact, like that of a postal worker informing me that a parcel had been delivered to my apartment by mistake.

"Why would they do that? Why would they bring Carlo here?"

"To give you a message."

I rested my forehead on the steering wheel. Here's the answer to Matt's question, I thought. What would make me stop pursuing this investigation? The possibility that I was responsible for the death of another human being.

"I get the message," I said.

THIRTEEN

MATT STAYED WITH ME until the RPD's large crime scene van turned into Tuttle from Revere Street. I knew he didn't want to leave Carlo's body unattended, but he wasn't about to send me upstairs alone either. I felt hopelessly stuck to the seat of the sedan, my legs pillars of stone, my breathing slow and heavy.

When I saw Rose and Frank pull up on the other side of the street, I was close to tears again, as if the sight of my dear friends amplified the awful scene in their driveway, and my part in causing it.

A uniformed officer who'd been directed by Matt to check out the building came back around the mortuary lawn to escort Rose and me to my apartment. I could hear Matt addressing a list of questions to Frank. What time had the mortuary been closed for the day? Had there been anyone suspicious hanging around? Any unusual phone calls? Was there anything he could offer to help the police as they started their canvass of the neighborhood?

For a change, I wasn't even curious about the questions or answers. It was a dark, moonless night, and my eyes and my mind were overwhelmed by the lights from the medical examiner's van and the flashing camera of the police photographer. Traffic on Tuttle Street slowed as it passed the crime scene, but pedestrians at least had the decency to cross to the other side as they approached. Since I couldn't turn back the clock, I wanted at least to be able to slip away and pretend that the gruesome sight in the driveway was part of the decor for a neighbor's off-season Halloween party.

UPSTAIRS, ROSE SAT ON the couch with me, looking as drained as I'd ever seen her. I waited for her to lecture me, but she was too wise and too good a friend to do anything but comfort me, alternating between making tea and holding my hands. I couldn't seem to straighten my shoulders or lift my head to stretch my neck, which was painfully stiff. The taste of Anzoni's house salad dressing was no longer pleasant, sending currents of acetic residue up to my throat.

I felt desperately sorry for Carlo. Another janitor I will now think of on a first-name basis, I thought, and for a terrible reason. I could not let go of the feeling that I'd caused his death.

Except for me, the police wouldn't have known about Michael's letter to Francis. And if I hadn't interviewed Carlo, they might not have thought of checking for a receipt. In my chain of reasoning, Carlo was about to bring me or the police the evidence, and Michael's killer knew it. But I couldn't imagine who else would care except Francis, who was the addressee, and, strangely, his gun-waving threats had done more to convince me of his innocence than otherwise.

I remembered that Sylvia had walked by the door while Carlo and I were talking. I couldn't clear Sylvia in my mind as easily as I'd cleared her husband, but maybe that was because of my history with female killers.

"Some very vicious person killed that man, Gloria," Rose said, as if she were reading my thoughts. "Not you. You did not kill him. You were doing your job."

"It wasn't really my job."

"Your intentions were to help find Mr. Deramo's murderer. Don't you think the police go through this all the time? Wondering if they're stirring up trouble as they try to solve crimes? You see it on TV all the time—people helping the police sometimes pay the price. But the police can't stop investigating, now can they?"

"Thank you, Rose," I said, genuinely moved by her attempts to soothe me in spite of her overall anxiety about my police work. I wondered if Matt would be as forgiving. I hoped not, since I wasn't ready to be cheered, or to abandon my mental self-flagellation.

I guessed I presented a scary picture, bent over on my couch, my eyes red, shreds of tissues all around me. When Matt came into the apartment, he had a look of concern that I'd seen only a few times before, notably when I'd been shot while in his employ. He'd brought his manila folder in from the car and placed it on my coffee table, sat down on a rocker across from Rose and me, and waited until I raised my head.

"I'm sorry," I said.

"She thinks she caused this," Rose said.

"That's always tempting when we're involved in an investigation and a seemingly innocent bystander is killed. You can't control everything that's going to happen while you're digging around, Gloria, and it's not a good idea to dwell on it."

Rose smiled for the first time that evening, as if she'd just been told she passed the police academy entrance exam.

"I dragged Carlo into this," I said. "What else could it be?"

"A lot of things. For one, what if Massimo realized the value of the receipt he had and tried to bargain with someone? It's a possibility. It seems dumb, given what happened to Deramo, but you never know what people will do if they think there's a lot of easy money to be had. If people didn't do stupid things, I wouldn't have a job."

"Carlo didn't seem the type."

"Probably neither did Michael Deramo. But Hammer's story confirms it. We don't even know if Massimo was involved from the beginning."

"He wouldn't have told me about the letter then, would he?"

"Who knows? The point is, there are a lot of possibilities for why Massimo was murdered."

I breathed deeply and smiled, but I was a long way from feeling relieved of the burden I had given myself.

Rose walked to my living-room window and looked down on the street.

"It seems to be clear of flashing lights down there," she said.

"I've ordered an unmarked car around the clock for a while," Matt said.

"I don't need—"

"It's done," Matt said, sounding like a military sergeant addressing unruly recruits. I hadn't heard that tone from him in months, not since the last time he disapproved of my overzealousness on a case.

"Matt, I'm sorry."

"I know you are. Try not to think about it. Maybe take something to help you sleep. There's just one more thing and then I'll let you get some rest."

He opened the folder on the table and took out a sheet of paper. While Rose and I watched, Matt tore the paper in half, then in half again and again until my contract was in sixteen pieces. His face muscles were tight, his chin drawn up. He put the pieces in his pocket, gave me a quick pat on my shoulder, and left my apartment.

I KNEW IT WAS USELESS for me to try to sleep. After Rose and Frank left the building, I made a bold attempt to do something normal, booting up my computer to pay some bills on-line. The "ta-da" sound emitted by the speakers seemed an especially inappropriate theme for the evening, and I wondered if I should look into programming a mournful hymn or a funeral dirge, given my current lifestyle.

I tried in vain to find an intelligent television program that might capture my imagination, not a cop show or an inane comedy.

My dirty clothes had been piling up, but going to the laundry room in the mortuary basement was out of the question. Even when my home wasn't a crime scene I had trouble doing my wash across the hall from the prep room. My strategy was to do it when, number one, it was a bright sunny day; number two, there wasn't a dead body on site; and number three, some of the living Galigani staff were around. This combination didn't come up with great frequency, and I'd had to adjust by buying extra underwear and towels.

At midnight I checked the unmarked RPD car for the sixth time. Not for the first time, my apartment had the luxury of special police protection, thanks to my meddling. I looked down at the dark, otherwise deserted street and wondered who was on duty. Maybe someone else who needed company, I thought. What I wanted to do most of all was call Matt or Rose and talk, not necessarily about Michael Deramo or Carlo Massimo, but just to have human conversation.

I lacked the courage for that, however, so I paced and puttered until about one in the morning, when I felt tired enough to go to bed.

My dreams, which came off and on throughout the night, were too predictable to make anything but a dull freshman psychology textbook. First I was in St. Anthony's Church with Carlo, who'd looked so much like my father in real life, and then we walked to Revere Beach Boulevard, which, of course, had ten times as many amusements as it had boasted even in its heyday. Matt's face appeared now and then, too, amid the saltwater taffy and dodgem cars, but I could never get close enough to see if he was smiling or frowning.

WHEN MY PHONE woke me up at ten o'clock on Sunday morning, I rolled over and let my answering machine take over.

By the time I left my bed to make coffee, at close to noon, I had three messages waiting for me.

Both Rose and Peter had called to check on me. Rose expressed her usual concern, but it was a new Peter, I noted, paying attention to my feelings.

"It must have been terrible, finding a body on your doorstep. I heard it on the news. If you want to cancel Tuesday's talk, I'll understand perfectly," Peter had said to my machine.

And a new Matt, I noted reluctantly, not calling at all. We usually spoke on Sunday morning and planned our afternoon together.

The third call, from Andrea Cabrini, who apparently wasn't as up-to-the-minute on news as Peter, was the most interesting.

"I forgot to tell you this the other day," she said to the tiny computer chip in my answering machine. "There's a seminar you might be interested in at the lab. Laughton and Hammer—the lithium program guys you met—are going to report on their research at a special meeting. It's tomorrow, Monday, so maybe it's too late for you to change your plans, but I can get you in if you want. And also, I was wondering, what should I wear to your party? Not formal, I hope. Ha. Ha. But I'll be there no matter."

How could Andrea know that I had no plans for the rest of my life after the events of the evening before? And I certainly didn't need to be reminded who Laughton and Hammer were. I told myself that I was off the Deramo case in a big way, so there was no reason for me to go to a lithium program seminar. There was no ambiguity about a contract destroyed before a live audience.

On the other hand, I thought, there was no reason for me to avoid a technical seminar. I didn't need to give up physics just because I'd retired from police service, did I? This was a good opportunity to keep up with a field I'd once been active in.

On my way to my rocker with a mug of coffee, I looked out my window at the unmarked car, then allowed my eyes to stray to the spot on the driveway where Carlo's lifeless legs had been. I resolved to do nothing more about the Deramo murder investigation. I'd call Andrea and tell her yes on casual dress, and no on the seminar invitation.

To cement my resolve, I pulled out my notebook and binder on the case and created a hanging folder, marked DERAMO, in the cabinet where I keep files labeled INACTIVE. I clipped together the copies of the police report and sketches of the crime scene—the first of two crime scenes, I realized with regret.

I came to the copies of the photographs of Michael lying on the ground of the pavilion and paused for another look, maybe to convince myself that I needed to leave police work to the professionals, but more likely to check one last time for a sign from the victim. I hadn't had a chance to review the package since Matt had given it to me at the Galiganis' on Friday night.

I picked up the close-up of Michael's face, which also showed his hand resting in the patch of new cement. I took out my magnifying glass and held it to the spot on the print where I'd seen the mark that had piqued my interest at the crime scene. Looking closely, I saw that the figure most resembled a triangle, but with rounded corners. The sides were uneven in length, the longest no more than an inch.

I thought about Matt's theory that the markings had been made earlier in the evening, a minor act of vandalism. It seemed to me that Michael's fingers were in exactly the position he'd use for writing, as if he'd anchored his palm in the cement and moved only his index finger to trace the shape. It was beyond my power to consider this a meaningless gesture—I couldn't accept that a dying man had used his last ounce of strength to engage in idle doodling.

Telling myself that this little task hardly constituted working on a nonexistent contract, I made a list of triangle shapes that Michael would have come in contact with. I thought of sails, rooftops, stylized trees, brackets, trusses. I even included the pyramids of Egypt and the triangular Transamerica building that dominated the San Francisco skyline, though I doubted that Michael had ever been to either Egypt or the West Coast.

Maybe it's a building or coat of arms in Italy, I thought. After all, Michael translated Hammer's name into Italian, he belonged to the Sons of Italy, and the only decorations in his home were prints of Italy, all indications that he still had strong attachments to the old country. I piled up all the books I had on Italy and pored through them looking for a triangle.

I noticed how often triangles appeared in Italian architecture—the shape identified the top of the Pantheon, the best-preserved temple of ancient Rome, which I'd visited with Rose once, and many campaniles throughout the large cities of the country. Some cathedrals and basilicas had triangular tops also, often with a rose window set inside. The corners of Michael's triangle were more round, but this was the last drawing of a man at death's door, I reminded myself.

I kept at the figure until I was too hungry to concentrate, my eyes weary, my mind ready to give up on the triangle and think of it as a weird circle. I hadn't had anything to eat since Anzoni's early-bird special the day before. I closed up the package of photographs, put it on my desk, and made a sandwich. As I ate raisin bread and peanut butter, a special recipe from my comfort food-file, I looked at the envelope from the distance of my rocker and knew I'd be returning to it. I thought of Carlo, and persuaded myself that if I could identify Michael's message, I'd be solving two murders at the same time. For a moment it seemed that might make up for causing Carlo's death, but only for a moment.

Fifteen minutes later, I did something else that I'd known I'd succumb to. I made a phone call to Andrea Cabrini.

"I'm calling to tell you casual dress is fine for the party, Andrea. It might be pretty warm by then, so wear something comfortable."

"Oh, great, and thanks again for inviting me, Gloria. I can't wait."

"I'm looking forward to it."

No sense telling Andrea every truthful detail, I thought.

"And what about the seminar? Sorry for such short notice. Are you free?"

I looked at the phone, a habit I'd developed since returning to Revere. I didn't remember ever treating my phone as a debating partner in California.

"What time does it start?" I asked her.

"Ten o'clock. If you come to the badge office around nine-thirty, I'll meet you and we can go to the conference room together."

"Nine-thirty is fine," I said, looking around as if I might be overheard. "I'll be there."

FOURTEEN

I KEPT MYSELF BUSY for a couple of hours, catching up on apartment maintenance and reworking my presentation for Peter's class to sound more like a graduation address. I'd identified a comment by the nuclear physicist Enrico Fermi, an Italian-American, that I'd use to open the talk: "Whatever nature has in store for us, unpleasant as it may be, men and women must accept, for ignorance is never better than knowledge."

Fermi hadn't included women, but I figured it was acceptable to do the gender-editing that would bring the quote into the 1990s.

As I went about my tasks, I wondered where Matt was, feeling like a teenager waiting for a phone call from the boy in the second row in math class. I checked the unmarked car on the street below every hour or so, and considered taking coffee to the duty cops as an excuse to ask about Matt.

"Has Sergeant Gennaro checked in recently?" I might ask, casually.

Each time my phone rang, I expected to hear the voice of either Carlo Massimo's murderer asking me if I'd gotten the message or an angry Matt Gennaro reminding me that I was off the case. Both prospects made my heart leap. All the calls were friendly, however, one being from Rose, who sounded surprised that I answered.

"I was going to leave a message," she said. "I thought you'd be out with Matt, but I guess this isn't your usual Sunday, is it?"

"No, it isn't."

"Do you want some company?"

"I have a lot to do," I said. I looked around at my clean kitchen counters, my dusted bookcases, and my notes for Tuesday's talk, polished and ready to put into my briefcase. I thought I sounded convincing, but apparently the catch in my voice betrayed me.

"I'm coming over," Rose said.

That was enough to cheer me, and I headed for the coffee-maker. I thought I'd put my good humor to use by taking drinks and a snack to the hardworking employees of Revere's Pride sitting below my window. I arranged a tray of crackers, cheeses, and dried fruits from a package Elaine had sent me, holding fast to her theory that only West Coast foods were worth the calories.

The sky was overcast, and the temperature had dropped to an unspringlike sixty degrees, below the threshold for my summer wardrobe. I put on a gray-and-blue Griffins sweatshirt from Golden Gate University in San Francisco, where I'd been an occasional lecturer, and walked down to the curb to deliver my treats. I couldn't avoid a glance at the bushes by the garage, now marked by yellow tape, as if they'd been infected by a strange bug and were now quarantined.

I raised my arm to knock on the window of the surveillance car, but the driver rolled it down as I approached.

"How are you doing, Gloria?" Matt said.

Through some glitch in the laws of physics, I managed to keep my balance, hold on to the tray, and scan Matt's face for signs of displeasure at the same time. His grin told me he knew I'd be surprised to see him and also, I hoped, that he wasn't angry with me.

"I thought you might like a snack," I said, trying to sound as though I'd planned our Sunday this way all along. Matt was not in the pool of officers who usually pulled security duty, and I wondered what his motive was in sitting out a shift in front of my apartment. One reason that I could think of was positive and optimistic—he cared about me and wanted to be personally involved in my safety. Another intention was suggested by the pessimistic voice of Josephine— *He'd rather do this than visit with you; you're just part of his job.*

Matt's partner on this assignment was a uniformed officer I'd seen around the RPD building, a young Asian woman with a short, dark ponytail. I tried to read her name badge as she gave me a brief wave and a smile, and thought I saw "M. Chan."

Matt gave a mug of coffee to M. Chan, who had already helped herself to the contents of the tray, now on the seat between them.

"I'm starving," she said. "We've been here since seven o'clock this morning. Thanks so much for the treats, Dr. Lamerino."

"You're welcome."

"We go off at three," Matt said.

I ignored the specter of Josephine and took a big risk.

"I'll see you then," I said, and went into my building.

I UNLOCKED MY DOOR and made it to the phone in time to answer a call from Elaine Cody. Before I'd thought it through, I told her of the good use I'd just made of her package of California-grown edibles.

"Why is there police surveillance on your house?" she asked, ignoring the compliment I'd paid to her taste in gifts.

"There's been some trouble here."

"Trouble?"

"Uh, another murder."

I heard Elaine gasp, and realized that I didn't need to tell her everything. She worried enough about my living arrangements and RPD contracts without hearing every gory detail, literally.

"Putting a car out there is just routine, for a day or two," I said.

"You never even liked mysteries on television when you lived out here. And now there's a murder right on your doorstep and you don't even seem concerned."

"I am concerned, but I also know I'm not in any danger. Let me read your flight number and time back to you to make sure I have it straight."

"I think you need me."

"I do. And then you can see for yourself how safe I am. Are you packed?"

My diversionary tactics worked at least for the moment, and Elaine gave me a rundown of the wardrobe she'd planned to bring, including a new outfit for my party. I promised to keep safe until I could meet her at Boston's Logan Airport, and she promised to bring pictures from the latest Berkeley lab picnic, at which I was sorely missed, in her words.

At about two-thirty, just before Elaine and I hung up, Rose and Frank came to the door. I shook my head in amazement as I considered life in my apartment—it seemed that I was either by myself with morbid thoughts and a police guard, or entertaining people by phone and in person at the same time, while expecting another guest any minute.

When I opened the door to the Galiganis, I realized that I was not the only stop on their Sunday-afternoon itinerary. They were dressed for a benefit dinner for the Sons of Italy scholarship fund. Rose wore a soft blue linen dress, Frank a dark Gucci suit, not too different from the one I'd seen on Barry Richards, Esquire.

Frank came in behind Rose, giving me a hug and a bag of cookies. Although his well-toned body didn't show it, Frank carried on the tradition of our parents' generation, using food as a universal panacea. A salami sandwich was an accepted cure for a cold, a bowl of pasta made up for a string of bad luck with the numbers, and a bag of cookies could soothe jangled nerves.

"The last man I saw in a suit like that was an arrogant

lawyer," I told Frank. "How come you don't look pompous in yours?"

"Remember the undertaker bees," he said. "The elite."

Frank never let us forget an article on bees I'd given him from a science magazine. The authors described a study of the bees that were responsible for removing dead bodies from the hive. According to the researchers, these "undertaker bees" were a small cadre of elite, developmentally advanced workers, only 1 percent of the bee population.

"Truthfully," he said, "I think the difference is Rose." He looked at his wife of four decades as if a priest had just announced that they were husband and wife and he could kiss the bride. I enjoyed watching Rose blush for a change.

"You have some high-priced help out there, I see," Rose said, shifting the spotlight to me.

Frank walked around and straightened all my pictures, a chore he took upon himself about once a month.

"We're glad you're in good hands. Rose worried all night," he said.

"I'm fine."

"And you're definitely off the case?" Rose said. Her tone took a slight upward turn toward the end of her sentence, more like a plea than a normal question.

"I'm off the case."

As I made this reassuring remark about my retirement from homicide investigations, I glanced at my phone, as if it might betray me by replaying my phone call to Andrea through my living-room speakers. The announcement echoed in my guilty ears—*Gloria is going to the lab tomorrow to snoop around some more, and face her alleged murder suspects.*

The Galiganis declined my offer of refreshments, staying only long enough to convince themselves that I was ready to move past the events of the night before.

BETWEEN THE Galiganis' exit and Matt's entrance, I barely had time to brush my hair and stuff the DERAMO file into my desk drawer.

When I opened the door to him, I realized that for the second time in a week, I'd be serving Matt coffee while holding back information about meeting Andrea Cabrini at the lab. I rushed to take control of the conversation.

"You look exhausted," I told him. "If you've been with Ms. Chan since seven o'clock this morning, you couldn't have gotten any sleep at all."

For some reason, my voice came out singsong, as if I wished that I'd been the one who got to spend all that time in the car with him.

"I am exhausted."

With only a brief word of greeting, Matt walked past me to my couch. He took off his jacket, stretched out on the sofa, and breathed a heavy sigh that came close to a moan, causing an enormous maternal swelling in my breast.

"I hope you don't mind," he said.

"Not at all. Can I get you anything?"

"This is all I need right now, thanks. I can hardly keep my eyes open."

Within a few minutes, I heard his low, gentle snores, another first in our dating life. I stifled the urge to tuck him in with my blue-and-beige cotton throw.

I SAT IN my glide rocker across from the couch where Matt slept. Although I had a book on my lap—a new biography of Ada Lovelace, Lord Byron's only legitimate daughter and the world's first computer programmer—my head was reeling with questions, some of which Matt could answer if I dared ask. I wondered if his falling asleep in my living room on a Sunday afternoon gave me the right to drill him later.

I wanted to know about the Federal Express trace, for one thing. And since Carlo's body had been deposited on my doorstep, I reasoned, I deserved to know some basics, like how, when, and where he was killed.

Matt woke up after about thirty minutes, in a much better mood than I expected. I was glad to learn something new about him, putting him in an enviable category—those who are refreshed by forty winks in the middle of the day. I myself had never mastered the art of the nap, waking up as groggy and listless as if I'd had a poor night's sleep.

"Do I smell coffee?"

"You do. It's waiting for you."

Matt poured his own coffee and a mug for me, after smoothing out the large crater his body had made in my sofa. He insisted that he felt rested and energized and suggested we do our jazz supper club routine as usual.

"We could try that new one in Everett," he said.

"Don't you have work to do?" I asked. What I meant was, How can you think of anything but the double murder you're investigating?

"There's not much more I can do today."

"What's next?"

"What's next is, I go home and change and come back and pick you up at six."

I wondered how many more rounds to go before ending the word game. None, I decided.

"Matt, Carlo Massimo's body was left in my driveway. How can I not be a little curious? You could at least tell me how he died."

I hoped I didn't sound as whiny to Matt as I did to myself, but whatever works, I thought.

"You're right. I'm trusting that you're only as curious as a normal person would be. Not as an investigator. Correct?"

"A normal person. Correct."

"Massimo was shot once, back of the head, probably about an hour before we found him."

"Someone was taking a big chance that we'd catch him in the act in my driveway. How did they know I was out?"

"It doesn't take long to dump a body, and it was dark."

"Anything else?"

"That's all a normal person needs to know, Gloria."

"One more question."

"One more."

"Can't you search places for blood, like Francis's car, or Hammer's, for example?"

"Not enough to go on. It was a different MO from Deramo's murder, for one thing." Matt rinsed his mug and straightened his jacket. "And I believe that's your last question," he said with a smile.

"I wonder when he'll be waked," I said as I held the door for him.

"Don't even think about it, Gloria."

I was about to give my "I live here" speech, but Matt was way ahead of me.

"Massimo is going to be waked at Cavallo's across town, and you have no reason to go there."

"But he lived in this parish. And this is the closest mortuary. Do Frank and Rose know about this?"

"It was their idea."

THE EVERETT JAZZ VENUE proved not as nice as the clubs we'd been to in Revere and Cambridge. The smoke density seemed much higher, the room more crowded, and the musicians not up to our standards.

"They're too young," Matt said, and I agreed.

Except for my rambling private thoughts, murder did not intrude on our evening. Now and then as I sipped a ginger ale, I wondered about the duplicity of my supposed friends and landlords, not telling me that they'd declined to provide funeral services for Carlo. I decided not to quiz them on it, realizing they had my own good in mind.

As energized as he thought he was, Matt showed signs of fading by nine o'clock. He blinked his eyes more often than usual, holding them shut for a few seconds at a time. We agreed to make it an early evening, and I was home before ten. He still hadn't told me his plans for finding the murderer, but then neither had I told him mine.

FIFTEEN

MONDAY MORNING'S weather report sounded a lot like what I'd heard almost every day in Berkeley. Early morning overcast, clearing later in the day, highs in the seventies. Nearing my one-year anniversary back in Revere, I'd survived the worst—a hot, humid summer and freezing winter storms, my rewards being a glorious fall in between and now these beautiful Massachusetts spring days. Two great seasons out of four isn't bad, I thought.

As I chose my outfit for my appearance at a professional meeting, I was conscious about how Matt would judge my decision to go to the lab seminar. I felt like a released convict ready to commit a parole violation. Whether out of sympathy for the prison population or because it was at the front of my closet, I put on a gray-and-white-striped shirtdress with long sleeves and a matching plain gray jacket. In keeping with the theme of incarceration, I pinned a small pewter replica of San Francisco's Alcatraz Island to my lapel.

I looked out the window to see if my home was still on the surveillance duty roster for the day. I couldn't see any vehicle that I recognized from the RPD fleet and guessed that a day and a half of police presence had been all Matt could arrange. I wasn't used to being afraid to leave my house, and considered getting a pit bull or some other large dog, until I realized that I'd never taken care of anyone or anything in my adult life, not even plants. I decided I owed it to the animal kingdom to leave them alone.

I was dressed and ready to go by eight-thirty, although I wasn't due to meet Andrea, ten minutes away, until nine-thirty. So I must have known all along that I'd end up driving by Michael's house on the way to the lab—not exactly on the way, I had to admit, unless you considered a large triangle the most direct route to any location.

I left the building through the garage. The crime scene tape had been removed, but still I held my breath as I drove out past the place where Carlo's body had been dumped. I pictured him alive and animated, talking to me about Michael's stamp one minute and cold and dead in my driveway the next. I pushed away the image with the select button on my FM station, allowing generic classical music to soothe me.

As I drove along the Boulevard, it seemed like months ago that I'd visited Michael Deramo's bungalow with Matt. Between then and now, our only progress had been to translate a note from Michael's refrigerator and to find another body. So, I told myself with a sarcasm I tried to keep in check, we've succeeded in eliminating the suspicious-looking Carlo Massimo as Michael's killer. I wasn't sure what this second visit would get me. Perhaps I was hoping for another clue on the lawn.

I pulled up in front of Michael's driveway, which really belonged to his landlord, Joe Bargello. I walked toward the back, where Michael's small cottage was, surprised to find the door open and some of Michael's belongings strewn about the backyard. Quick to action, I thought, as I saw Bargello moving a kitchen chair toward a pickup truck parked along the side of the house. An old Malibu that I hadn't noticed the first time I'd visited was parked next to it, on the gravel.

"Can I help you?" Bargello asked, as he saw me approach. Near at hand, he looked closer to Michael's age than he had at Galigani's. He also seemed heavier in his work clothes than he had in his mourning suit. The mortuary lighting gave everyone a gauntness and dullness that added to their years, I decided, probably to even things out with the deceased. I realized that although he'd been pointed out to me at

Michael's wake, he'd have no way of knowing who I was. He hadn't been around the day I'd come by with Matt.

"Good morning. Mr. Bargello?"

"Yes?"

I introduced myself, in my usual vague way.

"I'm Gloria Lamerino. I'm looking into Michael Deramo's case with the police."

"Looking into" seemed as good a phrase as any when I didn't have a formal contract. And "with the police" didn't seem as arrogantly incorrect as "for the police."

"The police have already been here," Bargello said, pleasantly enough, but squinting at me as if he knew I was a fraud.

"Yes, I know. But I thought I'd come and take another look. Also, you were away when I was here last time."

"I went to visit my nephew on the Cape that day. He came to get me. Nice boy."

"He sounds it. Looks like you're busy here."

"Yes, I want to clear the place out. Have to do it sooner or later. I called Francis, but he said do what I want with the stuff."

Bargello, who seemed tired already at eight forty-five in the morning, took a seat on a living-room chair—one of Michael's matching pair, upholstered in brown—and motioned me to the other.

I was sure we looked like models for a surreal painting. An odd couple sitting on living-room furniture arranged on the lawn, a few feet from a pile of appliances. Michael's small television set was surrounded by his toaster, iron, and microwave oven and a variety of tools, like an abstract sculpture of the kind that I walked by quickly at a museum.

"I'm loading it up to take to the Salvation Army," Bargello said. "The car, too. It's all junk, really. Still, you'd think his son would want to look through it. I found some photographs, mementos. I guess Michael was right."

"What do you mean?"

"You know, he always said Francis didn't have any use for him anymore, once he married North Shore money. Poor guy. You want some coffee?"

"No, thank you. I won't be long. I just have a few questions if you don't mind?"

"Shoot."

I wished I'd predicted and prepared for the possibility of this interview, one of the most cooperative subjects of my career. Maybe because he was a very unlikely suspect? I hated to miss an opportunity for information that might prove valuable later, so I kept Bargello awhile longer.

"Were you and Michael good friends?"

"We were friends, yes. He called me his chief," Bargello said with a smile.

"His chief?"

"In Italian, *bargello* means chief of police, or sometimes it can mean police headquarters." Bargello laughed as Michael's friends tended to do when they thought of his word games. I wondered what Michael would have done with my name, which has no direct translation, but can be thought of as a corruption of words meaning "the sea." I couldn't think of what Deramo might mean in Italian, and made a mental note to ask Peter if he'd heard of it other than as a proper name.

"I wasn't born in the old country like Michael," Bargello said. "My mother and father were from Naples, but I was born here, went to school here. But I know a little Italian and I liked to hear Michael talk."

"How long did he live here?"

"Oh, thirty, maybe forty years. He lived here before I bought the place."

"So Francis lived here at one time?"

"He did. Yes."

I had a hard time picturing the dapper Francis Deramo,

Esquire, living in the shabby cottage with his father. Probably it was before he had to bring Sylvia home.

"Can you think of anyone who would want to hurt Michael?"

"Nah, why would anyone? He paid his bills. He worked hard. Michael minded his own business."

That was the second vote for a Michael Deramo who minded his own business. He'd obviously put up a good front for that. But if he'd really minded his own business, he might still be living here, I wanted to tell his landlord, and you wouldn't be piling his sparse estate into a pickup for recycling.

"Do you have a new renter?" I asked, mostly because I was out of significant questions.

"No. I think I'll turn it back into a garage. Store some of my own junk."

I stood to leave and Bargello leaned back in his chair, as if he'd already finished work for the day. I reached down to shake his hand.

"You find his killer, huh?"

"We'll do our best, Mr. Bargello."

I walked back to my car, and on the way I noticed the set of prints that I'd seen on Michael's wall. The four photographs were lined up, spread out over the bulkhead door that led to Bargello's cellar. I stood looking down at them, thinking of their previous status as a shrine to Bari, Italy. Like their owner, they'd now been relegated to the ground. They were no longer useful, no longer admired by anyone.

"Do you want those pictures?" Bargello called out to me, probably mistaking my reverie for art appreciation.

For a moment, I considered adopting the set of photographs, as if they were Michael's orphans, needing a home.

"No, thank you," I said, and went to my car.

DRIVING TO THE LAB in my Cadillac, I was able to convince myself that there was nothing inappropriate about my appearance at a technical seminar. I made a mental list of what I would look for in Hammer and Laughton's presentation—how they'd handled the waste issue, and whether they'd solved their bonding problem, for starters. My guess was that Michael's death and all the publicity surrounding it had forced them to clean up their act, both literally and figuratively.

Andrea met me in the lobby of the physics building. She held out a bag of chocolate candy and invited me to take a piece.

"Not before noon," I said. "Like my father's rule about alcohol."

Andrea laughed and ate another chocolate, causing me to lick my lips.

"This is my breakfast," she said. "I had to take my roommate to the airport really early this morning."

"I hope you didn't rush back on my account?"

"Oh, no. I wanted to come to the seminar anyway. And I wanted to see how your investigation was coming. I can't believe there was another murder. I didn't know about it when I called you yesterday, but it's been all over the news. My roommate thinks I should find another job."

"I can see why."

"Are you getting close to finding the killer?"

"Well, I'm really here for the seminar, Andrea."

"Oh, of course. I should know better—you can't talk about the case. I'm sorry."

I didn't have the heart to tell Andrea my contract had been terminated in a dramatic way by a police sergeant of our acquaintance. I had the feeling she was living vicariously through what she perceived to be my exciting adventures.

By nine fifty-five, Andrea and I were headed for seats toward the back of a large, modern auditorium, equipped with screens, writing boards, and video displays that moved into place at the touch of a button. The seats, upholstered in mauve to match the carpets, were arranged theater style, set up to accommodate at least two hundred people.

I'd expected to be an anonymous observer, but a man in a dark brown suit by Uomo interrupted that plan.

"Interested in lithium, Dr. Lamerino?"

I turned to find Barry Richards close enough to brush his shoulder against mine in a gesture that he probably considered playful, and I thought annoying. For one thing, he'd pronounced my last name the way most non-Italians did, with a longish *a,* instead of the *a* that sounded like "ah." My name came out "Lamberino." He probably says "Eye-talian," too, I thought.

"I'm interested in all physics, Mr. Richards," I said, wishing I could have come up with a way to mispronounce his name.

I followed Andrea into one of the few available clusters of seats, and, without asking permission, Barry took a place next to me.

"How's the investigation coming along?" he asked. "I hear it's now a double homicide."

"Do you know Andrea Cabrini?" I asked him, in a tone meant to reproach him for lack of common courtesy.

Andrea leaned over and offered her hand, but Barry gave her a perfunctory wave that looked more like a dismissal than a greeting.

I wondered why Barry Richards without a weapon intimidated me more than Francis Deramo waving a gun at me, and decided it was his crooked smile and the nagging memory of how he'd seemed to know the exact hour of Michael's murder when Matt and I had interviewed him in the cafeteria. I also noted with interest that he'd referred to the Deramo and Massimo murders as a double homicide, as if he knew they were committed by the same person. Not nearly incriminating enough to arrest him, unfortunately, but definitely something for my notebook.

"Have they caught the mugger, or whatever hoodlum was responsible?"

"Of course, I'm not at liberty to talk about an investigation," I said. I tried to imitate his smile, but had the feeling I came off looking simple-minded rather than devious.

Fred Laughton's appearance at the podium spared me further conversation with Barry Richards. Laughton was wearing a dark suit and tie, and both he and Hammer, who was standing next to him, were considerably better groomed than they'd been when I'd first met them.

Laughton's introductory transparencies were mostly boilerplate about the advantages of lithium batteries in portable computers, like notebooks and palmtops. Several photographs of the process of lithium recovery from the brines of lakes in California and Nevada added color, if not substance, to the talk.

Laughton and Hammer took turns presenting the status of their research, neither one giving any indication of trouble on the workbench. As far as anyone could tell from the sixty-minute talk, the battery was ready for the patent attorneys, who I understood to be the law firm of Barry Richards and Francis Deramo.

During the question-and-answer session, a young woman near the front asked about the results of the task force studying the environmental impact of the lithium waste program.

Laughton gave a nonanswer, as if he'd been prepped by an expert in meeting the media.

"Lithium production in the United States is still in its infancy," he said, "and so it has safety challenges, like all new technology. We're doing more than required to be sure our citizens are protected from undue hazard."

Thanks for sharing that, I thought, smiling at his use of the word "challenges" instead of "problems," a typical public relations ploy. I'd kept my firm resolution not to voice my comments in this public forum, but couldn't help wondering if this seminar would have been different if Michael Deramo hadn't been eavesdropping, or if he'd gone to a proper authority, like the research director of the lab, with what he'd overheard.

Other than a few technical questions on the voltages and physical dimensions of the new product, the audience appeared satisfied and packed up to leave the auditorium. I walked out of the row in the opposite direction from Barry, an unusual choice for me, since I usually maneuvered to talk to murder suspects, not avoid them.

My tactics didn't work, however, since Barry caught up with me at the back of the auditorium. He maneuvered around people filing out, arranging himself in a position to talk to me.

"So, what do you hear from the police?" he asked me.

Taking a cue from Laughton's presentation, I summoned up my own meager media training and pushed forward with a nonanswer.

"Did I tell you Andrea here is a second-level technician?" I said. "She has her hand in just about every lab program."

I knew I sounded more like a proud grandmother than a smooth talker, but I was counting on the crowded conditions to dissipate the effect. "She's been talking to me about impurities that could be trapped in your battery."

"Not exactly my battery. I'm afraid you two know more about that than I do, Doctor. I must say I'm impressed with your knowledge."

Barry scratched his head as he spoke, and I was startled by what appeared to be a heartfelt sentiment. Either Barry was genuinely unaware of any problems, or they'd all been taken care of, or I was easily flattered into dullness, I decided.

"Do you want to grab some lunch?" Andrea asked as we made our way into the lobby.

Barry declined and, this time, shook both our hands.

"Some time we'll have to get together and you can both give me a tutorial on what it is I file papers on for a living," he said, and disappeared into the noisy crowd.

SIXTEEN

My instant mental replay of the conversation with Barry Richards left me confused. I tried to determine what had come over him during Laughton's seminar. I ran down a list that included guilt on his part and false stereotyping on my part.

"Lunch?" Andrea said, with an emphasis that told me she'd been trying to snap me into the present.

"Good idea. Is there someplace nearby that you like?"

"I usually bring my lunch or go to the cafeteria, so I don't know what's around here."

"There's a new place on Squire Road that I noticed as I drove over here. We could try it." Leave to it me, I thought, to know all the eating establishments even better than long-time workers in the area.

"Sounds good to me. Let's go out the back," Andrea said, and led me down a flight of stairs through the laboratory infrastructure. The long corridor in front of us was without the embellishments of carpet and false ceilings, or even fresh paint. I could see the delivery dock ahead of us as we passed storerooms, a copy center, and the mail room.

The mail room. I stopped in my tracks.

"Do you mind if we stop here for a minute?" I asked Andrea.

"Do you have something to mail?"

"No, I need some information."

Fortunately, Andrea Cabrini was one of my biggest fans and never questioned my motives. As far as I could remember, she'd never refused an invitation I'd extended, nor challenged anything I'd told her. This day was no exception.

"Okay," she said. "Lucia's on duty this morning. She's

really nice. I'm sure she'll help you.'' Andrea hit the bell on the counter, and a short woman in her forties, with thick dark hair, appeared almost immediately.

"Hi, Andrea. What's up today?"

Lucia leaned over the counter, both hands extended and clasped together as if she were in a church pew. The piles of boxes and overflowing canvas bins behind her were in enough disarray to give me stress, but she seemed to have all the time in the world.

"This is my friend Dr. Lamerino," Andrea said. "We're going out to lunch."

"How nice."

"She wants to ask you something first, though."

I thanked Andrea for her introduction, awkward as it was, and addressed Lucia.

"I need to know how Federal Express works, Lucia. Can you tell me the procedure, and perhaps show me a sample receipt?"

"Sure, I can do that," she said, in a pleasant Hispanic accent.

Lucia pulled a mostly white cardboard envelope, like the one Massimo had described to me, from a drawer under the counter and began her explanation.

"First I find out who it's going to. Then I find out who it's from. Then I go to the computer and type it in and print out a label. I put one on this side and one on this side." Lucia seemed to have had experience with day-care children—her sentences were short and clear. She pointed to the two blocks in the upper half of the envelope to show me where the labels would go.

"Then I peel off this little strip—this is the tracking number—and I give it to the customer."

I was a little distracted by the possibility that Lucia kept her nails a good half inch longer than mine just to make it easier for her to lift the small purple tab of the tracking strip.

"What happens on the other end, when the envelope is delivered?" I asked.

"The driver gives the person the envelope, and whoever receives it signs on the clipboard."

"Does the person who receives it know where it's from before he opens it?"

"Yes, it's right here, remember?" Lucia pointed to the imaginary "from" label she'd already explained. I was sure she thought Andrea had a dense friend.

"Of course," I said. "Sorry."

Lucia made a quick recovery from my dumb question.

"That's all right. It's confusing at first. The last thing is, the driver enters the day and time and the signer."

"Is there a record of who signs for a letter, other than on the driver's clipboard?"

"When the driver gets back to his truck, he enters everything into a central computer right there. And I had to get trained on this part. It's called PowerShip, and I get a printout of all the transactions every day. If I have the number, I can get information on any package."

I could have stopped right there, thanked Lucia, and moved on to lunch, but I seemed to have lost the power to abort this line of questioning.

"Is there any way you could know who signed for a particular package sent from this mail room, say, ten or eleven days ago?"

"Sure. But I couldn't give out that information," she said, straightening up, as if to illustrate her moral uprightness.

I was ready to accept Lucia's pronouncement and move on, almost relieved that her regulations were preventing me from getting into trouble. Andrea, however, had other ideas, and I feared I'd created another monster snoop.

"Dr. Lamerino works with the police," Andrea said. "She's trying to solve Michael Deramo's murder, and maybe

Carlo Massimo's.'' Andrea looked at me with what I took to be admiration.

''I feel so sorry for those men,'' Lucia said. ''My husband can't believe all the people at this place that have been murdered. He wants me to get another job.''

Andrea nodded her head in sympathy and told Lucia about her roommate's admonition just that morning.

''I can understand how you'd both feel that way,'' I said. ''But the police are doing their best, and I'm sure the killer will be caught soon. I suppose the other people in the police department already questioned you, Lucia?'' I resorted to my usual white-lie cover-up by coughing slightly at the words ''other people in the department.''

''No, they haven't,'' she said.

I couldn't think why not, except that the mail room was closed on weekends and they hadn't gotten around to coming this morning.

''Dr. Lamerino solved Eric's murder last fall,'' Andrea said.

''Imagine that,'' Lucia said. ''I would like to help you, but what would I know?''

I convinced myself that I was now under obligation to answer Lucia's questions.

''Well, for one thing, you might have been on duty the day Mr. Massimo came in to mail a letter for Mr. Deramo?''

''I was,'' she said, with a guarded look that told me she thought she might be under suspicion herself, if not for murder, then for some infraction of the rules in her employee handbook.

''Do you remember anything about that transaction?''

''I could show you the records, if you're police.''

Even I couldn't bend the rules that far, as much as I wanted to see the printout.

''I don't want you to be uncomfortable, Lucia,'' I said. ''Why don't I just have the other officers come and get it.

That's really their part of the investigation." And that's doublespeak on a par with Fred Laughton's and John Hammer's, I thought.

Andrea and I turned away from the counter to continue our trip to the back stairs, but Lucia called after us.

"One thing I remember that's different," she said.

"Yes?"

"I remember we had to use Carlo's—we always call each other by our first names...."

Lucia's voice cracked, as if she'd just come to a more personal understanding of the deaths of two people she knew and liked. I put my hand on hers.

"If this is too hard for you..."

"No, I want to help," Lucia said.

"We had to use Carlo's return address because he didn't know Michael's exactly."

I swallowed and hoped my involuntary groan was not audible.

"That could be important, Lucia. Thank you."

"So, whoever signed for the letter knew Carlo mailed it, not Michael?" Andrea asked when we'd left the counter for the second time.

"Right."

"Not that it's any of my business, but why does it matter? What was in the letter?"

"I don't know exactly, and anyway, probably we shouldn't be talking about it here."

I looked around, remembering how my indiscriminate discussion with Carlo might have contributed to a motive for killing him. I didn't want Andrea to be next. She put her chubby index finger to her lips to indicate silence, and we walked to the exit without another word. I wasn't sure what Andrea was thinking, but my mind was busy trying to figure out a way to get the real police to talk to Lucia without giving myself away.

THE PERIODIC TABLE was a new restaurant on Squire Road that was run by three retired lab chemists. The pale brick walls were covered with chemical equations, written graffiti-like in bright colors, and the glasses and dishes and vases were right out of a scientific supply catalog—beakers, oversized petri dishes, and tall graduated cylinders. The decor was close to what I would have chosen myself if I'd been inclined to retire to food service, but I'd had my fill of restaurateuring, stuffing hot dog rolls and spinning cotton candy on Revere Beach as a teenager.

We took seats under a large poster of the periodic table, and I saw a whole new side of Andrea Cabrini as we read the menu, which of course was decorated with symbols from physics and chemistry.

"I wonder if they have hydrogen soup," she said, then roared with laughter as we saw that it was the special of the day. I'd never seen Andrea so relaxed, and I entertained the thought of adding her to my short list of friends on the East Coast. Or any coast, for that matter.

"I'm glad you'll be coming to my party," I said, in a burst of camaraderie.

"Maybe I'll try to make one of these dishes and bring it along," she said, apparently unaware that Rose Galigani ran her kitchen like a kosher deli—no outside food allowed.

For a few minutes we forgot that what had brought us together in this delightful setting was a double murder. Andrea seemed to remember at the same time that I did.

"I can't believe they're gone. Michael and Carlo. They were both so nice. What could they have done to deserve to be killed?"

"We may never know, Andrea. But that doesn't mean we can't find and punish the killer."

"Do you think it was the same person?"

"I do, but that's just my opinion. How well did you know Carlo Massimo?"

"He came around at least once a week to talk to Nino Sartori, the guy who cleans the wing I usually work in. He was Nino's boss, too, besides Michael's."

"Maybe it's time for me to talk to Nino," I said, in what I thought was an internal mutter. It was loud enough for Andrea to hear, however, and she treated it like a request.

"He'll be at Cavallo's, at Carlo's wake," she said, looking at her watch. "In fact, I'm going to meet him there in about a half hour. Do you want to come? I could introduce you."

"I'll have to start paying you as my press agent," I told her.

"I'm so glad I can help. I don't have a lot going on right now."

It took much less time than it should have for me to brush away the image of Matt's unhappy face and decide to go to Carlo's wake. I considered what I'd do if I ran into Matt at the funeral parlor. I couldn't use the "I live here" defense at Cavallo's, and it was too late to apply for a job there.

I tried to remember what exactly I had promised Matt with respect to keeping out of the murder investigation—surely I hadn't promised not to comfort the grieving? I wished I hadn't thrown away all my old catechisms, in case I had to document my motivation.

ANDREA AND I had driven both our cars to the restaurant, and planned to reconnect in the Cavallo Mortuary parking lot.

On the drive to the mortuary, I pushed in a cassette tape of Neapolitan folk songs, which I'd selected in memory of Michael Deramo and Carlo Massimo, two men I'd never known alive, except for my brief conversation with Carlo. Alone in my car, I took the opportunity to organize my thoughts so I'd be ready for Nino, and for other spontaneous interviews in case any of the suspects showed up.

I started with my version of how the crimes came about. My favorite scenario was that Francis Deramo had received the Federal Express letter from his father, put it together with information from Laughton and Hammer that Michael was expecting a payoff, and decided to kill his father to protect his company's patent interests. Carlo was then the innocent victim of circumstances, one of which was his talk with me at the Galigani Mortuary. In this version Sylvia was an accomplice—she'd overheard us and told her husband that Carlo was a threat.

I knew that Francis should be the top of my list of candidates for two good reasons. One, he had pointed a gun in my general direction; and two, he was a lawyer, not a scientist. But for all his tough-guy bravado, as I recalled the interaction, I thought Francis was a pitiful sight in front of me in Martha's office, as if he wanted desperately to scare me away, but was more scared himself.

As for the lithium team, I still had trouble acknowledging the dark side of men and women who chose to study the lofty fields of science and mathematics, and I was quick to excuse them as suspects in a murder. I tried to make even young Andrew Palmer a more likely candidate than Laughton or Hammer. How trustworthy was an alibi from members of one's club, I wondered—especially a race car club. Without benefit of FBI profiler training, I decided that race car enthusiasts were wild, debt-ridden young philanderers, certainly more capable of murder than Ph.D. physicists.

With a little effort, I was able to concoct a plausible scenario: Michael had already been collecting money from the scientists and Andrew knew about it. He needed money for his expensive hobby and murdered his step-grandfather in a failed attempt to cut in on the blackmail scheme. This meant that his tears at Michael's wake were phony, designed to throw me off. Elaborate as it was, I couldn't rule it out. No one said murder plots had to be simple, I reasoned. I wished I'd asked Andrew more questions at Michael's wake, and I made a mental note to figure out a way to talk to him again.

In another scenario, Barry Richards and his sister, Sylvia Richards Deramo, both conspired to help Francis, for both business and personal reasons. After all, to Barry, having a father-in-law like Michael anywhere in the family took away from his social standing. While it wouldn't stand up in court, there was also Rose's report—whatever her reinterpretation of her words, Sylvia had referred to ''playing with the big boys,'' just as Francis had.

In a final gesture towards objectivity, I considered the possibility that Laughton and Hammer had helped Francis, perhaps by encouraging him.

I was frustrated by my lack of knowledge in the case, and the certainty that I wouldn't be getting any more information from Sergeant Matt Gennaro. I still didn't know what Sylvia's alibi was. What had she been doing while Francis supposedly passed by his father's house and drove on when he saw no lights? And how had Barry Richards been able to give an alibi for what was the most likely hour of Michael's murder?

In a flight of fancy, I imagined how Matt and I could help each other. I could tell him what I'd learned about the Federal Express process, and he could give me all the police reports on both murders. And a fully equipped laser lab for my spare room, I added, to complete the dream.

Arriving at Cavallo's with my theories as full of holes as a semiconductor, I turned my attention to parking my Cadillac and scanning the other vehicles in the lot for signs of an RPD unmarked. When I didn't see any of the two or three cars I'd ridden in during my tenure with the department, I unclenched my jaw and let out a long sigh.

SEVENTEEN

I ENTERED THE Cavallo Mortuary with Andrea, feeling like a traitor on two counts. First because I was disobeying Matt's official orders, and second because I was in a rival funeral parlor. I hadn't been to a wake other than at the Galigani Mortuary since my return to Revere. I wondered if anyone lived above the parlors at Cavallo's, and hoped I'd remember not to climb to the third floor myself out of habit.

The mourning rooms at Cavallo's were darker than those at Galigani's, with no relief from heavy brown drapes and a deep burgundy flocked wallpaper. Although Galigani's was dark by California standards, Frank had recently had the parlor walls painted an off-white, to balance the brown mahogany woodwork.

"Robert tells me it's the new style," Frank had said, sounding unconvinced himself. "He reads all those magazines that we never had when I was coming up in the profession. I guess the emphasis is different these days—not like when the organist played dirges and the priests wore black vestments."

"Like the changes in the Catholic Church itself," I'd said, matching Frank's grimace with my own.

The visitors at Carlo's wake looked very much like the group at Galigani's for Michael's viewing. I could have believed that they were a traveling troupe of professional mourners, hired for the funeral circuit in Revere.

Andrea seemed not to understand why I walked by the guest book without signing it, but then she hadn't been present at the tearing up of my contract. We went straight to the older woman in the front row, a sad figure in black, who I guessed was more in the mood for an old-time funeral dirge than a homily on the joys of heaven.

I gave my usual eloquent condolences, following a man who addressed her as Mrs. Massimo.

"I'm sorry about your husband. I'm sure this is a difficult time for you, Mrs. Massimo," I said to her.

Mrs. Massimo nodded and continued passing the steady stream of tissues from her boxlike black purse to her nose. Andrea repeated my remarks almost verbatim, and we moved on without further conversation.

Andrea pointed out Nino Sartori, whom I recognized as one of the visitors at Michael's wake. We walked toward him, a small, dark man, hunched in his seat in the last row of chairs, just in front of the heavy drapes that divided the parlor from a corridor along the back of the room. I saw on his face what looked like sadness mixed with fear. It hadn't dawned on me until then that Nino might think he was next in line for murder, and that he might be considering a different employer, if not a complete career change.

"Nino, this is Dr. Gloria Lamerino," Andrea said. "She's sort of with the police, working on the cases for Michael Deramo and Carlo Massimo. She might want to ask you a few questions about the murders."

I stiffened at Andrea's candor and found myself engaged in an involuntary scan of the room for true law enforcement officers.

"Mr. Sartori, I'm very sorry about your friends," I said.

Nino's greeting was so respectful I thought he was going to kiss my hand. He looked at me with his drooping brown eyes as if he were seeking my protection, confusing me with a holy Doctor of the Church, as some of the saints were known.

We were still holding hands as I sat down beside him. I wondered how to determine if Nino had any useful information, conscious that Matt or his partner might arrive at any moment. Andrea left us to talk to a woman her own age, who'd just entered the parlor. I patted Nino's hand and launched into my query.

"Mr. Sartori..."

"Please, signora, you call me Nino."

I smiled at Nino's assumption that I was married or widowed, instead of an unmarried signorina, but I didn't care what it took to get him talking.

"Nino, do you feel like talking a little bit about Michael and Carlo?"

"Sure. Sure. I have a lot of stories."

"First, I wonder if you'd remember this—did a triangle have a special meaning for Michael?"

"A triangle?"

His version of the word was only one syllable, prompting me to rummage in my purse for a piece of paper. I took out the little notebook I always had on hand and drew a triangle about the same size as the one I thought Michael had drawn. I showed it to Nino.

Here I am interviewing again, I realized. I wasn't supposed to cross-examine people on my own even when I had a valid contract, one that wasn't in sixteen pieces in my boss's pocket. But that applied to suspects, I countered, in my self-debating mode. It shouldn't keep me from talking to Nino, an innocent janitor, certainly not the killer of two of his colleagues in the sanitation profession.

Nino shook his head at the sight of my black-felt-pen triangle. I tried making it look more like a crooked circle, but still got no positive response. I put the drawing in my purse and took another tack.

"Tell me about Michael," I said. "What do you remember most about him?"

"Ah. Michael loved Bari," Nino said.

"Did he ever go back to visit?"

"Oh, yes, yes. He went to Porto Vecchio especially. And

he sent me postcards. It was his boy, Francis, he sent him back many times. He was very good to his father before he met this new wife and her brother.''

"You mean Sylvia and Barry Richards?''

"Richards,'' Nino said, moving his lips in an exaggerated way to get the right sound for the vowels. "It didn't used to be Richards.''

"What do you mean?''

"Francis wife and the brother, they used to be Ridano, but they change it.''

Nino's grammatical errors were like music from my past, his mistakes the same ones I'd heard growing up, from my parents, aunts, and uncles.

"Sylvia and Barry used to be Ridano?''

"Yes, yes. Francis, he told Michael, and Michael, he told me. Way back, their parents, they change their name so they don't sound Italian anymore. I guess it's not so good to sound Italian where they live.''

"But Sylvia married a Deramo,'' I said.

"Right, right. Michael tells me how when they get married, she doesn't want to change her name.''

As one who had never understood why a woman would ever change her name to her husband's, I was faced with one who wanted to do the right thing for the wrong reason. I supposed Sylvia had adopted the Palmer name willingly at her first marriage, selective feminist that she was.

"But finally she did,'' Nino said. "But she always say Sylvia Richards Deramo, just the same.''

"Did her family have a problem with her marrying an Italian?''

Nino shook his head and laughed in the way people do when they're about to tell you a joke.

"Just Barry had a problem,'' he said, dabbing his watery eyes. "See, Barry never learned to say Italian words right. He said Bari like it was Barry. So, Michael used to say Barry like it was Bari.''

In spite of Nino's mixture of laughter, tears, and broken English, I knew what he meant—it was the *a* problem, like the one Barry had with my last name, pronouncing the *a* in Lamerino like the *a* in "back," instead of like the *a* in "barn."

"Isn't that funny, like you say, a coincidence?" Nino said. "Barry and Bari."

"It surely is," I said, joining in his laughter. But I had a strong feeling that it was more than a coincidence, that it had to do with Michael's message, if I could just fit the pieces together.

"He call me 'tailor,'" Nino said. "*Sarto* is Italian word for tailor. We have such good times with these games."

Nino and I talked for a few more minutes, about sharing his lunch hours with Michael and Carlo. Nothing struck me as significant in his stories, but one did make me laugh, at Barry's expense.

"Barry, he has a—what do you call it—on his neck?"

"A birthmark."

Nino had turned his own neck to show me where the blue patch was on Barry's neck. He made no attempt to be subtle, and I gave a nervous look around the room to see whose attention we might have attracted. As far as I could tell, the twenty or so mourners were still facing front, and no new ones were coming into the parlor. Fortunately also, Nino spoke in a whisper. It was only his hands that were loud.

"Birthmark, yes. Well, Michael said it was the shape of Italy. The boot, you know, long and skinny. Michael told me Barry would have a fit whenever he said it."

I managed to convert a laugh into a wide but quiet smile, not revealing just how amused I was at the thought of Barry, with his Americanized name, wearing the map of Italy on his neck. I wished I'd paid more attention to it when he sat next to me at the seminar.

"Thank you, Nino. You've helped me a lot."

"Thank you, signora. You help me, too."

As I got up to leave I thought I heard a rustling of the heavy drape behind us. We moved the curtain, but no one was there, and I chalked it up to an overreaction to the similarity between this visit and the one I'd had with Carlo before his death. I seemed to be looking for stalkers everywhere these days.

Or maybe I'm not paranoid, and my alter ego is lurking behind the curtain, I mused—another amateur sleuth who lives on the third floor of the Cavallo Mortuary and is destined to solve the murders of the victims waked here. It was a nice piece of symmetry, I decided.

Before I went too far with that fantasy, I resolved to take my friends' advice and give myself a rest from intense police activities as soon as possible.

AFTER TALKING TO NINO, I was ready to go home and contemplate the great Italian-American coincidence. I knew in my heart that the clue to two murders was somewhere in Nino's reminiscences of Michael Deramo. Not that I had anything firm, just the feeling that I was getting closer to Michael's way of thinking.

I looked around for Andrea, to say goodbye, and saw her talking to Cavallo's newest guests, in the center of the parlor. They were my three top suspects—Francis and Sylvia Deramo and Barry Richards—and they'd managed to walk right by me while I was talking to Nino.

Andrea caught my eye and tilted her head in a "come on over" gesture. She'd make a good recruit for police work, I thought, and lifted my eyebrows in a response meant to convey "I'm on my way."

Weaving among the chairs in the back rows, most of which

were empty, I thought about the common wisdom that murderers always show up at the wakes and funerals of their victims. It never occurred to me that the Deramos or Barry Richards would have come to Cavallo's out of respect for Carlo Massimo, even though he'd been Michael's boss.

At the front of the room, fussing with the flowers next to Carlo's body, was a Cavallo Mortuary staff member with the telltale dark suit and posture of a funeral parlor employee. His handling of the floral pieces sent a fresh infusion of gladioli fragrance into the air. The first time I looked over at the man, I expected to see Frank or Robert Galigani. I have to get out more, I told myself.

"Dr. Lamerino," Barry Richards said as I joined them. "We meet again."

Barry ran his hand along the lapel of his jacket, which looked brand-new, although I couldn't imagine that he would have had a chance to change his clothes since I'd seen him in the lab auditorium.

"It seems we have the same interests," I said, straining to get a look at the Italian brand on his neck without being obvious.

"Did you know Mr. Massimo well?" he asked. Richards pronounced the first syllable of Carlo's name as if it were the word "mass." When I heard it, the same clicking went on in my brain that I'd heard while I'd been talking to Nino. It sounded like the soft ticking of a bedside clock, and I was waiting for the alarm to go off and wake me up.

Both Francis and Sylvia gave me polite nods and turned to face Andrea as if they had serious business to discuss with her and I'd interrupted.

I nodded back and got ready to play the doublespeak game with Barry.

"I think I neglected to congratulate you on the lithium battery report today," I said, ignoring his question about my connection to Carlo. "It looks like your patent schedule will be marching right along as scheduled."

"We've been confident of the product from the beginning. We had no reason to anticipate any problems."

"I didn't notice any hard copies of the transparencies," I said. "I was surprised that no written material was handed out. I usually like to look over data at my leisure."

"That's right," Andrea said, turning back to us and earning a dark look from Francis. "We always have copies printed out for the audience at seminars."

"I'm sure Dr. Laughton would give you a copy if you requested one," Richards said to me. "Call his secretary. In fact, I'll call her for you and have them sent over."

"Thank you, Mr. Richards, that would be good of you."

It was all I could do not to call him Signor Ridano, but I'd already pulled a similar stunt in his presence, with Il Martello, the Hammer.

I've got to move this conversation, I thought, preferably toward issues like alibis and motives. We'd been talking in hushed tones, as if we were in church, but still our voices were the loudest in the room.

I'd started to formulate a question for Barry about the effect of an environmental violation on the patent process when we were all distracted by a small commotion at the back of the parlor. It wasn't so much that the new group entering the room was loud—they were attention-getters simply by being on the job, two of them in the dark blue uniform of the RPD, the third one my friend and sometimes boss Sergeant Matt Gennaro, in a suit of almost the same color.

Matt glanced at me and frowned, more from surprise than displeasure, I assured myself. The two officers with him stood back two or three rows while Matt walked up to the person he'd come for.

"Francis Deramo, you're under arrest for the murders of Michael Deramo and Carlo Massimo," Matt said, for the first time within my earshot. I'd never heard the words spoken in person by anyone, let alone by the man who had fallen asleep on my living-room couch the day before. And although I'd seen handcuffs before, as part of Matt's standard equipment, I'd never watched him use them.

From Andrea's gasp, I gathered that this was a first for her, too. I wondered if she'd credit me for bringing this new excitement to her life.

I felt as if I'd stumbled upon an old episode of the 1950s television show *Dragnet* as I heard Matt in his official role, reading Francis his rights. Although Matt's voice was soft, befitting the formal venue, the phrase "if you cannot afford an attorney…" had an especially ironic ring.

I let out an involuntary comment as I witnessed Francis Deramo, his hands cuffed behind his back, look helplessly first toward his wife, and then at his brother-in-law and partner in law.

"This is a mistake," I said.

I was lucky that only Andrea and Sylvia seemed to hear me, and not anyone carrying a badge. Sylvia gave me a look of surprise, and Andrea gave me what I took to be encouragement, as if to urge me to continue my protest, but I had the sense, for once, not to.

Sylvia and Barry remained more calm than I would have expected in such circumstances. I chalked it up to their early training in public behavior. Barry immediately assumed the role of lawyer and advised Francis to remain silent. Sylvia seemed to walk straighter than ever, her eyes maintaining an uninterested stare as she followed the men out of the room.

EIGHTEEN

BACK IN MY APARTMENT about an hour after Francis's arrest, I replayed the scene in my mind. It was as clear to my memory as if I were watching a videotape. The total recall I experienced might also have had something to do with the dramatic background music I'd chosen—the death scene from Verdi's *La Traviata*.

The whole event had taken only a couple of minutes, the tinkle of the handcuffs not that much different from the sound of the little bell the altar boy rings to announce Benediction at St. Anthony's Church. I wouldn't have been surprised to learn that the mourners in the front rows of the parlor had no idea what had gone on.

I sat in my rocker, the DERAMO file on my lap, its exile over as far as I was concerned. Contract or no contract, I had work to do. I wished I knew what had prompted Francis's arrest. And I wished I knew what had gone through Matt's mind when he saw me there.

Most of all, I wondered why I didn't believe that Francis had murdered his father and his father's supervisor. He was, after all, the only one of the suspects who had physically threatened my life, unless I counted the possible jogger/stalker, who'd seemed a lot heavier than Francis.

I figured it was the letter from Michael and the evidence that Francis had received it that had sealed his fate. It was hard to hold on to the thought that I was the only one who'd been able to determine how the Federal Express tracking system worked. I took some solace in the fact that I'd found the draft scrap of letter in the first place, on Bargello's lawn—the only shred of help I'd given the RPD. Balanced with what I saw as my role in causing Carlo Massimo's death, it didn't seem like much.

And I'd failed miserably in my real job, to uncover a scientific motive, if there was one. After hearing the seminar, I had to admit that Laughton and Hammer's technical data looked pretty convincing.

I thought back to my own years in physics research and how easy it would have been to present a false picture of my results—a small change in the recording of a temperature, a voltage measurement, or an energy deposit could mean the difference between the appearance of success and failure. All it would take in any laboratory facility would be conspiracy among a few colleagues, and no one would be the wiser.

Fortunately, it was built into the minds of most scientists throughout history that even the "failure" of an experiment provided enough information to qualify as progress. And for most of us, the integrity of scientific investigation was more important than any pressure for external rewards. Or so I wanted to believe.

If anything was suspect, I decided, it was the environmental practices of the lithium program managers. Often the harmful spin-off from research was considered negligible, a necessary trade-off for progress, and some scientists might not think twice about fudging that kind of data.

To give my mind a rest, I called sunny California, where it was just after lunchtime. I had to be satisfied with Elaine's answering service at work.

"Don't worry, there hasn't been another murder," I told Elaine's voice mail, hoping only Elaine would hear it.

I left the same message on Rose's answering machine at home. Having given over Carlo's wake to the Cavallo Mortuary, the Galiganis' business had a few days off, and I was without a friendly distraction, another reminder of my need to develop more options for conversation and relaxation.

I ruled out a call to Matt, since I assumed he was busy with paperwork for Francis Deramo. My last hope for a chat was with Peter. I had to firm up plans for my talk the next day anyway, and since his recent behavior had been so pleasant, I didn't even dread the call.

"Gloria. I was just thinking about you," Peter told me. "Looking forward to your talk tomorrow as usual."

"I'm all ready for it, I think. Do you still want me to wear my academic gown?"

"Yes, if it's not too much trouble."

"Not at all. I love wearing my robes. And I should be there about ten, is that right?"

"Right. The ceremony will be at ten-thirty, then we'll have refreshments. I just got off the phone with Luberto's. They're doing a tiramisu and a special cake for us."

"My mouth is watering," I said, without exaggeration.

"Did you need anything from me?" Peter asked.

"No, I just called to say hello and to confirm the arrangements."

My call to Peter was a good deal shorter than I'd hoped. Wouldn't you know, I thought, when I can use a pest, Peter doesn't come through.

I RECOGNIZED THE LEVEL of my loneliness when I felt a twinge of annoyance at Rose and Elaine for not returning my calls. I resolved to find a club to join in the next six months. Happily, before I did something drastic like pay dues to a health club or to the Women's Auxiliary of the Sons of Italy, my phone rang.

"Hi. This is Andy. Andrew Palmer," the young male voice said.

"Hello, Andrew."

Sylvia Deramo's son would have been among the last names I'd have guessed if I'd made a list of likely callers. I sat up straight on my rocker as if to increase my alertness.

"Do you remember me, Dr. Lamerino?"

"Of course I remember you. The champion race car driver."

"Yeah, right."

"And you pronounced my name correctly. I'm impressed."

"Yeah, Michael used to teach me a little Italian."

"Have you been thinking about Michael?"

"Yeah."

"I have, too. I suppose you've heard about his supervisor, Carlo Massimo—a second murder victim."

"Yeah."

"Are you feeling any better, Andrew?"

"Yeah, I'm okay."

So, I thought, what next? Is this how the younger generation carried on conversations? Talking all around the subject? I had to remind myself that Andrew had called me and not vice versa, so my best option was to wait him out to find out why. I walked around my living room with my phone, to keep myself occupied, thinking it would increase my level of patience.

"I'm glad you're okay," I said, getting into the groove of Andrew's special language.

"You gave me your card."

"I remember. I'm glad you called."

"You were asking if I thought someone might want my step-grandfather out of the picture?"

"Yes, that's right. Have you thought of something, or someone?"

"Yeah, my mother."

I drew in my breath and picked up a pencil from my desk, as if I needed to write down what Andrew was telling me. I couldn't tell whether he had new information or just felt like reiterating what we all knew about Sylvia Deramo's dislike of her janitor father-in-law. Maybe Andrew had had a fight with his mother and wanted to vent his anger this way, I thought. Or maybe he liked his stepfather, Francis, more than he liked his mother and wanted to distract the police from their current arrestee.

"What makes you say that, Andrew? It's a very serious accusation."

"I have some proof."

Well, there was my answer. Prudence told me I should immediately direct Andrew to call Matt, but I couldn't pass up a chance to redeem myself and the terrible job I done so far on this case.

"What kind of proof?" I asked him.

"I'd rather show it to you."

"Would you like to come over, or meet me somewhere?"

"So you're interested?"

"Of course."

Andrew's voice had taken on the tone of an informer at best, or an obscene caller at worst, and I wondered if I should trust him. For all I knew he was the killer and he was setting me up to be his third victim. I considered whether Andrew might be "my" jogger, but decided that he was not as tall nor as heavy as the person I'd seen. I'd also seen the jogger run when he heard my car alarm, and his gait seemed more like that of an older man than a twenty-year-old in very good shape. Not too scientific, I admitted, but my judgment was made.

"Would you like to come here?" I asked him.

"Maybe not."

"Where would you like to meet, Andrew?"

"I thought maybe my pad."

"Your pad?"

"Yeah. It's just a trailer, really. Over by Washington Avenue."

"Fine. Just give me the address and directions."

"Well, it doesn't have an address, exactly. But you go along Washington, then there's this dirt road right after St.

Mary's Church. Take a left there and keep driving and then you can't miss it.''

"Do you have a phone number in case I get lost?"

"No phone."

"Well, then I guess I'd better not get lost."

"So, tomorrow?"

"I have a speaking engagement in the morning. I could meet you around one o'clock. Will you be there?"

"Yeah. I'll see you then."

I WASN'T TOO COMFORTABLE with my arrangement with Andrew Palmer. Matt's voice had joined Josephine's in my ear, reprimanding me for a dumb move, and every now and then during the evening I had misgivings about meeting him on his turf—and a phoneless, addressless turf at that. I reminded myself that it would be broad daylight, and put my mind at ease by concentrating on Andrew's tearful moments at Michael's wake. The hardest thing was waiting so many hours to find out what Andrew considered proof that his mother wanted Michael out of the picture, in his words.

One cheerful, distracting task ahead of me was preparing for the mini-graduation in Peter's classroom at Revere High School. I took my long, black rayon gown and blue-lined hood from the plastic bag at the back of my closet, and thought about the many ceremonies they'd been through. After my own graduation, I'd worn them for alumni events, convocations at the laboratory, and annual commencement processionals—all joyous occasions, just as tomorrow's promised to be.

I'd bought my academic robes on the advice of my mentor, who assured me that I'd use them often enough to make a purchase more cost-effective than continual rentals. I brushed out the wrinkles and buffed the three velvet stripes across the wide sleeve. The hood needed pressing, but I managed to smooth it out with a damp towel.

Although it felt good to be preparing for something other than a crime scene or a wake, I had trouble pushing the image of prisoner Francis Deramo out of my mind. I pictured him in an orange jumpsuit, posing for mug shots, or trying to touch Sylvia's hand through a thick pane of glass. More than ever, since Andrew's phone call, I wanted to picture Sylvia in the prison outfit, confident that she'd ask for the designer version in size four.

I blamed my fantasies on my recent reading of an article in Matt's *Detective* magazine, on Alphonse Bertillon, who invented the mug shot and other photographic techniques of crime investigation in the late nineteenth century.

For the rest of evening I continued to succumb to the dating rule of my college years, which dictated that no self-respecting female initiates a call to a male. I invented good news about Matt's failure to contact me after our brief encounter at Cavallo's. He's busy, I told myself, closing out the case with Francis's arrest. For good news, he wasn't in my living room, as on other occasions, cursing me for continuing to participate in an investigation when it might be hazardous to my health.

Think hard, Josephine reminded me, *and you'll see what a bad sign this is that he hasn't called to check in and give you closure on your contract.* Never mind that Josephine wouldn't use a word like "closure"—her message rang true.

I finally tired of staring at my phone as if I could deposit enough energy to bring it to life, and started my bedtime ritual—turning off my computer, stereo, and living-room lights. I moved the curtain in my bedroom for a look at St. Anthony's tower in the moonlight.

Usually this was a settling moment in my nightly routine, but not this evening—across from my window on Tuttle Street, where occasionally there had been a patrol car, was a man in a dark jogging outfit, the white stripes down the legs of his pants shining in the glow of the streetlight.

I dropped the curtain as if it had suddenly burst into flames. I leaned back against my bed, my heart pounding. Through the thin fabric I saw the figure slowly take off at a trot toward Revere Street, as though he'd been waiting for me to notice him, and had made his point.

My first thought when my breathing slowed was to call 911. And what, I asked myself—tell the dispatcher about a jogger passing beneath my window? After a few minutes, I was able to convince myself that this was more good news. The murderer has already been arrested, I reminded myself, with a sudden confidence in the RPD's judgment, so the jogger is indeed a harmless neighborhood resident, one who regularly jogs past my house.

At midnight, I went to bed hoping to dream of Maria Agnesi's beautiful cubic curve with the graceful lines of a bouquet of flowers. Instead, I saw Francis Deramo's face in the Table of Facial Expressions, part of the metric photography scheme created by Bertillon a century ago to classify the physical reactions of criminals. In my half sleep, Francis was wearing a jogging suit, his face screwed up in layers of wrinkles like the ones in my academic hood, his tiny eyes reduced to dark lines beneath his brow. While I should have been hearing the victorious strains of *Pomp and Circumstance,* I heard the loud wail of Andrew Palmer pointing at his mother.

NINETEEN

SIX YEARS OF graduate school was good training for me in more areas than experimental physics. I'd also learned how to get through a day of classes or lab work on a few hours of sleep. If I could pass a quantum mechanics exam after only four hours in bed, I thought, I can talk to a group of seventeen-year-olds for a half hour on the same schedule.

As usual, I neglected to factor in the age difference—I was in my twenties in graduate school. I was surprised on Tuesday morning to find myself with a headache and heavy, tired eyes, having been kept awake by my dreams of murder and imprisonment.

As I dressed for the day, I checked on the street scene below my window. I thought of the jogger as a recurring presence, like the metal ducks eternally passing before the contestants in a shooting booth on the old Revere Beach Boulevard. This morning I saw no one passing by on Tuttle Street, however, except two nonthreatening retirees who lived down the block, out for their daily walk.

I put on a medium-blue dress and jacket, taking my cue from the old couple, whom I'd been using as a thermometer for several months. When they wore their light blue paratrooper outfits, I'd noticed, my unlined knit jacket was appropriate for the prevailing temperature. I wondered what they'd think of their role in my scheme to determine the weather without opening my window or going down three floors to the front door. I also wondered if I should tell them to watch out for a jogging murderer with stripes on his pants.

I hung my academic robe, in its plastic bag, on the hook in the back of my car and stuffed the morning newspaper into my briefcase. I planned to read it during breakfast at the coffee shop across the street from City Hall and not far from the high school. Before I left I'd checked my answering machine one last time, in case Rose or Matt or Elaine—my three friends in the world—had called during the four hours I'd been asleep.

I kept thinking about Sylvia as a murderer. It was hard to imagine her sneaking up on Michael with a wire. She was shorter than Michael and much lighter, for one thing, and for another, I didn't think garroting was her style. On the other hand, I wondered who else was in danger if she was a killer, since, unlike her husband, she was loose on the streets. I couldn't keep myself from trying to guess what Andrew's idea of proof was. Bloody designer shoes found in his mother's closet? A special-order debutante's gun with one bullet missing? A signed confession seemed too much to hope for.

I TOOK MY NEWSPAPER to Sabrine's Coffee Stop, hoping that the crowd had thinned out enough for me to occupy a whole table without guilt. It seemed a long time since I'd opened a newspaper to enjoy the science section or crossword puzzle, and Tuesday's was no exception—Francis Deramo's arrest had made the bottom of the front page of the *Revere Journal*, capturing my attention.

I read the few paragraphs that described how Francis had been taken into custody on suspicion of murdering his father and his father's boss, Carlo Massimo. In an attempt to convince myself that the RPD had the real murderer, I mentally resurrected the picture of Francis as he'd looked sitting across from me at Galigani's, his steel-gray gun between us. The presence of the jogger beneath my window after Francis's arrest did nothing to dismiss my doubts that the killer was still at large.

In the middle of this exercise, I felt my table shake and saw ripples appear on the surface of my coffee. I looked up from the newspaper and made a movement to head for the doorway, a reflex response from years living with earthquakes in California. Before I could rise, RPD's Sergeant Matt Gennaro took a seat on the rickety metal chair next to mine, setting his own drink down next to my plate of assorted mini-muffins and jam.

"Mind if I join you?"

It took a few seconds for me to swallow muffin crumbs and discard the notion of coming up with something clever.

"Not at all. Have a muffin." I nudged my plate toward him until it touched his hand, the closest I could come to giving him a big hug to let him know I was happy to see him. At the same time I tried to bury my newspaper, folded open to the Deramo story, under the sleeve of my jacket.

"Thanks, but I ordered a bagel," Matt said, pointing to the counter. He took hold of my arm and lifted it slightly, extracting the newspaper.

I smiled and took a sip of coffee.

"Do you come here often?"

"I'm following you."

"I'm flattered," I said, not far from the truth. In the past year, I'd come to rely on police presence beyond the ordinary "service and protection" that every citizen expected.

"You shouldn't be." Matt held the newspaper vertical between us, arranging it so that Francis Deramo's feet were planted firmly on Sabrine's table and his eyes stared out at me. "You were at Cavallo's because?"

"Another fill-in-the-blanks test? I'm on my way to school, so I suppose it's fitting."

Matt laughed, but I knew he wasn't happy with my response.

"It's over now," he said, laying Francis's newsprint body down on the table, "so I won't belabor this. But I have a feeling you haven't been following my orders."

I didn't like the sound of his voice, and I screwed up my

nose as if the word "orders" smelled funny to me, intruding on the pleasant aromas of coffee and pastries. At the same time, the young waitress brought Matt's bagel and cream cheese, and I hoped she didn't think that's what had prompted my reaction.

I need to remember, I told myself, that Matt is a law enforcement officer, in charge of my contracts when they're in one piece. From the immediate change in his demeanor, I gathered that Matt was also sorry about his tone.

"Gloria, I know it's difficult for you to…"

I felt obligated to help Matt out of his verbal quandary.

"Mind my own business?" I said. "I wanted to pay my respects to Carlo Massimo's widow."

This time Matt's laugh was pleasant and relaxed, close to his delightful "whoa."

"And that's why you quizzed the mail-room clerk at the lab?"

I sat back, slumped in defeat.

"You must be the best detective of all time."

"I could claim that, but the truth is that when we finally got to her, Lucia said she'd already explained everything to the nice police lady Andrea Cabrini brought to her."

"Oh dear."

"Right. Well, this case is over, so I don't have to worry for a while. I've thought about never hiring you again."

I chose to ignore Matt's threat and blurted out what was nagging at my brain.

"I don't think Francis is the murderer."

Matt sat back, and I figured he was taking a minute to suppress the law-and-order tone.

"You have something to back this up?"

"Not yet."

"Then not ever, since you wouldn't dream of continuing to investigate."

"I wouldn't dream…"

As I shook my head to indicate that I wouldn't dream. I opened my mouth to ask Matt what evidence he had against Francis that I didn't know about, but I got a look at his watch, handier to read than my own, and gasped.

"I'm supposed to meet Peter in two minutes. It's a good thing the school is right down the street."

Matt stood up and picked up my briefcase from the floor. I noticed he did not return my newspaper.

"Do you have dinner plans?" he asked. "Maybe we can celebrate the end of a case tonight?"

"Sounds good to me," I said, lifting my purse to my shoulder. "I'll even cook." And fill you with pasta so you'll talk about why you think this case is closed, I added to myself. "By the way, were you really following me?"

"In a way. I knew you were going to talk to Peter's class today, and figured you'd stop here."

I smiled and left the shop, happy that Matt could guess my movements. The fact that he made a living tracing the movements of criminals didn't spoil my pleasure.

IN LINE WITH his new persona, Peter made no fuss about my being eight minutes late.

"I'm just glad you're willing to do this, Gloria," he said, leading me to the faculty lounge.

I hooked my black gown closed over my dress and had Peter straighten my hood in the back so the bright blue lining showed. Like a man in a tuxedo, a woman in academic robes looks elegant, no matter what her age and size, and I was pleased with the effect I saw in the mirror above the faculty sink. I wondered how I would go about influencing the industry to make long, loose robes an acceptable fashion statement for everyday wear.

Peter's classroom was transformed for the day, with a small podium next to his desk and piles of parchment certificates ready to be handed out. His seniors had risen to the occasion by wearing normal pants and dresses instead of the array of oversized baggy shorts, miniskirts, and tennis shoes that I'd seen on every other visit.

Maria Agnesi came through for me, and the students seemed to enjoy my presentation of her life and accomplishments. Although I didn't necessarily recommend the specific paths she chose later in her life—abandoning mathematics to give herself to the works of the church—I wanted the students to appreciate the energy and enthusiasm which drove Maria to do things well, no matter how odd it made her look.

As I helped Peter hand out certificates to about two dozen young women and men, I realized that I hadn't seen so many Italian names on one list since my own days at Revere High School—Cerniglio, Guerrini, La Rosa, Tempesta—plus one lovely young woman with shiny black hair, named Gabriella Choy.

The most touching moment of the morning came when one of the students, Gina Imbriano, walked to the front of the room and handed me a package, beautifully wrapped in gold-toned paper designed to look like a map of the Old World.

"To thank you for everything this year, Dr. Lamerino. This is from all of us."

I looked over at Peter, who shrugged his shoulders and showed me his palms, managing to look helpless and proud at the same time.

"It was their idea," he said.

"You can open it," Gina said, apparently noticing that I was at a loss for both words and action.

I took a deep, controlling, breath, pulled at the gold ribbon, and unwrapped a large book, titled simply *Italy*.

"How beautiful. What a perfect choice," I said, touched by the students' thoughtfulness. "Thank you very much."

I wasn't prepared to have the attention shifted to me. I wished I could either think of a more memorable acceptance speech or disappear into the wide sleeves of my robe. The awkwardness of the moment was relieved by the arrival of rich desserts that kept us all busy for the next half hour.

"Thanks again," Peter said, after the students had left and we were sitting in the faculty lounge.

"I should be thanking you, Peter." I flipped through the pages of my new book, full of colorful plates. "I'll enjoy going through this—it'll bring back wonderful memories."

"I'm pleased to say that it really was their idea. All I did was give my approval when they asked what I thought. Paul formed a committee. They collected the money, chose the book, and wrapped it. Gina won the lottery to determine who would present it to you."

"Well, I love it."

"I hope you'll accept a little present from me, too."

Peter handed me a plain white envelope. His grin told me I'd find nothing as mundane as cash or a check inside. I opened it, conscious that he was waiting for a matching grin from me, but I couldn't work my face into anything but confusion when I saw the contents—two tickets to a concert at Symphony Hall, performed by the Academy of St. Martin's in the Fields, an all-time favorite of mine.

It was hard to find my voice, as I ran through my options—from an enthusiastic acceptance to "Sorry, I'm going steady with the cop." I chose a passionless, middle road.

"This was very thoughtful of you, Peter. I'll check the dates as soon as I get home."

Apparently Peter was tuned into the whole range of emotions I'd undergone, and wasn't happy with my final response.

"Yes, well, do let me know, Gloria."

"Peter..."

"I see from the *Journal* that they've solved the case of those two janitors who were murdered. Isn't that the one you were helping the cop with?" Peter said, his old self emerging in grand style.

"They've arrested someone."

"Did you have any interaction with him?"

"Him?"

"The killer, Gloria. Any wrestling matches or shootouts this time?"

Welcome back, Peter, I almost said out loud, but a young woman with an armful of books and papers entered the lounge, giving me a minute to compose myself. She nodded to Peter and turned on the small television set in the corner of the room. The noon news came on, at a very low volume, but I focused on the graphics behind the anchorman—a boring financial pie chart, but enough to calm me down.

"I didn't work on that case very much," I said, then switched to a more agreeable topic. "Isn't it wonderful that Gina was accepted at Middlebury?"

"Just because I haven't said anything lately it doesn't mean I'm not still worried about you, Gloria."

"I wish you wouldn't worry, Peter. By the way, I'm glad you'll be coming to my party at Rose and Frank's. I hear you're bringing Barbara Negri."

"I might invite her. This is your third murder investigation. I'm wondering how many cases it will take before you see how dangerous it is for you to be involved with the worst kind of criminals."

"About one hundred and nine all together," I said, thinking of beryllium, boron, carbon, and so on to meitnerium.

"What?"

"Never mind. It's just a joke," I said, smiling at my own wit, even if Peter didn't get it.

TWENTY

I LEFT PETER AT about twelve-thirty, both of us in a frustrated state, more typical of our meetings in the past year. I wondered how come Barbara Negri had been demoted to the "I might invite her" realm. My first, and uncharitable, thought was that Peter had simply used her in an attempt to tease me into jealousy and good behavior. My second, equally unkind theory was that Ms. Negri had no more tolerance for Peter's arrogance and sexist leanings than I had, and had refused his invitation.

I took out the paper with the directions to Andrew's trailer, giving less and less thought to Peter Mastrone as I drove northwest from Revere High School, toward the city limit on the Everett line. I remembered Andrew's warning that "it doesn't have an address, exactly," and drove slowly along Washington, passing St. Mary's Church at ten miles an hour so as not to miss the path.

Following Andrew's landmarks as best I could, eventually I drove through a gate in a chain-link fence into a gravel lot with a run-down trailer at its southeast corner. There were no other buildings in sight. Outside the trailer were an old pickup truck and an unidentifiable vehicle completely covered by a blue-and-white-striped cloth. From its long, low shape, I figured it to be a sports car, probably of the racing variety. Maybe it's a kart, I thought, with my newly acquired jargon.

I'd seen cars protected from the elements before, usually in simple canvas wraps, but this version was in a fabric nice enough for a party dress, in clear crisp colors.

The trailer's rusty supports and peeling paint gave it an air of abandonment. Its location was far from any busy thoroughfare, and when I stepped out of my car I heard nothing but the scraping of my shoes on the dirt and gravel.

Here and there the sunlight reflected off pieces of glass strewn among the small pebbles, casting a benign glow over the otherwise creepy setting. If it had been a rainy night instead of a sunny afternoon, I might have driven away immediately. I still wasn't sure whether I'd be brave enough to enter the trailer.

As I was rethinking the wisdom of solo sleuthing, a motorcycle thundered through the gate. I jumped back, pressing my body against my car, more from reflex than because of any real danger, since Andrew stopped at a safe distance from me.

"Hi," Andrew said in his customary talkative way.

I almost came back with "Yeah," but succumbed to the gravity of the situation—a meeting to look at physical evidence in a murder investigation.

"Hi, Andrew," I said above the roar of the bike. I noted with relief that he wasn't wearing a jogging suit with striped pants, although I was fairly certain anyway that Andrew was slimmer than the man hanging around my building.

Andrew pulled ahead and parked next to the pickup, motioning for me to follow. I wondered how the scene might look from above, to a police helicopter, for example. A pseudo-vacant lot on the outskirts of town, populated by a dilapidated trailer, an old truck, a Yamaha motorcycle, a new Cadillac with academic robes hanging in the back, and who knew what under a fancy drop cloth. Throw in a young man in black leather and an old woman in blue knit and you have a story, I thought.

"Sorry about that," Andrew said, watching me make my way across the gravel in shoes meant for city sidewalks.

"It's okay."

"Want to see it?" he asked, pointing to the covered-over car.

Without waiting for an answer, Andrew whipped back the cloth to reveal a kart, like the one I'd seen in the newspaper article. The bright yellow vehicle was even smaller than it had looked in the photo, very low to the ground and barely long enough to accommodate an adult. I wondered if Andrew's slight build might be a requirement for kart drivers. I was sure he'd be insulted if he knew how tempted I was to look for a cord in the front to pull it with.

"It has a motorcycle engine, a two-stroke, and it'll go to about one-twenty, no problem."

"One hundred and twenty miles an hour?"

Andrew nodded, seeming pleased that I was impressed.

"No problem."

"Is this the kart you drove when you won the regional title?"

It was Andrew's turn to be impressed. He lifted his eyebrows in surprise at my use of the technical term, and I gave silent thanks to my research assistant, Andrea Cabrini, who'd searched out the clippings.

"Yeah, I paid for it myself. Got it for less than eight thousand from a friend in the club. Paid my own fees and everything," he said, running his hand along the kart's sharp angles. I expected him to call it by name any minute, like some favorite pet.

Andrew covered up his kart and took a set of keys from his pocket. I nearly laughed out loud as he unlocked the trailer. It seemed to me that even I could have fit in through the other side of the door, in the space between the hinges and the frame of the building.

Andrew pushed the door open and stepped aside to let me enter first. Inside was another world. A clean and colorful world. Where I had expected black walls and neon psychedelic paint, the panels of the trailer were lined neatly with posters, each one of a different car and driver. The cars looked more like small airplanes, hugging the asphalt beneath them.

On the legends of the posters I saw names that were only
vaguely familiar to me: Mario Andretti, Michael Schumacher,
Paul Tracy, and what seemed to be a whole family of Unsers.

Where were Michael Jordan and Cal Ripkin, Jr., I wondered. As little as I knew about professional sports like bas-
ketball and baseball, I knew even less about race car driving.

I was struck by the number of advertising logos on the
uniforms of the drivers and on the cars themselves. I'd have
expected one brand name per car, but instead, each car had
an array of different corporate sponsors—a cigarette manu-
facturer, an oil company, big names in tires, electronics, and
soft drinks—the motif repeated on the uniform of the driver.

Andrew gave me a few minutes to look around, then acted
like any kid just out of his teens, still looking for parental
approval.

"Like it?" he asked, sweeping his arm across the expanse
of his domain.

"You have a nice setup here."

"Yeah, my dad owns this property. I persuaded him to
leave the trailer for me after they razed the buildings that were
here."

"Your biological father?"

"Yeah. He lives in Minnesota now. He bought me the
pickup, too, to move the kart around. "

"Are you close to your dad?"

"Close as we can be since mom got rid of him. I should
have been with him, but he's not married and she is, so she
got me."

I was intrigued by one poster that seemed to be a greatly
enlarged photo of Andrew himself, sitting on the edge of a
car that was much more elaborate than the kart in the newspaper article. An array of colored flags waved in the background.

"That's me," Andrew said, drawing himself up to about
five feet five inches. "That's a V-6, bigger than the little

125-cc kart I have outside. I had a scholarship to one of the best racing schools around, out in the Berkshires.''

"Did you go?"

"Yeah, and they said I was gifted—definitely Indy material, but—''

"Excuse me, but what do you mean by Indy material? That you could have entered the Indiana 500?'' I was proud of myself for knowing there was such a thing, but I was off the mark.

"It's Indianapolis 500,'' Andrew said with a polite smile, pleasing me with his diffident correction. "And no, I'm not ready for that for a while. An Indy is a kind of car. Bigger even than that one in the poster. But I would have had to pony up for about a year of training and local races. And my parents wouldn't support me.''

"Maybe they were worried about your safety. Or maybe they didn't have the money.''

"Yeah, right. They just didn't approve. They would have sent me to Harvard if I wanted to go, because that's their thing, you know? And I'll bet one year at Harvard would be twice as much as a year on the racing circuit.''

I wondered how I would have responded if a child of mine had Andrew's ambitions. Another blessing of childlessness, I thought, not to have to make those decisions. Looking at Andrew's smooth, young face, I decided to try a little parent-child counseling.

"You know, Andrew, most parents make choices like that. I have friends in California who paid for one son to go to Stanford—a very expensive private school, by the way—but refused to support their other son, who wanted to spend a year traveling around Europe writing poetry. It's hard not to impose your own values on your children, I guess.''

"Yeah, but I'm so close. I can see them making my customized seat—in my dreams.''

"Customized seat?" I asked, beginning to understand how Matt must feel during his periodic table tutorials.

"Seats and helmets are all customized for the big drivers. Those guys are basically molded into their cars." Andrew seemed to have left his tiny trailer for a large oval track with bright lights. "I'd make so much money I could pay them back big-time, if I could only get a start toward Formula 1."

I must have shown another sign of confusion, because Andrew clarified the term without my asking.

"And no, it's not chemistry. It's international competition. Faster. More class than Indy even." Andrew kicked the side of his table with his bulky leather boot, then gave me the apologetic look of a small child who really didn't mean to tell his mother he hated her. "Sorry," he said.

Like most sports enthusiasts I'd known, Andrew seemed to have put as much energy into his interest as other people put into doctoral studies, knowing every aspect of the field. But in spite of his intense ambition, if this was the angriest he got, I doubted he'd be capable of killing an old man he liked, even for money.

I did have one more matter I wanted to clarify, however, before I crossed Andrew off my suspect list. I felt I'd bonded with Andrew enough to be direct.

"Tell me about your drug use, Andrew."

I'd started to look around for signs of drug paraphernalia as soon as I'd entered the trailer, and realized I wouldn't know it if I saw it, unless it had a large label, FOR ILLEGAL DRUG USE. Although I'd lived through most of the 1960s in Berkeley, I was remarkably naive when it came to the drug culture. I'd also hidden in my lab rather than take a stand on the big issues. Another part of my life I should revisit someday, I thought.

"That was a onetime-only thing. My girlfriend—my ex-girlfriend—talked me into it. Uncle Barry believed me, at least, and got me out of it, and you're not even supposed to know about it. And that guy I knocked around? I hardly touched him. Anyway, it's about time we got down to why I asked you to come here.''

"You're right, Andrew. Let's get to that.''

Andrew cleared a spot on his tiny table, pushing aside racing magazines, pieces of a model car kit, and what looked like a uniform in shiny red and black fabric.

When we were settled, Andrew got to the point of my visit. He took out a piece of paper folded in quarters, held it between his thumb and index finger, and shook it at me.

"This is my proof," he told me.

He spread the sheet on the table and smoothed out its folds and wrinkles.

"This is the application form for the new club my mother wants to join. It's for the North Shore's finest women, you know? This is a copy she threw in the trash. She had a few of them around and kept redoing it.''

My, my, I thought, this case is an editor's dream, full of first drafts. I followed Andrew's finger down the page, past lines of information. Dates of birth, maiden names, addresses and occupations. He stopped at the section on father-in-law. Name: Michael Joseph Deramo. Occupation: Engineer. Status: Deceased.

"Engineer?" I said, with a smile. "This is pretty common, Andrew—many people refer to Michael's profession as sanitation engineer. I think it's amusing, but it doesn't prove your mother killed her father-in-law.''

"That's not the part I meant," Andrew said, tapping his thumb on the word "deceased" and stretching his index finger to the date at the top of the form. May 8. Sylvia had filled out the application two days before Michael's death.

I sat back and let out a long breath. After the initial surprise, I thought of many explanations and rattled them off for Andrew. She might have gotten the date wrong. Or she actually wrote in the information after Michael's death, but predated the application to meet some deadline.

"Why would she write this and incriminate herself, taking a chance that someone might check the dates?" I asked Andrew and myself at the same time.

Andrew had an answer ready.

"She realized it was incriminating and she wrote it over. I don't know what the one says that she mailed in. But, see, she was planning to kill him all along. If he was dead he couldn't mess up her life anymore."

Andrew's voice had an authoritative ring I hadn't heard from him before. Perhaps it only seemed so because we were on his territory, surrounded by his friends, the gods of race car driving. He ran his fingers through his hair, which seemed more red in the light from the dingy trailer windows than it had in the Galiganis' foyer. Maybe Sylvia's choice of hair color is close to her natural hue, I thought, in the circuitous, irrelevant way my mind usually works.

"How did you happen to find this?" I asked, remembering that I was there in the capacity of a police investigator, counselor, friend—anything but beauty consultant.

"It's a thing I do."

"A thing you do? Do you go through only your mother's trash, or everyone's?"

"I don't know. It started when she'd write letters to my teachers and counselors, you know, and I'd want to know what she was telling them. And lucky for me, she always practiced first. God forbid anyone would get a bad impression of my mother's writing."

"Andrew, I'll admit that this is strange. It's as if she knew Michael would be dead by the time the application got to the club. But it's nothing definite. I'm sure she can explain it away just as I did."

Andrew's face muscles were tight as a wing nut on a hubcap, his jaw moving up and down as if he were on his mark, waiting for the sound of the starter pistol. I could tell that my reaction had disappointed him, and we were at a standstill.

"Will you at least see what the police think?"

"Why don't you do that yourself, Andrew?"

"They won't believe me. I've been in trouble, like you said. And you said to call you."

I reached over and took his hand, conscious of how young he was.

"I'm glad you called me, Andrew, and I'm going to take this form home and think about it. But I want you to think about it, too. Try to be honest and ask yourself if there's some reason you want your mother to be accused of murder."

Andrew withdrew his hand and put his head on the table, supported by his crossed arms.

"Do you want me to leave?" I asked him.

"Yeah."

"Will you call me when you've thought things over?"

"Yeah," he said.

I DROVE AWAY from Andrew's nearly empty lot with a feeling of sadness, wondering why an intelligent, nice-looking young man from an affluent family wasn't a top-ranking freshman at an Ivy League college, going steady with a gorgeous pre-med student. Having had so little by way of material possessions when I was his age, I fell into the trap of thinking that money solved more problems than it created.

I was at a loss about how to help Andrew—I'd had so little to do with people his age, except for dealing with the Galigani children from a distance, which was quite different.

The longest contact I'd had with anyone even close to Andrew's age was with my godchild, Mary Catherine Galigani, when she was sixteen. She'd come to stay with me in California one summer when things were particularly stressful between her and Rose. Her disagreements with her mother paled in comparison with Andrew's, however, having to do with curfews and nail polish. She'd accused her mother of treating her like a baby and ruining her social life, but not of murder.

For the moment I was convinced that Andrew was acting out of resentment toward his mother and little else. It was clear that he preferred his father and blamed her for his parents' divorce and an unsatisfactory custody agreement. He might even have forged the document. And I couldn't rule out the idea that Andrew was covering for himself, distracting me by pointing to his mother. From what he'd told me, his hobby took a lot of money, which wasn't easy to come by with all the restrictions his parents had set up.

Anticipating dinner with Matt, I wondered if I should mention any of this to him. I knew I might be risking his intense disapproval of my actions with nothing to gain from the exercise if the lead didn't amount to anything.

I went through some scenarios in my head and calculated the likelihood that there was something to Andrew's suspicions and his trash-can find. The probability was small, but not zero.

TWENTY-ONE

I STOPPED AT A small market on Revere Street, not far from my building, to pick up ingredients for a penne and shrimp dinner. As I carried my basket up and down the aisles, I created a menu sprinkled with some of Matt's favorite touches—balsamic vinegar, garlic bread, biscotti without nuts. I questioned the normalcy of a woman who plans a strategy to seduce a man so he'll talk about a murder investigation, but I consoled myself that it meant I had professional integrity.

As I took a right onto my street, I saw a late-model black Lincoln Continental parked in front of the Galigani Mortuary building. Expensive cars were not a common sight on Tuttle, unless they were part of the funeral procession fleet, like mine. Has my jogger gone in for a change of tactic, I wondered, stalking me from a vehicle worthy of valet parking? Maybe we could order a stretch limo and have a luxury car chase, I thought, with a flight of whimsy that surprised me.

I drove into the garage as I usually did when I thought I was in for the night. I considered keeping my car door locked while I closed the garage door with the remote control. Then I'd be able to walk into the building without setting foot onto the street and with some level of protection at every stage.

Tired of feeling weak and threatened, however, I decided to walk around to the front door and face my guest. For all I knew the Lincoln was empty—I couldn't tell one way or the other through the tinted windows. Or maybe it was a new Galigani car after all. I was about to find out.

I walked toward the front lawn, laden with groceries, choosing to leave my academic robes and briefcase in the car for the moment, probably an unconscious desire to spare them any splattered blood should there be unpleasantness of the violent kind. I approached the walkway to the front door, apparently the signal for a uniformed driver to get out of the long, highly polished car and open its back door.

Sylvia Deramo stepped out.

She was wearing an olive-green outfit—matching suit, shoes, and handbag. Her hose was the perfect shade to blend the pieces into the ideal monochromatic image. On her it looked exquisite. In the same color, I would have looked like the subject of an army poster recruiting senior citizens. I wished Rose were present to see what I'd meant about who should be exiting luxury cars.

Surprised as I was, I managed to hold on to my groceries. I reasoned with some speed that if she'd come to kill me, she wouldn't have arrived in the middle of the day with her driver, both dressed for a fashion show. I ran my eyes along her chauffeur's jacket, checking for bulges, just in case.

"Good afternoon, Dr. Lamerino," she said, her voice without the shrillness I'd come to expect from her.

I was stumped as to how to greet her. "What are you doing here" seemed too crude for one who arrives with a chauffeur. "How nice to see you" would have been insincere. I held back on "I just came from your son's trailer. He thinks you're a double murderer."

"Mrs. Deramo," I said.

With one plastic bag of food in each hand, I felt as if I were her cook, caught out of the scullery and out of uniform.

"I wonder if we could have a few words?" she asked.

"Certainly. Would you like to come up to my apartment?"

"Thank you."

I wanted to warn her that the back of her Lincoln would have made a better meeting place than my living quarters. It probably had more plush seating, plus a full bar and stereo system. I tried to picture the condition I'd left my apartment in that morning. I usually kept a reasonably neat home, something between college dormitory mess and Josephine's operating-room standards. It was too late to run the vacuum, so Sylvia would have to take what we found up there.

"Follow me," I said, my nervousness depriving me of all verbal elegance.

Having had no experience with personal servants, I was conscious of my lack of understanding of the protocol. Should I invite Monsieur le Chauffeur? Were chauffeurs and maids to be ignored, treated as part of the landscape? Did everyone know this but me?

I took a middle road and nodded in his direction, raising my eyebrows at Sylvia.

"Mr. Westphal will wait here," Sylvia said, with a tone bordering on condescension, as if she were telling a small child how things worked in the adult world. I had the feeling she was holding back her full-blown patronizing attitude because she needed something from me.

I OPENED THE DOOR to my apartment and glanced around. Josephine would have marked it a B, I decided, taking points off for lint on the floor, unfluffed pillows, and a used mug on the kitchen counter. I didn't want to know what grade Sylvia gave it.

"Would you like a cup of coffee?" I asked, thinking the least I could do was to follow Josephine's rule of offering food and drink before anyone has even sat down.

"That would be nice. Thank you."

While I prepared coffee and arranged cookies on my best plate, Sylvia stood in front of my San Francisco poster. I couldn't tell if she was using its glass front as a mirror, as I often did, or if she was appreciating the artistic rendition of an omnipresent Bay Area theme—a cable car on a hill.

"You were in California how long?"

"More than thirty years."

"And you've been back?"

I wondered if this aborted speech was standard cocktail talk among the rich. Maybe Elaine could do a private grammar workshop for Rose and Sylvia when she visited.

"I've been back one year, almost to the day," I said, brushing aside a short-lived image of Sylvia at my anniversary party. If I had invited her it would have been to show off Rose and Frank's home.

"And what exactly is your status with the police department? Professional? Personal?"

I wasn't prepared for a quiz on my own territory, but something about Sylvia's manner softened me. For one thing, her eyes were red, in spite of what appeared to be a valiant effort to cover the signs of sleeplessness and tears. The words and music didn't match this time—although her words had a cutting edge to them, her voice was tired and almost pleading.

"Mrs. Deramo, I'd be happy to answer your questions, but my guess is you already know the answers. I'd like you to tell me the purpose of this visit," I said, trying to sound welcoming and firm at the same time.

"Fair enough. And please call me Sylvia."

We'd sat down across from each other on my rockers. For the first time, my favorite matching glide rockers, among the few pieces I'd brought from California, seemed tacky and low-class, as if I'd bought them, two for the price of one, at a garage sale.

"This is a very comfortable chair," she said, either from a mind-reading trick or because she'd never sat on ordinary furniture before.

She glided back and forth, like a kid from another planet learning the wonders of a playground swing. I admired my own patience as I watched her struggle to keep her composure.

"How is Mr. Deramo doing?" I asked, hoping it would help if I opened the topic of her prisoner husband.

"Not well, as you can imagine, even after only twenty-four

hours. My brother Barry is doing his best for Francis, but he's a patent attorney, not a criminal lawyer.''

"Do you have a defense attorney now?''

"Yes, Barry found us a good one, I think. Thomas P. Warner from Boston.''

I shook my head and acknowledged that the name meant nothing to me, nor would that of any other criminal lawyer.

"They won't release him on bail, because of the nature...''
Sylvia stopped to sip coffee and calm herself.

"I know,'' I said, filling in. "They don't usually allow bail in cases like this. It must be very hard on all of you.''

"I had the feeling that you don't think Francis is guilty,'' she said, her voice wavering. "From what you said when he was arrested.''

"You're right, I don't believe he's guilty.''

"I'd like to know why that is. First of all, since I know Francis was less than courteous to you. And, of course, I'd like to know if there's anything you can do for him. Through your connections to the police.''

I had the strongest urge to tell her one reason I didn't think Francis was guilty was that I thought she might be. And so did her son. I looked around for my briefcase containing the potentially incriminating social club application, almost relieved when I remembered I'd left it in my car. I wouldn't want Sylvia to find it, if it turned out she was really here to search my apartment at gunpoint.

"I don't know exactly why I think Mr. Deramo is innocent,'' I said. "Maybe because he could have been meaner to me than he was, given his advantage in the situation.'' That is, his gun, I said to myself. "I'm afraid I have little more than my instincts.''

"But you do have an inside track with the police, don't you, Dr. Lamerino?''

"I guess you could call it that. And please call me Gloria. Maybe if we brainstorm together, we'll make some progress.''

"I've been going over and over this with Barry and Tom Warner. It's true that I can only vouch for the time Francis came home that night after his meeting in Winthrop—around midnight. But I have no information on the critical time of his father's death, nor that other man's."

"Carlo Massimo," I said, wanting to give him status as a person.

"Yes, Mr. Massimo. They think the same person killed both men."

"Do you know when Carlo was murdered?" I asked, realizing that Sylvia might know more about Carlo's death than I did, since my inside source was protecting me from useful information.

"Well, the police are asking me if I know where Francis was around noon on Saturday, so I presume that's the time Mr. Massimo was murdered."

"And do you know Francis's whereabouts at that time?"

She shook her head.

"No. He says he was home swimming. We'd given everyone a day off, in honor of my father-in-law, so no one was with him. And I was at my club."

Skeptical of the calculus of the North Shore elite, I wondered about the meaning of the Deramos' gesture to the common folk, giving servants a day off in memory of a janitor.

"What about other alibis?" I asked, aware that Sylvia had already given me hers.

"They're not much better than Francis's, I gather, but it was his gun that was used. Many people had access to that gun, however. He kept it in his desk usually."

Does every patent attorney keep a gun in his desk? I wondered. And do you know, Mrs. Deramo, that I have intimate knowledge of that gun? I held back my sarcastic questions, however, since at that point Sylvia was giving me more information than I could give her.

I weighed the idea of sharing with Sylvia my thoughts

about what I considered to be Michael's last message. Her next comment settled my mind.

"I was hoping that you had some other leads, something that points away from my husband," she said, her voice low and deliberate, as if she wanted me to understand that I was her last resort.

I told Sylvia about my theory that Michael had left us a clue with the last tiny movements of his fingers.

"I'm convinced Michael told us who his killer was. It has to do with what he scratched out in the wet cement, and it has to do with Italian."

"Italian?"

"The language. Something about Michael's playing word games with the language. It's not clear to me yet. But I know I'm close. I wish I could give you more than that."

"You're giving me hope, Gloria," she said, causing a guilty shiver to run through my body. I hadn't meant to mislead her as to the progress I'd made. I wondered if she was misleading me, away from thinking of her as a killer.

Sylvia stood to leave, and we shook hands. It was far from the warmth Rose and I shared when we parted, but it represented a quantum leap on the friendship scale between Sylvia Deramo and me, considering I'd started out as her nosy personal flower arranger.

"I didn't hate my father-in-law, Gloria. And Francis loved him. We had the problems many families have, but we wouldn't have killed him."

I took in Sylvia's words, trying to keep in mind that nothing she said was necessarily the truth. More than anything, I wished I had evidence, one way or the other, and not just strong feelings telling me who was or was not the killer.

"I'm glad you came by," I said. It was all I could say with sincerity.

"Thank you very much," she said. "Barry will be happy to have my report. He said you'd be able to help."

about what I considered to be...

"Barry said that?"

"Yes, I must admit, it was his idea that I come. Barry and I have always been very close, and this terrible tragedy has pulled us together even more. I'm very glad I took his advice and came to you."

"I am, too," I said, not knowing quite how to feel about the sudden confidence all the Richardses had in me.

TWENTY-TWO

IT WAS NEARLY four o'clock by the time Sylvia left. Matt had said he'd be over for an early dinner, since he was expecting to be called out to work later in the evening, giving me about an hour before he was due. I sat down to answer my phone messages, starting with Rose, the only caller in the same time zone.

"I've been sick," she said, taking me by surprise.

"What's wrong?"

"Some twenty-four-hour thing with my stomach. I'm fine now."

"I wish I'd known. Can I bring you something? Soup?"

Too little, too late, Rose's best friend comes through, I thought. I felt pangs of guilt as I remembered my annoyance that Rose hadn't immediately called me back the day before. She never complained, and could beat out any baseball player for consecutive days at work. In my selfish way, I always assumed she didn't need anything from me.

"No, no. Thanks. I'll be back at work tomorrow. Anyway, you may have noticed, we're slow right now, so it's a good time for me to be out."

"How thoughtful of you to time your sickness with a slump in business. A slump you brought on yourself, I might add."

"It was the right thing to do, Gloria. You don't need another wake in your house with personal connotations."

I listened with a smile to Rose's unique grammatical constructions and the peculiar word choices that made her speech seem so charming to me. I hoped Elaine, my professional editor friend who was due to arrive on the scene from California, would be able to resist editing her on the spot.

"I saw the son was arrested in the Deramo case," Rose said. "And how did the talk go for Peter's class? I feel like I've been out of touch for weeks. Talk to me, Gloria."

I gave Rose an update of events—my presence at an arrest and at a graduation, my lunch with Peter, my visit from Sylvia, all while she was at home, prostrate and fasting.

Rose seemed most impressed by my personal witnessing of a real-life arrest.

"Do they really read the Miranda thing? And handcuff them?"

"Both."

"Wow."

"It was pretty upsetting, actually."

"Why? No, don't tell me. You don't think he did it."

"Right," I said, feeling more certain every time I thought about it.

"Gloria, you're not still investigating."

"Uh, is that a question?"

Rose sighed loudly, causing her to cough. Her slightly weakened condition on the tail of a flu worked in my favor. She didn't pursue the controversial topic of my unsanctioned activities, and neither did I, not wanting to slip up and reveal my unauthorized visit to Andrew's one-room, multivehicle one-trailer-park home, for example.

I'd deliberately left my visit with Andrew Palmer out of our conversation, although I was desperate to share the information and get another person's view of the twist he'd put on the case. I wanted to spare the indisposed Rose from worrying about my Deep Throat–like trip to a vacant lot.

I shifted to a more pleasant tale.

"The best part of the day was being presented with a gift by Peter's students at our ceremonies this morning."

"I know how much that would mean to you. What did they give you?"

I looked at my new coffee-table book, in a front-and-center space specially cleared for it.

"A beautiful book on Italy. A new one that I don't think you even have yet. Wonderful color photographs, some history, famous personalities. There's a whole section on Rome."

"Mark the pages we've seen," Rose said. "Maybe it's time for a return visit."

We reminisced about a week-long trip we'd taken together to Rome in our fortieth-birthday year, just the two of us. It was one of several trips Rose and I had taken during my thirty-odd years away. When I was fortunate enough to attend professional conferences in Europe, Rose would join me, sometimes with Frank.

I realized Rose had made the major effort to keep our friendship alive, meeting for long weekends in New York City or Washington, D.C. She'd also visited me in Berkeley, but I'd returned to Revere only once, when my father died and was waked in the Galigani Mortuary. I was always grateful that Rose never quizzed me about why I chose not to appear in my hometown until I was ready to return for good. I wasn't completely sure what my answer would have been if she'd asked.

"I should let you go back to bed," I told Rose, hearing her cough again.

"I think I will. Oh, I knew there was something I wanted to tell you. Frank was out with Jimmy Falzone last night."

"The big developer?"

"Right. Some benefit dinner that I had to miss. Well, he was bragging to Frank that he'd just signed a huge deal to buy Michael Deramo's property."

"Michael didn't own property."

"Right, right. It's Bargello's, but Michael's house was on it."

"Michael rented what used to be a garage."

"Evidently the whole lot packaged together is prime real estate, on the beach, so Bargello made out really well. Falzone's going to put up another one of those white concrete monsters with a million apartments. Anyway, what a coincidence, huh?"

"Yes, what a coincidence," I said, my mind wandering back to my conversation with Bargello. He had told me he was going to convert Michael's little place back into a garage. I was sure of that. I just wasn't sure why he'd lied to me.

"Are you there?" Rose asked me. "I think I will go back to bed now. What are you doing this evening?"

"Matt's coming for dinner. To celebrate what he thinks is the end of the case."

"I wish you hadn't said it that way."

"Me, too. Sorry."

"Don't go poking around, okay?"

"Just in my mind," I said, as if that would put anyone at ease.

FROM HANGING UP with Rose, I went directly to my bedroom to change my clothes. I kicked off my shoes, the worse for their trek through dusty gravel, and dumped my dress and jacket onto a pile in my closet for dry cleaning. I put on slacks and a bright red sweater, succumbing to Rose's influence even though she wasn't watching.

Since dressing took little mental effort, I was able to construct a new scenario at the same time. Bargello wants to sell his property to Falzone for big bucks. Michael doesn't want to move out. Bargello kills Michael. Very neat, but it was hard to picture Michael with any clout over Bargello. As a renter, the most he'd have over his landlord would be emotional power, and no one kills just to get rid of a little whining.

Factoring in that Bargello was with his nephew when Michael was killed, I was running out of steam in my new script. Of course, there was the Falzone connection, with influence that probably stretched up and down the East Coast. It wouldn't be the first time I'd heard of murder at a distance.

And I had to deal with the fact that Bargello had lied to me. Surely he'd already started negotiations for the sale thirty-six hours ago when I'd sat with him on his lawn. My final thoughts were, number one, Bargello had lied because it was none of my business until the ink was dry and it became public record, and number two, it was a coincidence that the ink was dry a week after Michael's murder. I formulated a plan to call Bargello and congratulate him on the sale of his property, but wasn't sure I had the gumption to do something so blatant.

I headed for the kitchen, and stopped short when I saw a large envelope on the hallway floor in front of my door. I hadn't yet brought my briefcase upstairs, so I knew it wasn't something I'd dropped. Besides, Sylvia had been with me, so I'd inspected the carpet before entering and would have seen it. I could see that there were no stamps in the corner. I walked towards the manila package as though it were hazardous material and I'd been caught without my protective jumpsuit and booties.

My police involvement had brought threats before, and my stomach reacted to the memory of them. A fine point I've come to in my life, I thought, when the last thing I consider is that this might be a harmless note from Martha, the Galiganis' longtime secretary, deposited as she left work for the day. For a moment I even considered calling for help—a letter bomb came to mind. Too thin, I reasoned, trying to remember whether the Unabomber had ever slipped anything under a door.

Finally, I picked up the envelope. My name was typed on a package label affixed to the center. The preprinted return address said simply "University Physics Laboratory, Charger Street Mail Stop, Revere, Massachusetts." I pulled out a sheaf of pages, eight-and-a-half-by-eleven, that were set up like transparencies, with bulleted items and an occasional photograph or chart. I recognized them as reproductions from the Laughton and Hammer lithium seminar I'd attended with Andrea on Monday.

My first wave of relief was dampened by concerns about their method of delivery. There was no question that they knew where I lived—they'd been in my building for Michael's wake—but that didn't give them the right to sneak up on me. Why didn't whoever brought them call first or ring my bell? My initial fear gave way to annoyance that the scientists had chosen an intimidating way to answer my legitimate request for copies of their talk.

I picked up my reading glasses and sat down to look over my special delivery. A handwritten note was clipped to the pages of text. "Dr. Lamerino," it read, "I hope this meets your needs for closer examination of our lithium project." It was signed "Fred Laughton and John Hammer."

The team again. Did they hold the pen together? I wondered. While I'd planned to use the next half hour to start dinner, the transparencies won the contest for my time.

I went through the set twice from beginning to end. It was much easier to follow the logic of the presentation with hard copies on my lap than it had been when I was straining to listen to Laughton and Hammer in the lab auditorium, conscious of Barry Richards sitting next to me. The smell of his cologne came back to me, as if it had permeated the transparencies.

As far as I could tell, the particular battery design that Andrea had told me about and that I'd read about in the clippings she gave me—the design that caused impurities to appear at the tops of the batteries—was not included in the current program offerings. Either they'd pulled the design from the market proposal or they were burying the problem, I reasoned, hoping for the former.

The environmental problems also seemed to have been addressed. The lithium program managers showed a cycle of waste management that included chemical treatment before any disposal into the ground. They already had a contract in place, the text said, with a waste treatment plant on the Mystic River.

I put the transparencies and the notes I'd made back in the envelope, satisfied for the time being that Laughton and Hammer were not trying to put one over on me or the public at large. Moreover, I saw nothing worthy of a blackmail attempt, which left me confused about what Michael had in mind. I wanted to believe the researchers had no role in the two murders, thus keeping alive my vision of the purity of science and those who practice it.

By THE TIME MATT ARRIVED, I'd buried the seminar pages and my notes in my bottom desk drawer and had made progress in the kitchen. My apartment smelled of shrimp, tomato sauce, and bread loaded with garlic and Parmesan cheese, and Matt gave an appreciative sniff as he set down bottles of sparkling juices on my counter. I'd decided to play my CD of Neapolitan folk songs again to put him in a mood to discuss the deaths of two Italian-American janitors. I was pleased to hear him hum a few bars of ''Torn' a Napoli.''

With me in my bistro apron and Matt setting the table, the scene was seriously close to ''Hi, honey, I'm home.''

We settled on my matching blue glide rockers, the same ones Sylvia and I had used that afternoon. They seemed more comfortable when I was sitting across from Matt, sipping pretend champagne while the water for the pasta was heating. Except that this time I'd had two meetings—one with Andrew and one with his mother—that I was keeping from him. I couldn't have felt more guilty if they'd been adulterous trysts.

''How was your day?'' I asked, earning a laugh from my guest, the homicide detective.

''Same old, same old.''

"Matt, you know I need some answers."

Matt sighed, put down his glass, and folded his arms across his chest. His grin told me that he knew exactly what he was doing.

"Open-minded and receptive to questions, are you?" I said, crossing my own arms.

"The case is closed, Gloria. That's why we're here."

"That's it?"

"Well, no, I might be here anyway."

"I mean, that's it, the case is closed?"

"I know what you mean."

It was hard to ignore the sound of the boiling water, spitting molecules over the range top, and I got up to take care of it.

"I have an idea," I said from the kitchen. "How about giving me until the pasta is ready—seven minutes—then we'll eat, with no more talk of the case."

"Seven minutes?"

"Starting now. I'll set the timer."

Matt had uncrossed his arms and nodded, appearing to get into the spirit of my request. I punched in the numbers on the pad of my microwave oven, the most accurate timer I had on hand.

"First, what evidence do you have that Francis is the killer, other than that he signed the Federal Express form for the letter?" I was conscious of the need for care, not revealing what I'd learned from Sylvia.

"His gun matches the one that put a nine-millimeter hole in the back of Carlo Massimo's head."

I let out a soft grunt and asked myself if I really wanted all the details. I knew that gun and shuddered to think of its being put into operation. Then I remembered my shrinking seven-minute limit and recovered.

"But that doesn't mean he did it," I said. "Anyone could have used Francis's gun. He kept it—"

"Is that a question? And how would you know where he kept it?"

Matt got up to face me in the kitchen, his look seriously close to angry.

"Matt, please cooperate. You can quiz me later. This is my time."

"All right. I'm going to assume you're behaving yourself, for now."

"I've tried to explain. You can't engage me in a case, then leave me hanging. Did you search his house or car or office?"

"Yes, the letter gave us probable cause, so we searched. That's how we found his gun."

"Any physical evidence around the crime scenes? Footprints, fingerprints, anything like that?"

"No. The Boulevard pavilions are among the worst places to pick up anything. Besides the masses of people that tramp around there leaving debris and touching everything, you've got the sprays of salt water, the wind blowing the sand around—way too messy. And, of course, we don't know where the second crime scene is. Massimo's murder could have taken place anywhere."

"Nothing in my driveway?"

"Nothing in your driveway."

"Was there any blood in Francis's car? Remember, Carlo's body had to have been in someone's car. And if we think the same person killed both…"

Matt held up his hand as if he were stopping runaway traffic. I looked at the clock on my microwave. I imagined how people on a television game show felt, with thousands of dollars at stake.

"You'll have to slow down if you want me to answer," Matt said. "His gun was in his desk drawer in his office, which you probably already knew. There was no blood in his car."

"What about everyone's alibi? Do they all check out?"

"We verified that Sylvia was at a committee meeting while Francis was with a client in Winthrop the night Michael was murdered. The guy he was meeting supports Francis's time frame in part, but that doesn't mean Francis didn't go into his father's house later, instead of driving off as he said."

"But Michael wasn't killed in his house."

"They could have gone to the pavilion together. Francis might have seen his father walking to the spot where he'd collect his money. Who knows? The point is, nothing really clears Francis at the time of his father's murder. And he has a strong motive—enormous potential gains from the patent. You said so yourself. And his place in the law firm and the whole new life he'd built around North Shore society were in jeopardy."

"And his alibi for the time of Carlo's murder?"

"Francis was at home alone, reading at the time."

I gave him a funny look that spelled my doom. Although I hadn't given anything away by my words, I might as well have said I thought he was swimming. Matt's skills as a professional lie-detector were hard to fool.

"Aha," he said. "I thought I'd catch you. As I'm sure you know, he was swimming."

I tried not to succumb to his charming grin.

"What about Barry Richards?" I asked, struggling to use up my time wisely.

"He says he was at home alone. His wife was asleep upstairs, but says she'd know if Barry had left the house. The car is a diesel, makes a lot of noise."

"Hmm."

"You didn't ask about the scientists. The Holy Innocents."

"Oh, right. What about the scientists?"

Matt often teased me about my predilection for ruling out scientist suspects, but I hoped he knew I could be objective when it came to research of any kind, including murder investigations. It occurred to me that this would be a good time to bring up the delivery of the seminar transparencies and my review of them. I decided against the idea, since I'd learned nothing new from them.

"At this point there's no physical evidence to link them to either crime. Hammer's story that Michael was dead when he got to the beach is as good as any. And the other two guys in the conference room that night are from some other state— Montana, Minnesota, one of those—and they took the red-eye home that same night. Hammer says they never knew there might be a problem with an eavesdropper. And even if those guys did something wrong in their research, it's not a crime. It's up to the lab officials to take care of it."

"They fixed it, actually."

"And you know this how?"

"Uh, never mind for now. And I think this part of the conversation should not be charged to my account, since you brought up the Holy Innocents."

"Okay. Duly noted."

"Did you search anyone else's car or house?"

"No, did you have someone in mind?"

"Maybe Sylvia?" I asked, putting her well-behaved visit out of my mind and thinking of my meeting with Andrew.

"We checked Sylvia's car on the grounds that Francis had access to it. Clean."

"Hmm," was all I could say to that.

"Anything else?"

"Not yet."

"There's that 'not yet' again," Matt said. "Why do I think you're still working on this case?"

I had one more thought to squeeze into my interval, and with no time to spare for a response to his remark.

"What about Andrew's alibi?" I asked, simultaneously with the high-pitched beep of my microwave oven.

"Time's up."

TWENTY-THREE

I GAVE IN TO Matt's wishes and dropped the Deramo-Massimo murder talk for the rest of the evening. We had no trouble coming up with other topics, including a minor disagreement over the city government and the current mayor-city council structure at Revere City Hall. We reviewed the significance of Wonderland dog track's still being the city's largest employer in spite of the presence of nearly 250 retail establishments.

We did agree on most matters of politics, both of us among the 62 percent of the population who voted Democrat most of the time. As for entertainment, neither of us cared much what was showing at the fourteen-screen movie complex, preferring live musical performances.

Looking forward to the summer, we planned a visit to Matt's sister, who lived in Falmouth, a town on Cape Cod. Jean, a real estate broker, was ten years younger than Matt and still had children in school. I'd met the family at Christmas and felt we'd all gotten along very well, though I hadn't heard from them since.

There was nothing unpleasant in our conversation, and I enjoyed deepening our understanding of each other. At the back of my mind, however, was the unsettling feeling I had when I was working on a puzzle. It might be over for the RPD, but this case certainly hadn't been solved to my satisfaction. I was also distracted by all that I had not told Matt Andrew's claim, his mother's visit, the lithium transparencies and the jogger, to name the obvious.

I might not have been able to hold out on my promise of

no police work if our time hadn't been cut short by Matt's pager going off.

"Sorry," he said, responding to vibrations at his waist. "I've been expecting this. Berger said he'd call when he brought someone in for questioning."

I looked at him with widened eyes and raised eyebrows.

"It's another case," he said, getting up to leave. "And it's about jewelry, not science."

I'D JUST CLEARED AWAY the dishes when my phone rang. With a towel in one hand and the phone in the other, I clicked the on button, expecting to hear Rose or Elaine. Instead I heard a male voice that was only vaguely familiar.

"This is Fred Laughton. I hope I'm not calling at a bad time."

"No, not at all," I said, thankful he hadn't phoned thirty minutes earlier while I was discussing his character flaws with a homicide detective.

"I assume you received the package we sent you?"

"I did, thank you. I was surprised, however, that you left it as you did and didn't wait to speak to me."

"I sent my secretary," he said. "I don't know how she chose to get it to you. Sorry for any inconvenience."

"I see," I said, embarrassed at my whiny remark, and at my initial fright over the package, as if he could tell the color of my cheeks from a distance.

"Have you had a chance to go over the material?"

"Yes, as a matter of fact, I've looked through it. I see that you really have paid attention to the problems that needed to be addressed."

"I'd like to explain further, but I'm a little uncomfortable saying any more on the telephone, Gloria. May I call you Gloria?"

"Gloria is fine."

"Would you be willing to meet with us? John Hammer is with me."

Of course he is, I thought. And here comes one more little rendezvous I can't share with Matt, another private meeting, with two murder suspects at once this time. Two that are still on my list at any rate. Is this wise? I thought of how angry Matt was the last time I'd entertained people who were candidates for a murder-one conviction. At least this time it's not in my own apartment, I reasoned.

"I'd be happy to meet you," I said to Fred Laughton.

"Do you know Sabrine's Coffee Stop across from City Hall?"

"Yes, I go there often," I said. Like early this morning, I added to myself.

"They're open till at least nine. Can you meet us there?"

"Certainly. I'll be right over."

I hung up the phone and shook my head, as if to assume the attitude that Matt would have taken if he were present. I'll never learn, I told myself.

ONE PROBLEM WITH meeting near Sabrine's was that it was just one block up and across Broadway from the police station, and only a few blocks from Matt's Fernwood Avenue home. I parked as far past the coffee shop and Matt's addresses as I could and still feel safe, since the streets were deserted.

They wouldn't have been empty at eight-thirty in the evening in the 1950s, I thought, when the city's one movie theater had been located here. I'd watched the last of the good films that came out of Hollywood in that theater, in my opinion. June Allyson in *Little Women,* Gary Cooper in *High Noon,* and a dazzling array of Bing Crosby *Road* movies and Gene Kelly musicals. Although I wouldn't dream of owning a less than state-of-the-art computer, and fully embraced the technology of the late 1990s, for movies I thought 1959 was the last good year.

Thinking of the auditorium of the old theater brought back another memory—Revere High School graduation ceremonies used to be held there, and I'd given a valedictory speech from its stage. My success wasn't enough to win approval from Josephine, however, and I remembered getting less attention from her that day than the football players who squeaked by with all D's got from their mothers.

Before I entered Sabrine's, I looked down Pleasant Street toward the police station, hoping Matt wasn't out for a late-evening stroll. That end of Broadway was one of my favorite parts of Revere, second only to the Boulevard that ran along the ocean. The police station, City Hall, and the post office were beautiful old buildings, clustered within a block of each other, enhanced by rich lawns and large pots of flowers. A path that ran in front of City Hall, in matching red brick, was lined with benches that faced the traffic on Broadway. I liked the way the newly constructed fronts of nearby establishments like the *Journal* office were designed to blend in, having a slightly lighter hue than the deep red of the old structures.

Laughton and Hammer were at a table when I walked into the coffee shop.

"Thanks for meeting us," they said, almost in unison.

They stood to greet me and shook my hand in turn, behaving more and more like a vaudeville team each time I saw them. I imagined them rehearsing while they waited for me. No wonder I didn't perceive them as serious threats.

I'd taken the envelope of transparencies with me and placed it on the table between us, in case they were needed for reference. Having reached my caffeine quota at dinner, I ordered a mineral water and sat with an attentive look on my face, my hands folded, as if I were waiting for a performance.

"It bothers us that you might have suspicions about our procedures, Gloria." Laughton tapped the envelope with his index finger. "Our paths may cross again," he said, "and we don't want any lingering doubts about what we've done here."

This meeting had a distinctly different flavor from our first one in the cafeteria—Laughton was treating me like a professional equal this time, and I wondered why.

"There were some, uh, problems with our original approach," Laughton said. "At first we did think we could rush it past the regulators. But we knew the task force would eventually find out, so we decided to pull back and market only the portion we were sure of."

The Hammer, as I preferred to think of him, apparently not embarrassed by the admission, had been nodding elaborately while Laughton spoke.

"Of course, we would have preferred not to wait for the vacuum process to reach a useful stage. We're looking at applications to automobile batteries, for one thing," Hammer said. "It's a huge market, plenty to go around, but whoever gets there first is going to be the real winner."

It crossed my mind that there were more honorable ways to carry out research than to think of it as a contest with "real winners" and losers. I wondered about scientists who did the right thing because they knew they'd be caught if they didn't, but I decided not to voice that observation.

"What Michael heard was—well, preliminary thoughts we had," Hammer said. "Right after we approached him about keeping quiet, we decided to work out the plan to change the bonding process. We tried to explain this to Michael, but he insisted on keeping our appointment. He probably thought we were trying to put one over on him."

"So you didn't go to the Boulevard with money?"

"No, no. We realized that was completely off base. We had to take care of the problem eventually anyway. I went to meet him just to satisfy him, try to explain again that there was nothing he could tell anyone that we weren't already willing to disclose.''

Poor Michael, I thought, trying to raise his stature in a world he knew nothing about. I thought of the crime scene photographs I had copies of, and imagined him dressing in a shirt and tie to feel important and worthy of doing business with the big boys.

''Why didn't all of this come out before?'' I asked. ''You've made it sound as if the lithium program was never in any trouble.''

''It's the government connection,'' Laughton said.

I conveyed my ignorance by a serious frown.

''We're involved in special projects.''

Special projects. Code phrase for work sponsored by the Central Intelligence Agency in Washington. Laughton and Hammer as spooks?

''The idea is not to call attention to the work until it's absolutely ready for transfer to the industrial sector,'' Hammer said. ''We had to be really careful how we recalled something that had already been out there, so to speak. It was like playing a card we shouldn't have played, and now we take it back, but the other guys have seen the card.''

''The card being the particular bonding process you tried.''

''Exactly,'' Hammer said, appearing to be happy that I'd said the phrase so he didn't have to. Just like the CIA, I thought, nodding heads instead of talking.

''We didn't even tell our lawyers everything,'' Laughton said.

''Barry Richards and Francis Deramo didn't know there were problems?''

''Not at first. I guess eventually Michael told Francis, and then, well, you know the rest.''

So far no one had mentioned out loud that one of their patent attorneys was in jail on suspicion of murder.

"Who knew that you were going to meet Michael?" I asked Hammer.

"Only Fred here, as far as who I told. But gosh, who knows? I mean, literally, who knows how many people Michael bragged to? Not to speak ill or anything, but he wasn't the most discreet man."

"Really," Laughton said. "It sort of defeats the purpose of a payoff if you're telling everybody."

I tried to see the situation from Michael's point of view. Probably it wasn't the money itself, but the idea of having money that was important to him. I guessed he got it into his head that money would gain him respect from his son's new family and the likes of the people he saw every day at the lab. I'd have bet a lot that his dreams of wealth extended only to a decent home and car, not to servants, Learjets, and trips around the world, unless it would be to Bari.

Michael was an Italian-American of the same generation as my parents, so I thought I understood why he might want people to know he was coming into money, even if his boasting ran counter to the money-making scheme he thought he'd fallen into. I guessed that he was like Josephine and my father, who'd had little money during the depression years of the early 1930s. I'd heard their stories over and over—how they'd sat on fruit crates until they'd saved enough to buy chairs. No one who grew up in a credit card economy would know what they were talking about, I realized.

When there was finally enough work and income to feel comfortable, my mother filled the narrow shelves of a hallway closet with canned foods—meats, vegetables, soups, fruit. She told all our neighbors and relatives about the larder, not so much to brag, but to claim her place in the world of those who had some measure of security.

I figured that Michael would act in much the same way, and therefore, in Laughton's words, had told "everybody" that he'd soon be rich. I still didn't know who "everybody" was, but apparently I'd gotten all I could from the Laughton and Hammer twins. Not wanting this meeting to be solely a public relations ploy for the lithium team, I made one last attempt at a useful interview.

"Do you think Francis killed his father?" I asked.

"We don't know what to think," Laughton said, shaking his head.

"We just know we didn't do it," said his sidekick.

TWENTY-FOUR

LAUGHTON AND HAMMER were still sitting in Sabrine's when I left, and I had the feeling that I'd be the subject of their conversation for a few minutes of debriefing at least. I wondered how much the attention I was getting from the suspects in the case had to do with my association with Sergeant Matt Gennaro of the Revere Police Department. Ninety-nine and forty-four one-hundredths percent, I figured.

I walked toward my car at a quick pace, only slightly uncomfortable at the emptiness of the sidewalks and the darkened doorways, since there was still a moderate amount of traffic on Broadway.

My comfort level took a sharp decrease, however, when I saw a figure approach from the opposite direction. About two cars away from my Cadillac was a man in a dark jogging suit. With impeccable reflexes, instead of walking faster to reach my car, I stopped in my tracks, waves of fear flowing through my body like current through a lithium battery, until I was light-headed and unable to focus.

The man was four doorways ahead of me, hands in his pockets, walking at a slower, more relaxed pace than I'd ever seen from him—that is, if he was the same man I thought of as my stalker. He seemed to be strolling, enjoying the perfect spring evening, causing me to doubt that he was there to kill me, until he passed in front of a streetlight and its rays reflected from the shiny white stripes on his pants.

I shook my head to clear it, and ran through my choices, remembering again the advice in the police brochure—if you're being attacked, cause a scene. I could pull my panic-button trick again and send my Caddie into attention-grabbing spasms. I could cross the street in the middle of traffic and call attention to myself and risk getting killed that way.

Among all these action-filled options, I chose to duck. I stepped into the doorway of a deli, closed for the night, the small area cluttered with newspapers and flyers. I had barely enough room to stand without having my hip jut out onto the sidewalk, another belated reason to lose weight.

I stood facing the direction of the jogging suit and looked around me for something that could serve as a weapon. I tried to picture myself strangling a full-grown man with a piece of string from the bundles of newspapers at my feet. Hurling the brick that was holding down the flyers presented an option, but it was small, meaning I'd have to have very good aim and apply a great deal of force, and I couldn't count on either.

What else could I do? Break the glass of the storefront with my briefcase and hope an alarm would go off? Trip him and run for help? And if he turned out not to be ''my'' jogger, I could hurt an innocent person, I thought, with a sudden unwarranted sense of my own strength.

While I was thinking, the jogging suit was closing the gap. Out of ideas, my heart pounding, I stood in the doorway and held my breath. I clutched my briefcase to my chest, as if to create a bulletproof vest as one line of defense.

Pressed against the deli window, face to face with a sign advertising knishes, I made what I hoped was a perfect act of contrition as a preparation for death. I couldn't keep the jogger in my line of sight without projecting myself farther onto the sidewalk, so I had lost the sense of how close he might be. Besides that, I had my eyes closed.

So I was surprised to realize that he was standing next to me, a few inches away. I was even more surprised when I heard his voice.

''Gloria?''

I opened my eyes and dropped my briefcase to the ground. ''George?''

Facing me in a dark jogging suit was George Berger, Matt's young partner and the father of little Cynthia.

"What are you doing here?" we asked together.

"I just came from Sabrine's," I said, answering first. I noticed the bulge of Berger's gun in his waistband, inadequately hidden by the flimsy fabric of his jogging jacket.

"Why are you hiding in a doorway at this hour of night, Gloria? I couldn't tell who it was trying to duck out of sight— didn't know what was up. You really scared me."

You're the cop, and you have a gun, I thought, but kept it to myself.

"I—I thought you were someone else," I said. "Someone, maybe, following me."

I looked at Berger's face, lit by passing headlights just enough for me to see a sheepish expression. It came to me like a bright idea in the shower.

"You're the jogger," I said, seeing a match between Berger's short, heavy physique and that of my stalker. "You *have* been following me."

"Not tonight, not yet, anyway," he said, looking at his watch, as if to see if he was going to be late for his stalking session with me. "But yes, I've been hanging around your house."

I took one of my first breaths of the last few minutes, feeling my body struggle for relaxation.

"That was you coming out of the bushes? Jogging down my street? Outside my window?"

"That was me. Matt asked me to keep an eye out, you know? Nothing too intense, he told me, just to be sure nothing bad happened, especially after the second guy bought it—uh, was murdered."

Feelings of relief and anger fought with each other for control of my body. Should I be flattered at the special attention of the RPD, or insulted at being treated like an untrustworthy teenager? I needed more information before I could decide how to feel.

"Did you follow me here?"

"Naw, I never followed you anywhere. Like I said, it wasn't supposed to be intense. I was going over to Galigani's about now. See what was going on."

"But you've arrested Francis Deramo, the person you think is the murderer."

"Right, but Matt worries, you know. Said I should stick it out another few days to be sure. And I can use the extra hours, with the baby and all. So everything was cool."

"Really cool," I said, making it easy for Berger to pick up on my displeasure.

He ran his hands through his hair, thinner than Matt's although Berger was a good deal younger. Well, I'm over doing anything to stay in your good graces, I thought.

"It's not like we're spying on you, Gloria," he said. "Really. Matt has only the best intentions."

"I know. I should be thanking you, George," I said, about 50 percent sincere, since he was only doing his job.

"Why don't I take the night off? I'll just walk you to your car," he said, providing a welcome laugh.

What interested me most in my encounter with Berger was that Matt had decided to keep up the surveillance on me even though Francis was in jail. Maybe he wasn't as convinced about Francis's guilt as he let on.

I PULLED INTO my garage feeling a little lighter, minus the burden of worrying about a stalker. I knew I needed time to think about how to approach Matt on the surveillance issue, and I made an appointment with myself to design the strategy the next day.

It was still only a little after seven o'clock in California when I got home, a good time to reach Elaine Cody. At first I let her think it was an everyday kind of call.

"I can hardly wait," I told her. "You'll be here in two days."

"I hope I'm going to meet your cop."

"You sound like Peter, but, yes, you'll meet Matt. He was here this evening as a matter of fact."

"Dinner and…?"

"Dinner and a page from his office."

"Too bad."

"Elaine, I'm not calling to discuss my love life."

"You never do."

"Seriously, I need to talk to you about these cases. I just need someone to listen, or else I'm going to have to talk out loud to my empty apartment, which always makes me feel crazy, unless it's just a sentence or two."

"Gloria, what's wrong? Are you sick?"

"No, no. It's this double murder. I have facts and theories swimming around my brain and I need to sort them out, out loud. I'm supposed to be off the case, so I can't talk to Matt or Rose. They'll just worry."

"And I won't worry? It's worse for me—I'm worrying all the way across the country."

"Right, so you can't tie me up or take away my car keys."

"Not until Friday anyway."

"Deal. Here it is. You know almost everything except what happened today."

"In one day there's enough to confuse you?"

"Yes, just listen."

I started with the most recent encounter, with Laughton and Hammer.

"They work for the CIA?" she said, impressed as I was. "What does the CIA want with lithium?"

"It's lithium for batteries, remember. They're always looking for the best DC power sources for surveillance devices."

"I get it. If they toss a camera or tape recorder over a fence in Libya, they want to know it's going to operate for a long time."

"Something like that."

"So now you're sure that neither of them is the killer, because they're funded by the CIA? I'd think that would make them more suspect."

"It's just the way they approached me. Of course, they could be setting me up, to make sure I don't look any more closely. But right now, I think they're telling the truth."

"But you said it was the first janitor, Michael, who could have brought everything into the open. Wouldn't that have made them angry?"

Elaine was giving me exactly what I needed—a devil's advocate. I considered asking her to move to Revere and be my partner in fighting crime.

"They would have been angry, but why kill him? They had to solve the problem anyway. What Michael knew was anticlimactic. The most he'd have been able to do was say he overheard them trying to get away with something, but it would be his word against theirs."

"Okay, so we're ruling them out. Who's left?"

"Well, there are still the lawyers, Barry Richards and Francis Deramo, one of whom is already in jail. That's Francis, the first victim's son."

"I'm following."

"And there's his wife, Sylvia."

"The one with the flower paranoia."

"Right," I said, dazzled by Elaine's ability to follow the case from a distance. "But she's redeemed herself a bit, as I'll tell you in a minute. There's also a funny interaction I had with Michael's landlord yesterday. And last—I think—there's her son, Andrew."

I gave Elaine the substance of my meetings with Bargello and Sylvia, and ended with Andrew and his alleged proof that his mother killed Michael.

"Hmm," I heard on the other end of the line, Elaine's heavy-thinking mode.

"You have an idea?" I asked her.

"Were Andrew and his mother both at the wake?"

"Yes."

"And you kept this club application form he gave you?"

"Yes."

I couldn't see where Elaine was headed, but she sounded excited, as if she'd hit on something. I held my breath.

"Galigani's has a guest book, doesn't it?"

"Yes," I said, holding my breath and wishing I could hurry Elaine along.

"Well, just compare the handwriting."

I exhaled, and focused on Elaine's idea.

"That's brilliant, Elaine. Even though it can't work exactly that way. Rose and Frank always give the guest book to the family right after the wake."

"So, it's not so brilliant."

"It's still brilliant, because there must be something else with Sylvia's writing, if not Andrew's. She made the funeral arrangements with Rose. I can at least check her handwriting against the form Andrew gave me."

"Great. You just need to wait until Rose comes in the morning."

I looked across the room at my desk drawer and squinted as if I had X-ray vision and could see inside to a set of keys to all the rooms in the building.

"I may not have to wait," I said. "I think I have a key. I'm on my way. Thank you, Elaine."

"Wait. Is it dark there or anything?"

I knew Elaine's problem with walking around a mortuary, especially at night. When she'd visited me and we came in late, she'd insisted on turning on all the lights as we went through the foyer and up to my floor. She also whistled a happy tune the whole time.

I decided to tell her the false-alarm jogger story to make her feel better. For some reason, it had the opposite effect.

"Matt thinks you're in enough danger to warrant having someone shadow you?"

"Now there's a term I haven't heard in a while. Be careful, Elaine, your age is showing."

"I'm sorry I suggested anything. Why don't you wait till morning?"

"Don't worry. The building is locked."

"Call me when you get back upstairs."

TWENTY-FIVE

I HUNG UP THE PHONE and went to my desk. Rose and Frank had given me keys to all the rooms in the building, but I'd had little reason to use them up to now. I rummaged in my top drawer, not sure where they were, pricking myself on a staple remover in the process. Finally, I located a couple of loose keys with plastic tags attached, one labeled "R," the other "C."

I figured the R was for Rose's office. I had no idea what C was for, but I didn't need to know at the moment. I wondered vaguely where F for Frank's office and M for Martha's were, but I had the key I wanted, since Rose kept the current files.

For all the warmth of my friends who ran the business, and all the bright touches they had added by way of leafy green plants and fresh paint, the Galigani Mortuary was creepy at night. Even with no bodies in the parlor or the prep room as far as I knew, the building seemed to shudder on its own, as if death calls were being made from its walls and carpeted stairway.

"You next," I heard in my mind, and shivered.

I nearly talked myself out of the mission, but curiosity kept me going until I reached Rose's office, unlocked it, and stepped inside. With the lights on, reflecting from happy family portraits on her credenza, things looked brighter, giving me confidence that I'd finish the job alive. I focused on a three-paneled brass picture frame with the high school photographs of Robert, John, and Mary Catherine. I noted the sensible jackets and ties the boys wore and wondered why

Mary Catherine had agreed to the fluffy pink boa around her neck.

With the fear dissipated, guilt took over as I acknowledged what I was doing. Trespassing. A small photograph on the wall from a trip I'd taken to Rome with Rose—loyal, trusting Rose, I mused—increased my uneasy feeling. This was not the reason Rose had given me a key, so I could sneak around in her office late at night. Maybe I should look in her drawer for spare change to steal while I'm at it, I thought.

I made an effort to think of my visit not as a violation of friendship but as an efficient tactic to solve a double homicide. Even if I could clear Sylvia of the words on the application Andrew gave me, it didn't mean she was innocent, I reminded myself. But if the handwriting pieces did match, then I'd have something tangible to bring to Matt.

Next I asked myself, What handwriting pieces? I only had Andrew's version of Sylvia's handwriting, and I didn't really know where to find a second for comparison. I went to Rose's tall four-drawer filing cabinet, marveling again that she was able to find one in mahogany to match the décor of her office. Like her wardrobe, Rose's office furniture was exquisite, with new pieces carefully chosen to complement family heirlooms.

To my dismay, the filing cabinet was locked, as was the center desk drawer where the key to the cabinet might have been. A lot of good it does to have the key to your office, Rose, I said to the photo of her and her family in front of a Christmas tree, if I can't snoop in your files. I was about to abandon the project and head upstairs when I saw another possibility. The in-box at the corner of Rose's desk. Michael Deramo was a new client, quite likely not filed away yet. At least not his paperwork.

I flipped through the papers in the in-box and stopped at a manila file marked DERAMO, M. I took it as a sign that I was meant to be there, without even having to break and enter Rose's filing cabinet. I opened the folder and found not one but three documents with Sylvia Deramo's signature, all in the same bold, broad strokes. A wide S, an elaborate D, a prominent dotting of the *i*. I didn't need a magnifying glass or a certificate in handwriting analysis to determine that this was not the same signature that Andrew had showed me. The country club application form, which I now believed to have been filled out by Andrew, had been signed in a small, pinched script, as if the writer were wrapped as tightly as a race car driver in his fire-resistant suit.

I checked the room to see that I'd left everything as I found it, still uncomfortable being there. I wasn't quite certain whether I would tell Rose what I'd done, although I had no doubt that she would forgive me. I wasn't sure I forgave myself, in spite of how profitable the venture had proved.

I climbed the stairs to my apartment, undecided about what to do with my new information. Tell Andrew I'd uncovered his trick? Tell Matt that one suspect was trying to frame another? I took out the key for my own door, which I'd locked even though I was only one floor below. I'd had enough unpleasant encounters in the Galigani Mortuary building, and took pains to protect myself against surprises.

When I got inside my apartment, I realized I'd locked the key in Rose's office, probably right beside the in-box. Obviously, I needed education in how to cover my tracks. Not the only reason I wouldn't make a good cat burglar. Just as well, I thought, that takes care of whether to tell Rose or not. She'll know in the morning.

I TOOK A FEW MINUTES to process what I'd concluded about Sylvia's handwriting, even pulling out the form Andrew had given me to be sure I'd remembered correctly. It was too late to call Andrew or Matt, but not to call Elaine back as promised.

"It's not Sylvia's handwriting on that form," I told her. "I'm as sure as I can be without professional help."

"What does that tell you? Do you think Andrew did it?"

"I think he created the information on that form. I can't imagine why he didn't do a better job of forging his mother's signature, unless he just never thought anyone would check."

"He's pretty young, isn't he?"

"Very young. Twenty."

"Doesn't mean he didn't do it."

"No, but after spending some time with him today on his own turf, I can't believe he's a murderer. He's really just a kid who wants to be a big-time sports star, and his rich parents want him to go to Harvard. What's new about that story?"

"Sounds like a few movies I've seen."

"Exactly."

"So what are you going to do about it? And who's left?"

"Technically, everyone is still left. For now, I'm not going to bring this up to Matt. I may talk to Andrew. Maybe I—"

"Oops, there's my call-waiting signal," Elaine said. "Can you hold?"

"Sure."

"It might be Bruce."

I hadn't heard about Bruce yet, but I was sure I would. It was easier to keep up with advances in biotechnology than with Elaine's dating life.

"This is just a fling," she'd say, after mentioning Mel, the man who'd come to lay her new carpet. Or Stanley, the FBI agent who'd interviewed her to update her clearance. Or Wayne, the mechanic who'd done her last smog check. Elaine had never given me her exact definition of "fling," and I didn't ask.

While I was on hold, I flipped through my new book on Italy, turning the heavy, glossy pages, admiring cathedrals, palaces, and seacoast vistas. I stopped at color plates of Taormina, where all four of my grandparents had been born. They'd come to the United States at the turn of the twentieth century, not knowing a word of English. I wondered what

they'd think of the extent of my education, just two genera-
tions later. I could hear Josephine behind me, standing on the
threshold of my kitchen, wiping her hands on a flowered
apron. *Don't think you're better than they were, just because
we sent you to school.*

"I don't, Ma," I said out loud to my empty apartment. "I
don't."

I noticed a narrow red ribbon meant to be a bookmark, and
opened to the page where it was wedged tightly into the binding. The book fell open to a full-page photograph of the seaport town of Bari. "Next to Naples," the caption read, "Bari
is the most important city in Southern Italy, the capital of the
Puglia region."

It was impossible to suppress a wave of sadness as I
thought of Michael Deramo once again. The large photographs in the Bari section featured modern apartment buildings along the sea, the landmark Petruzzelli Theater, and the
dome of San Nicola. One of the smaller shots was nearly
identical to one that had hung on Michael's living-room wall.

Still on hold while Elaine entertained her other caller, I
examined the picture as if I were seeing it for the first time—
the aerial view of Porto Vecchio, with its triangular center
architecture. A triangle with rounded corners, just behind the
seawall.

I'd known all along I needed to see things as Michael saw
them. Now it was as clear as if he had written Barry Richards's name out in full in the Boulevard's newest patch of
cement. A triangle at the center of Bari—or Barry, if you were
playing a game with Italian vowels.

I offered a silent apology to all the others I'd suspected, in
alphabetical order from Joe Bargello to Andrew Palmer. I
imagined Michael in the pavilion, waiting for his money from
Hammer. I saw him recognizing Barry and having one final
joke as he drew his symbol for Bari. I wished there were some

way I could tell Michael that his little Italian word game had paid off—in a strange, sad way, he'd won the last round.

Elaine came back on the line, and I barely heard her report on Bruce, the plumber who'd come out on a weekend to unclog her toilet.

"It's over with Bruce," she said. "I finally figured it out."

"And I've figured out what Michael Deramo was trying to tell us, Elaine. I think I've just solved the murders."

TWENTY-SIX

ELAINE WAS RELUCTANT to hang up.

"Don't do anything foolish," she said, a touch of panic in her voice.

I wouldn't have been surprised if she'd called 911 and told them to get a car to Tuttle Street in Revere, immediately. I wondered how quickly a Berkeley, California, dispatcher could communicate with one in Suffolk County, Massachusetts.

I paced around my apartment, walking from living room to kitchen to bedroom, piecing the story together—at least, my story. Barry's motives were clear, partly the same as Francis's, except that he was apparently more ruthless and didn't have any filial connections to overcome. And Michael seemed to make a career of taunting Barry, making fun of his birthmark and his pronunciation.

I counted other points in favor of Barry as killer. A sleeping wife was not a convincing alibi. He'd seemed to know the exact time of Michael's murder when we talked to him in the lab cafeteria. Most significant to me, however, was the undeniable message that Michael had left for us.

Why Barry would have killed Carlo was harder to figure. I was certain, however, that Sylvia had overheard my conversation with Carlo about FedExing Michael's letter. It wasn't a big leap to think she'd told Barry. She'd told me how they kept each other informed. The thought of Sylvia and her brother sharing information brought another frightening realization—I'd told Sylvia that I was close to finding the murderer.

It was time to move—no more risks. I'd call Matt immediately. I was convinced that I had everything in order for a presentation to him, as if I were submitting my final exam.

Late as it was, I picked up the phone to call Matt at home. I heard no dial tone. One of those telecommunications glitches, I thought, or maybe Elaine hadn't hung up soon enough after I did. I pushed the power button on and off several times, and even shook both the base and the receiver—a decidedly nonscientific approach, I mused, but sometimes it worked.

My hands were shaky with the excitement of my enlightened state, so I had a hard time removing the battery, which was my last troubleshooting hope. I inserted a new battery from my charger and pushed the power button again and again.

Nothing.

When I banged the phone against my leg in frustration, I knew I had to calm down and think clearly. Mine was not the only phone in the building. There were phones in all the offices below me—Rose's and Martha's on the second floor, and Frank's on the first floor.

It was nearly midnight. I thought about putting off my call until the morning when the staff arrived and I could also call the phone company about my dead line, but I knew I'd never be able to sleep until I'd reported to Matt.

I went for the key to Rose's office and remembered that I'd left it in there during my last outing through the building. All I had was the C key. I still couldn't think what the C stood for, although the handwriting looked like mine. It's a good thing I didn't run my research lab this way, I thought, or I'd have been out of business long ago. And for a woman devoted to technology, I hadn't taken very good care of my connections to the outside world.

The only thing I could think of was to try the C key in all the office doors. I left my apartment, ready to tackle Rose's second-floor office first, in case it was a duplicate. Maybe C meant copy. But halfway down the stairs I remembered what I'd meant by C—the casket showroom on the first floor.

Heartened by this bit of progress, I flicked on the overhead lights on the landing and continued past the second-floor offices, down to the foyer. I knew that the casket room didn't have a phone, but I remembered there was a door at the back that connected to Frank's office, which did have one.

I breathed the sigh of relief and excitement that comes with having a plan.

My relief was short-lived. As I crossed the foyer, key in hand, I saw a man's shape through the narrow window next to the front door of the building. I stopped in my tracks, telling myself it was just Frank or Robert coming back to check on something, but that fantasy didn't last long. The man was working on the doorknob in a way that suggested he didn't have a key, or any right to be there.

I made an enormous effort to shake myself from the sudden paralysis that had taken over my body and my mind. I managed a quick calculation and realized I probably didn't have enough time to make it back upstairs to my apartment. I wasn't exactly in two-stairs-at-a-time shape, and my apartment had no working phone anyway.

I had a fleeting, useless feeling of dissatisfaction with the security measures at Galigani's. Every time something happened to threaten my life, we'd add a feature—a peephole, a state-of-the-art lock, an upgrade to the alarm system. Then a whole other weak link would appear, as if we were pushing down on one side of an inflatable mattress, only to have the other side pop up. This time the weaknesses were my fault—failing to set the alarm as soon as I was in for the night, and neglecting to keep my phones in working order.

Except that it finally dawned on me—there was nothing wrong with my apartment phone or my battery maintenance practices. Someone had cut the wires, and that someone—my money was on Barry Richards—was now trying to get into the building.

I clenched my teeth and had a sudden longing for my jogger/stalker—if I hadn't exposed George Berger he might have been outside my door this evening, gun drawn, catching Barry in the act. Instead I pictured Berger at home reading a book to baby Cynthia. One more example of my being what Josephine would have called too smart for my own good.

Probably I'd foiled Barry's plan by coming down here instead of waiting for him to break in upstairs. Probably all the phones were dead, and probably I would be, too, if I didn't do something to prevent it.

I wondered how he chose his weapons. Did he select them on a rotating basis—wire for the first one, gun for the second, back to wire for the third? Or maybe according to the acoustics of the crime-scene-to-be? I remembered that the police had confiscated Francis's gun, the one used to murder Carlo, and found a little comfort in that fact. As if there was a shortage of guns for people like Barry.

I knew it wouldn't be long before Barry could enter the building. If picking the lock failed, he could always break the glass, reach around, and open the door from the inside. And I was still in the brightly lit foyer. I realized with horror that if Barry had a gun instead of the wire he'd used on Michael, he'd have a clear shot.

I made a quick decision and ran the few steps to the three-way switch that controlled the lights. Thank heavens for redundancy, I thought, grateful that I didn't have to go all the way back to the switch on the landing. With a swift motion, I threw the building into darkness. It would make it harder for me to unlock the showroom door, but also more difficult for Barry to see me.

Back at the doorknob, I brought my left hand over my right one, to keep it steady as I felt around, attempting to cover the surface of the knob in a systematic way. I had a flashback to the hours I'd spent in my laboratory darkroom, feeling around for the edges of small lenses and photographic plates. The stakes seemed higher now.

Although I'd half expected it, the crashing sound of glass on the tile floor startled me. By the end of my gasp, Barry was at my side, his arms raised in a position to come down on my throat with his wire. I swallowed hard and lashed out at him as hard as I could with my right hand, on the wild chance that the key I held would scratch him enough to hurt him and slow him down.

Since I'd closed my eyes—I'd never been able to strike a person while looking at him—it was only luck that directed the key right to Barry's eye, with my full weight behind it. I heard him scream in my ear. He pushed me away, and I landed against the door of the showroom. I bumped into the handle and knocked the door open. Brilliant as I am under stress, I'd never thought of testing whether the door might be unlocked.

Inside the showroom, I pushed the door closed and locked it, breathing harder than if I'd run the Boston Marathon a month earlier. In the last second before I entered the room, I'd felt the coldness in Barry's steely eyes, even though his wide hands covered the one I'd gouged.

Now what, I asked myself, trapped in the casket showroom, without benefit of technology—no phone, no red panic button. I looked around at the caskets, the variety of woods and stains a blur, as if I were lost in an eclectic forest of mutated trees.

I found the light switch and saw the door to Frank's office, with its large pane of clear glass, at the back of the room, past rows of caskets. I wasn't sure the door would be unlocked, and I knew that if I had to smash the glass, I'd need time. I wasn't counting on Barry to take a long time to recover from an injured eye and break through the door, which had only a weak lock in the knob. I could hardly blame Frank for not installing more potent safeguards against an intruder who might carry off his inventory of caskets.

I could hear Barry already working on the doorknob on the other side. In all the time since he'd entered the foyer, he hadn't said a word, except to scream in pain when I dug at his eye. He hadn't tried to explain himself as so many TV killers do, nor was he yelling at me or cursing as he worked at the lock on the showroom door.

I set to work to barricade the door. The first casket I chose was a high-priced bronze number near the entry. It was mounted on a metal stand with wheels—Frank had called the apparatus a "truck," the same contraption that was used to move the casket down the aisle in a church. I pushed the heavy box off its support and shoved it against the door, hoping Frank would forgive me any nicks and gouges on the beautiful finish.

At the side of the room, Galigani's had caskets on a two-tier display rack, the lower-priced maple and poplar boxes on the bottom and the more expensive woods and metals on the top. I pushed and pulled at all the ones I could budge, regardless of price. I moved a plain pine box and a five-thousand-dollar solid mahogany one, with pale ivory silk lining.

Busy as I was, I did a double take at a pink one, with a sign that said "Special order for Simone." Then I remembered Frank's stories of unusual color requests—around every St. Patrick's Day, he'd said, at least one family came in wanting a green casket for a departed Irishman. I paused long enough to worry that the pink casket might be for a little girl, then continued my undertaking.

When I thought I had created enough of a blockade for Barry, I took a moment to examine my construction project, which closely resembled a surreal painting—a haphazard arrangement of sample caskets in a brightly lit room. I was nearly out of breath from the strain of the project, but I finally heard some sounds from Barry on the other side of the door. The loud thumping told me he was throwing his body against the door, but still the only sounds from his mouth were groans, and not curses or threats in any language that I recognized.

I thought I'd recovered my strength and hurried to the back of the room. At the same time, I became aware of an intense throbbing in my arm, near my wrist. I remembered its being trapped for a minute or so between a casket and the top surface of the rolling truck. When I found the door to Frank's office locked, everything conspired to bring me nearly to tears, but I clenched my jaw instead, biting back the pain, and surveyed the scene.

Through the glass, I could see Frank's certificates. I'd always thought it amusing that the credential that allowed him to embalm the dead was from an institution called Applied Arts and Sciences. Frank had consistently maintained that his profession was a little of each. Frank had also mounted his licenses—since he'd passed both state and national examinations, he could practice his art/science in any state in the nation. Great, I thought, Frank can embalm in any of the United States, but I'm going to die outside his office in Massachusetts.

What sounded to me like a gunshot reminded me that my job was to break the glass, not read a wall. I couldn't imagine why Barry would have waited so long to use a gun if he'd had one all along, unless he was concerned about the noise. Although I knew his shooting at the door lock wouldn't go far toward moving the casket blockade, I tensed at the sound and refocused on my situation. I wasn't sure enough of the mortuary layout, and worried that there were other ways Barry could reach me.

A strange image came to my mind—a mother experiencing a sudden burst of strength, lifting an automobile to save her child pinned underneath. I hoped the phenomenon didn't apply to murderers, having faith that our biological makeup wouldn't yield extraordinary powers in the service of violence.

More banging and thumping from the foyer brought me to another level of panic. I could see the phone on Frank's desk, and felt like a kid looking in the window of a candy store that's closed for the weekend. Frank's phone might also be dead, I reminded myself, but buried that idea until I had to face it.

It seemed a dreadful irony—now that I knew who had murdered Michael Deramo and Carlo Massimo, I was helpless to tell anyone who mattered and I might be his third victim.

I turned around to find something smaller than a casket that I could hurl at the glass, and I saw another door in back of me. I was thrilled when the knob turned easily, and for a moment I thought it might lead to the outside. Instead, I found myself in a tiny closetlike workroom with a counter full of office equipment, including a telephone.

It took only a few seconds to determine that this telephone was in no better shape than mine. I felt the energy drain from my body, ready to march out to Barry with my hands up. But, with any luck, I thought, the caskets formed an impenetrable barrier for anything but explosives or tanks, and I should engage my brain to work on my behalf.

I breathed deeply and looked at each of the other items on the counter in turn, as if I could convert one of them into a weapon, or a working telephone. A simple countertop photocopier, an old ink-jet printer, a small paper cutter, a binding machine, a fax machine.

A fax machine, I said out loud, with all the strength I had left. Wires. A connection to the outside world. Had Barry been smart enough to look for a separate fax line? Evidently not, because I saw the welcome glow of the green "ready" message on the display panel.

In his thrifty, low-tech way, Frank had chosen a brand with

no independent phone feature, but I was undeterred. Tacked to the wall behind the machine, enclosed in a plastic sleeve, was a neatly typed list of frequently called names, telephone numbers, and fax numbers. Thank you, Martha Franklin, I said out loud, noticing the information in the corner. MF/revised 1/92. I hoped emergency teams didn't change numbers annually.

Unlike the lists parents leave for baby-sitters, this one had no doctors or dentists. Instead, I found all the support personnel I could have wanted at that moment, and in the next few minutes, I sent a fax to everyone on the list.

Ignoring the pain in my arm, I worked quickly. I scribbled a message on Galigani's letterhead, underlining the address, and sent it to 911, to the main police station, the Shirley Avenue substation, the fire station, and the hospitals in Lynn, Chelsea, and Malden. Redundancy is key, I'd learned in my earliest science classes.

HELP, I wrote, in giant letters. FROM GLORIA LAMERINO. I'M IN THE WORKROOM. BARRY RICHARDS DID IT. AND HE'S AFTER ME.

Without editing the prose, more like Rose's than Elaine's would be, I closed the door to the small workroom and sat on the floor, trying to remember the statistics about how long one could go without food and water. In a moment of optimism, I thought maybe my reserve of fat and cellulite would save my life, as if every cannoli I'd ever eaten was working toward the happy resolution of my current predicament.

I had no idea whether my faxes would reach any living person. I knew in theory the places I'd faxed were open all night, so to speak, but I'd never tested them. In my panicky mode, I pictured them all taking a break at midnight—nurses, dispatchers, paramedics, firefighters, all uniformed policepersons going off duty—just missing my call for help.

After what seemed an impossibly long time, I stood up and looked at the fax machine. Did I really expect 911 to send a return message? I tried to remember where the police department fax machine was located. Certainly not where it should be at this hour—next to Matt Gennaro's bed.

I wondered where Barry was, but had no intention of leaving the meager safety of the workroom to find out. I leaned against the cupboards under the counter, trying to determine whether my arm was broken. As a last resort, I made a stab at creating soothing images for myself. Rose in this very room, photocopying a funeral program for a grieving family. Martha trimming the edges from a copy of a death certificate. Frank picking up a purchase order from the ink-jet printer— a dozen caskets and thirty gallons of embalming fluid. Nothing very comforting came to mind.

My body ached all over from pushing the caskets around, and from tension. I rubbed places on my ankles and my arms, where I'd bumped into sharp edges on my journey to the workroom. I could hear nothing that told me whether help was on the way or how far Barry had gotten.

Before my new career as police consultant, my most serious occupational injuries, as a researcher, had been a rash from photographic developing chemicals and a few paper cuts. And once I'd hurt my eyes by accidentally looking into a germicide lamp, but a few hours in the dark had reversed the process and repaired the injury.

The brushes I'd had with killers since returning to Revere, on the other hand, were terrifying—this wasn't the first time I'd been the target of a murderer. But the other two experiences had ended quickly, high-stakes encounters from which I had miraculously come out ahead. This time my plight seemed worse, because I couldn't see the end of it. I couldn't even see the killer.

I remembered the prayers of my youth at St. Anthony's. 'd petition before a test—"Let me get an A and I'll make he Thirteen Tuesdays novena services." I'd ask for help finding an after-school job—"Let them hire me at the hot dog stand, and I'll put ten percent of everything I make in the Sunday collection.'' Even then I thought in terms of mathematics. I didn't know what to pray for now, except for my life, and I didn't know what would be an appropriate offering in return. I'd found the economics of adulthood more complicated than those of adolescence. Maybe I wasn't as sure anymore whom I was bargaining with.

I wondered where Matt was, where Rose was, and probably most critical, where Barry was. With the workroom door closed, I couldn't hear how he was doing in his attempts to break through the casket fortress.

Having some confidence that I'd have heard him if he'd gotten through, I decided to peek out.

As soon as I opened the door, I heard the faint but unmistakable sounds of police noise—a siren, a scratchy, garbled dispatcher sound, and the shuffling of too many feet to be Barry's alone. Under the mound of caskets at the other end of the room, I saw the blue-and-red blur of police lights, more festive to me than the reflections of a dazzling disco ball.

Moments later, I heard the booming entrance of Revere's Pride, as they were dubbed on the side panels of their patrol cars. After a thunderous collapse of the mountain of caskets, an army of uniforms climbed over the boxes and into the room. The next thing I heard was a chorus of "RPD. Freeze.''

I COULD HARDLY believe that I'd been trapped in my isolated chamber for less than a half hour. Later, safely cradled by Matt in the back of a patrol car, I learned that the police had taken Barry into custody easily. At the sound of the sirens, he'd run from the mortuary, literally into their arms. But the police, not willing to read too many assumptions into my fax, had no way of knowing if one or more accomplices might still be in the building. They'd come in with their battering ram ready for a showdown.

When they found me coming out of the workroom, I had my hands high over my head in surrender.

TWENTY-SEVEN

HAVING LIVED ALONE all my adult life, I didn't realize for a while that the smells of breakfast were from my own kitchen. Elaine Cody, who had arrived a few days after my adventure with Barry Richards, brought me a tray of scrambled eggs, coffee, and orange juice. Rose trailed after her, carrying mugs for her and Elaine, ready for a sorority meeting in my bedroom. We ate muffins from a batch Elaine had made from the scrapings in my cupboard.

"I didn't even know I had any flour," I said.

"I did have to make a staples run." Elaine wore a teal-blue velour sweatsuit with a matching headband, and tennis shoes that looked brand-new and expensive. "I'm glad I'm here," she said. "I hate having to take your word from three thousand miles away that you're all right."

"Barely a scrape," I said, striking a pose with my left arm raised to show off my short cast. A simple fracture, according to the doctor. Otherwise I thought I looked healthy and energetic, even if I was still in bed. I neglected to mention the serious aching in all my muscles as a result of my casket-room romp.

Elaine and Rose had been taking turns treating me as if I'd had major surgery. It was hard to accept attention I didn't think I deserved, but I welcomed the company. With Elaine's California stories and Rose's soothing company to distract me, the memory of a frightening hour with a double murderer faded. Except when they both wanted details of my latest brush with a killer.

"You can thank Frank," I said. "He had the building upgraded to get more electrical power. The modern codes call for the new wires to go underground, and since he was also adding a fax line at the same time, they put the fax wire underneath, too. And they're all on the other side of the building.''

"Thank heaven Barry didn't think to walk all around the house looking for more wires," Rose said.

"He thought he had them all when he found the first group," I said.

"I guess Barry felt he had to kill Mr. Deramo, with his career and a lot of money at stake," Elaine said.

"I think it was personal, too," I said. "Barry saw Michael as the one keeping him and his sister from the position they aspired to in North Shore society."

"I thought ethnicity was a plus these days. It is in Berkeley," Elaine said.

"Not everywhere," Rose said. "In some places it might as well still be the turn of the century when they put 'Irish Need Not Apply' signs in retail-shop windows. Then the Italians came over right after that and got the same treatment. And in some circles things haven't changed much at all."

"Michael didn't do a lot to endear himself to the family, either," I said, recognizing at last that Michael was not a saint. "He embarrassed them at parties. And apparently he made fun of Barry a lot. His name. His birthmark. This pseudo-blackmail attempt was the last straw."

"And the son wasn't involved at all? The one who nearly shot you?" Rose asked.

"I don't think Francis Deramo ever intended to shoot me. From what Matt's told me, Francis suspected it was Barry who killed his father, and he was upset with himself for giving in to Sylvia and showing Barry the Federal Express letter. But the letter wasn't the only thing that tipped Barry off—he' learned about the payoff money from Fred Laughton and John Hammer. Because of the secrecy around the patent, not even the lawyers were sure what Michael knew or whether he was a threat.''

"Then there's Sylvia Deramo," Rose said with a frown. "The in-charge lady who wanted to tell us how to run our business? Her own son thought she was guilty."

"Poor Andrew was trying to get even with her for breaking up their home, as he saw it. She was technically innocent, except that she set the stage by rejecting Michael."

"So, essentially, everyone else fed Barry information and reinforced his own motives. I still can't imagine how anyone could commit murder," Rose said.

"Evidently you have a happy marriage," Elaine said.

Unfortunately, it still hurt when I laughed.

MATT SENT ROSE and Elaine out one evening and took over, preparing dinner and playing cards with me, with only the slightest sign of censure.

"How come you keep doing things that make me worry?" he asked.

"How come you didn't tell me you had Berger staking out my house? He scared the life out of me."

"So I heard. I'm sorry about that. I can't believe he isn't better at blending in."

"Well, he didn't blend. He acted like a stalker," I said, examining a losing hand of cribbage.

"Curious that you never told me you thought you were being stalked." Matt studied his cards, not revealing how he felt, either about the hand he'd dealt himself or my failure to tell him about the jogger.

"Good thing I didn't bother you about it, because I was wrong, wasn't I? I wasn't being stalked."

"But you thought you were... but, never mind. I felt you needed some protection, and I wasn't wrong about that. Looks like we cut it off a little too soon, though."

"I guess that was my fault."

"It was Berger's fault for getting busted on his way to work."

"Did he report to you on my activities?"

"No, no. He was just supposed to keep an eye out."

"Thank you, I guess."

"You're welcome. And by the way, that was some trick you pulled with your car alarm. Pretty impressive."

"I thought he didn't report... well, I do my best," I said, as we both laughed at the image of a wrought-up Cadillac. Matt claimed he could picture it perfectly.

"I wonder when you'll have had enough of this," he said, moving his wooden peg to the end of the board, and winning the game.

"Enough cribbage?"

"Right, Gloria. Cribbage. Notice I'm getting better at accepting your, uh, perseverance?"

"You can say stubbornness," I said, with a laugh. "I did notice and I appreciate it."

"You know I do realize you're doing what you want. And you seem to be able to take care of yourself, in a bizarre kind of way. But I still worry. I don't want to lose you to some nut you're trying to track down. Not if I can prevent it by protecting you."

We both knew that Matt was also thinking of his wife, Teresa. He'd told me how helpless he'd felt as she'd suffered and died of genetic heart disease more than ten years ago. I'd heard that people in the medical and law enforcement professions always think they should be able to keep their loved ones from harm, even from death by a disease no one has any control over. I thought it must be a terrible burden.

"I was thinking of signing up for some classes in criminology," I said.

Matt dropped the deck of cards in the middle of a shuffle and looked at me, as if I were the subject of a psychological test he was conducting.

"What?"

"Maybe you wouldn't worry so much if I had some professional training."

"Isn't that what every retired physicist does? Enter the police academy? Fortunately, you're too old, if you'll pardon my saying so."

"I'm not talking about being a cop. Just learning a little more about how police work is done right. Maybe you could teach me a few things yourself."

"Maybe we could teach each other."

I blushed at my inadvertent overture. A lot had happened since our last necking session on the Boulevard right after Michael's death.

"Interview techniques. Fine points of the law. The criminal mind. That's what I meant."

"That's not what I meant," he said.

Matt looked across the table at me with an intensity I'd seen only briefly in the last few days—usually just before his pager went off, or just before I felt I had to make a confession to him. I had the vague memory of being relieved when this new level of intimacy was cut off. This time I felt there'd be no need to stall, but I still hadn't completely disconnected my brain.

"Elaine and Rose…" I said.

"They're out for a long time."

"How do we know they won't come back early?" I asked, my whole body in a state of tension. I'd locked onto Matt's eyes like the best laser in Reagan's Strategic Defense Initiative.

Matt grinned. He collected the cards and put them back into the box, closing the cover.

"I gave them tickets to the Boston Symphony." He looked at his watch. "They're doing their marathon Beethoven program, starting in a half hour."

"The one that's four hours long?"

"That's the one. And I suggested that since they'd be so late, it might be a good idea if Elaine went home with Rose tonight instead of waking you up."

"I need my rest."

"So, is there anything else in the way?"

I reached over and pulled at his collar.

"Just all these clothes."

We got up from our chairs at the same time, bumping the table and knocking the cards and cribbage board to the floor.

We had no further use for them anyway.

TWENTY-EIGHT

ROSE HAD OUTDONE herself with the decorations for my party, dressing her already beautiful living room in elaborate arrangements of flowers. Even the balloons placed around the edges of the room looked elegant in the Galigani home. She'd ordered them specially, with the imprint of the Massachusetts state flag—white, with a dark blue shield at its center.

Matt surprised me with an unexpected guest—he'd driven to Worcester in his personal car, a steel-blue Toyota Camry, to pick up Mary Ann and bring her to the party.

"Your young man is very nice," she'd whispered to me more than once during the evening.

The best part of having Mary Ann at the party, I realized with shame, was that I'd get to drive her home later with Matt. He'd suggested making a detour coming back and staying at a bed-and-breakfast in Chatham.

The dining-room table was set for twelve. Though I'd seen the Galiganis' home in festive decor many times, it still amazed me that anyone had enough equipment and supplies to serve dinner and set out matching plates, two kinds of glasses, and silverware for a dozen people at once. Robert's son, William, the fourteen-year-old computer guru, had prepared place cards using a font style that looked like the calligraphy of an illustrated medieval manuscript. He'd made cards for me and the extended Galigani family, and for Matt, Elaine, Andrea, Mary Ann, and Peter, who'd arrived alone.

"Barbara couldn't make it," Peter said.

He glanced at me briefly, and then at Elaine for a much longer time, taking in her model-like stature and her newest party outfit, in mauve silk.

Why didn't I think of that, I wondered, as I hurried to introduce them. They'd already started to look like a couple to me, both tall and thin, both clearly fashion-conscious in their elegant clothes. They appeared to have matching patent-leather shoes.

I questioned whether I wanted to wish Peter on Elaine, but who was I to predict what might work and what would not? Remembering Elaine's two husbands and one extra fiancé, I decided she could do worse than Peter Mastrone.

After dinner—an extraordinary feast of pasta and roasted meats and vegetables—we all found comfortable seats in the Galiganis' living room and successfully avoided the subject of my newly completed contract with the RPD. The younger guests had to suffer through fifties music—Johnny Ray, Frank Sinatra, and Perry Como among the vocalists. I didn't quite understand Rose's reason for choosing crooners for the party, but she claimed it was appropriate.

"It's the music that Gloria and I listened to on the radio when we first met," she explained.

"We used to hum along while we were ironing," I said.

"What's ironing?" William Galigani asked, pointing to his oversized T-shirt.

Long before Rose's party, I'd made my decision to stay in Revere. Sitting among my closest friends, and a man I was starting to love, surrounded by the landmarks of my youth, I felt that California was very far away.

Until Elaine spoke.

"I just remembered something," she said, with an apology for bringing up California folks, as she called them, in front of people who didn't know them. "I can't believe I forgot to tell you, Gloria—in all the confusion—remember Gary Larkin? He died last week."

I put down my glass of sparkling cider and leaned across the coffee table as if to hear better. "He wasn't even fifty years old," I said. "What happened?"

"I think they said it was an allergic reaction in the lab. He had an accident with some beryllium powder."

"An accident? I find that hard to believe."

"That's what the police called it."

"Gary Larkin is a beryllium expert. He'd never have an accident." I folded my arms across my chest in a gesture of certitude. "There must have been foul play."

The ripple effect started with Matt, who removed the jazz trombone tie clip I'd given him and used its pointed tip to burst the balloon nearest him. The state of Massachusetts, small as it was, was blown to bits, its rubbery pieces settling on the carpet at my feet.

As far as I could tell, each of Rose's guests found a pointed object—a pen, a paper clip, the edge of a piece of jewelry— and in less than a minute, the sound of two dozen balloons splitting apart drowned out my theory of a beryllium murder.

Enjoy the mystery and suspense of

POISON APPLES

NANCY MEANS WRIGHT

A VERMONT MYSTERY

"Wright's most gripping and satisfying mystery to date."
—*Female Detective*

"…Wright doesn't put a foot wrong in this well-wrought mystery."
—*Boston Globe*

After tragedy shatters Moira and Stan Earthrowl's lives, running an apple orchard in Vermont gives them a chance to heal. Yet their newfound idyll is short-lived as "accidents" begin to plague the massive orchard: tractor brakes fail, apples are poisoned.

Desperate, Moira turns to neighbor Ruth Willmarth for help. Ruth's investigation reveals a list of possible saboteurs, including a fanatical religious cult and a savvy land developer who, ironically, is Ruth's ex-husband. But deadly warnings make it clear that even Ruth is not immune to the encroaching danger.…

If great tales are your motive,
make Worldwide Mystery your partner in crime.
Available September 2001 at your favorite retail outlet.

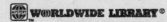

WNMW395

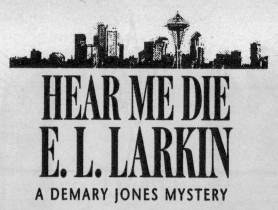

HEAR ME DIE
E. L. LARKIN

A DEMARY JONES MYSTERY

When private investigator Demary Jones gets a desperate message from friend Sara Garland, she begins to fear the worst. Her fears are soon confirmed when Sara disappears. Head accountant at the highly secretive Electric Toy Company, Sara isn't the only one in trouble—the office manager is a victim of a hit-and-run. Next, the eccentric head of ETC is found beaten to death.

Though the cops are convinced Sara is behind the killings, Demary believes otherwise and follows a trail of greed and desperation to a clever game where toys are more than child's play.

Available September 2001 at your favorite retail outlet.

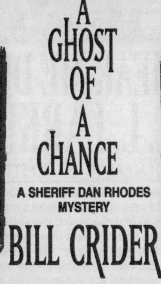

A GHOST OF A CHANCE

A SHERIFF DAN RHODES MYSTERY

BILL CRIDER

Sheriff Dan Rhodes of Blacklin County,
Texas, knows that times may change, but
most things can be explained with a little
common sense—even the "ghost" haunting his jail.
When the body of Ty Berry, the president of one of two
feuding historical societies, is found shot dead in a
freshly dug grave, Rhodes decides the crime is
of a more earthly nature.

The outspoken head of the rival historical society becomes
the second victim, putting Rhodes on the trail of a double
homicide…and of course, one irascible ghost.

Available September 2001 at your favorite retail outlet.

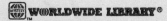

WBC396